The Travel Book

(A NOVEL)

MATTHEW PEACOCK

Gili Isles, Indonesia

Johnny made his way between the tall trees, snapping twigs as he ran, trying to catch up with the girl in front of him, but she was nowhere to be seen. A warm tropical breeze swept towards him as he made his way over a small sand dune and down towards the beach, where he stopped to stare at the ocean, transfixed by its calmness. He sensed Rachel behind him as she put her hands over his eyes, causing him to flinch.

'What were you looking at?' she asked.

'Trying to find you,' he replied.

She ran towards the water.

'Where are you going?'

'For a swim,' she replied, undressing to her bra and pants, revealing a petite and attractive figure.

'You want to swim now?' asked Johnny.

'Yes!' she said, entering the sea. 'You have to come in dude.'

Johnny removed his top, tiptoeing awkwardly on the pebbles that stabbed into his foot.

'You look really uncomfortable,' she said.

'Alright, I'll be honest, this is sort out of my comfort zone.'

'Why?'

'I don't like the fact you can't see what's below you which is ten times worst at night time. But I'm doing this. I just won't go in so deep.'

'We always used to go swimming at night back home.'

'Where was home again?' he asked, making his way tentatively through the water towards her.

'Brighton.'

'Cool. I like Brighton. You still live there?'

'My parents do. Dad's away a lot. He's a musician so he's always touring.'

'A musician. Wow. Is he famous?'

'He never really made it big. Mum kept convincing him to go into teaching but he never listened to her. Kept telling her that music was his life.'

'That's very Brighton, having a dad as a musician.'

'Meaning?'

'It's just very cool. I guess Brighton's a very trendy place to grow up. London by the sea don't they call it?'

'I guess. Where did you grow up?'

'York.'

'You're a northerner? I love northerners. Good sense of humour!'

'No rock star parents though. Dad's a solicitor and Mum works part time in insurance.'

'And you still live there?'

'No. Ended up moving to London after uni.'

'I was going to say, you don't have much of a northern accent.'

'That's what posh northern school does to you. Drills the accent out of you.'

'So what do you do in London?'

'I also work in insurance. Not very original.'

'You like it?'

'No. Not really.'

'What do you want to do?'

'I don't know. I guess that's why I came out here. To figure it out. To hopefully be inspired. What do you do? Sorry I hate that question. Like your job defines you.'

'So I just finished a graphic design degree in the summer.'

'You want to do something with that?'

'I wouldn't mind drawing one day. Maybe being an illustrator of some kind. But you never know what sort of job you're going to get.'

'I think you'd be good at it.'

'How do you know that?'

'You seem like the arty farty type. What sort of illustrations?'

'I wouldn't mind designing greeting cards one day. Owning my own business.'

'You should do it. Rachel Hortley Cards Limited. I see it now.'

Rachel lay back and floated in the sea, resting her head in the water while she looked up at the clear night sky above her.

'How do you do that?' asked Johnny.

'What?'

'Manage to float like that?'

'It's easy, just lay back, breathe out and relax.'

'I'm trying that,' he said following her instructions, with his legs sinking in the water, pulling the rest of his body with them. 'See I'm obviously just not a floater. I just turn into the bloody Titanic every time!'

Rachel tittered.

'So tell me something about yourself?' asked Johnny.

'I like tea!'

'I see you more of a tea drinker than a coffee type.'

'I am.'

'So how old are you?'

'Are you meant to ask a girl such a question?'

'Probably not.'

'How old do you think I am?'

'I'm guessing… early twenties?'

'Good answer. I'm twenty-three. You?'

'Old. Much much older.'

'How much older?'

'Twenty-eight.'

'That's a prime age. A good age.'

They moved to shallow water where they could stand. Johnny held his hand around Rachel's waist, moving his hands delicately up her back and through her long brown unkempt hair. He noticed her tanned flawless skin, assuming she was a girl who did not need make up, a girl who would still glow when nursing a hangover. He edged his head forward laying his lips on hers, but she broke the kiss, and headed out of the water.

'Where are you going?' he asked.

'Let's go for a wander.'

He did as she insisted. They both dried themselves in the warm nighttime air, dressed and walked north along the beach, past shut backpacker bars which still had their fairy lights on.

'So what do you think of the Gili Isles?' asked Johnny.

'I love them. No cars. No crime. No police.'

'There must be some police.'

'Nope. The Danish guy who runs the bar we were just in told me the last local person who stole an iPod off a tourist was made to return it to the owner. As a punishment, he was forced to walk around the village with a sign around his neck saying 'criminal.' Apparently he was so humiliated and ostracized by the experience he ended up leaving the island to go to live on Lombok.'

'Jesus. Never underestimate the power of humiliation. Maybe the London Met should take a few hints.'

She laughed. 'So what's your story? What made you want to come out here?'

'Well I was working in my hideously boring job in London and I headed to a book shop one lunchtime. The minute I walked in there there was this travel book, staring straight at me, asking me to pick it up, actually calling to me!'

'I take it you were off the meds that day?'

'Well clearly I was because the first page it opened at when I picked it up was this very place, the Gili Isles. So that very afternoon, I'd handed in my notice with a year long plan to travel the globe.'

'Sounds very spur of the moment. How did your work take it?'

'They were OK. My sister wasn't best pleased.'

'Why's that?'

'Well I was living with her at the time, and it meant she had to get someone in. She basically thought I should be getting on with a career instead of going partying around the globe. In all honesty, I think she was jealous.'

'Sounds it.'

They looked ahead at the bar where they had met earlier.

'We could head back to the party?' he asked.

'We could, though I've had my fair share of full moon parties over the last few months, so I'm good talking to you.'

They walked further up the beach, arriving by a fire where two local Indonesians were sitting down playing music with two tourists.

'Don't look but the local guy with the guitar on the left proposed to me the other night,' she said.

'He proposed to you? What, does he even know you?'

'We've chatted a few times. He works in my hostel. He told me he loved me.'

'I'm sure he meant it.'

Rachel sniggered. 'So where are you off to next?'

'I might head off to Lombok, then maybe head on to Flores. Then possibly Komodo, go see a few dragons. Then I'm off to Australia, going on a tour from Cairns to Sydney for two weeks, then to New Zealand, America, and when I run out of money, home I guess'

'Sounds like you've got it all planned out.'

'And you?'

'Not sure. My dad's got a few gigs coming up in Australia so I might go see him at some point.'

'Oh, so he has a bit of a following?'

'A small one.'

'Well he must be doing alright if he's known internationally. What sort of music does he play?'

'Mostly folk.'

'Does his band have a name?'

'The Conkers.'

'That's quite a cool name.'

'It's not bad.'

'I take it you don't approve?'

'I do think he's talented. He just didn't always put being a father at the top of his priorities. Music always came first.'

'Are you close?'

'Yeah. I probably have the best relationship out of all of us.'

'How many of you are there?'

'Older sister. Younger brother.'

'So you're the middle one? The troublesome one.'

'I can be when I want to be,' she said, shooting him a cheeky smile.

They arrived at the top of the island where Johnny stopped to look at the sun rising over the ocean.

'Would you look at that. We really are in paradise aren't we?' he said.

Rachel sat down, closing her eyes as the white early morning light shone onto her eyes.

'Listen, I don't want this to sound forward or anything, but do you fancy coming back to mine?' Johnny asked coyly. 'My hotel room is literally a few minutes from here.'

'I see. You've been planning all this all along. And did you just say 'hotel room'? I thought we were all staying in dingy old hostels in this place.'

'Thought I'd spruce out during my time here.'

'I see.'

'Then it's dingy hostels for the rest of the trip. What do you say? I mean you can come back for a cuddle? I'm going to shut up as I'm making this sound less appealing the more I mention it.'

She rested her head on his shoulder.

'Sure. I'd like that.'

Johnny looked at himself in the bathroom mirror, refreshed his face and short dark hair using the salt water from the tap, then dried it with a towel. He undid the top button of his shirt to display a glimmer of chest hair, then sprayed his neck with aftershave before returning back to the bedroom. Rachel was lying on his bed on her front, rubbing her crossed feet together, while looking at the black arrows he had drawn on the map in his travel book, planning out his journey around the globe.

'You're very organized. All these arrows going everywhere,' she observed. 'Where's your compass?'

'You may joke but I do actually have one.'

'Oh my God you really are Mr Organised!'

'Hey if we were lost right now you would be thanking me.'

'Lost in Johnny's room!' she said turning over.

Johnny looked into her blue eyes, moved his mouth to her lips, her ears, her neck, rubbing his hands over her slim delicate shoulders, cupping her breasts but resisting the urge to take things further.

'Listen. Let's just lay here tonight. It just feels different with you. I can't explain it. I mean, God, you're seriously, well, way out of my league. I don't normally do this, but I just don't feel like taking things further and screwing things up tonight. I have a feeling we'll see each other again. Does that sound weird?'

'No,' she replied. 'Not at all.'

Johnny sat up. 'Do you mind if I kill the lights?'

'Sure.'

He removed his shirt and trousers, and got into bed wearing his boxers that smelt of seaweed. Rachel undressed to her underwear, got under the thin sheets allowing Johnny to put his arms around her, and the room fell silent with only the sound of the waves crashing in the distance.

'Rachel?'

'Mmm?'

'I had fun tonight'

'Me too,' she replied.

Byron Bay, Australia

Johnny's body tensed up as he looked out of the small plane window with unease as it rose above the clouds. A lively Australian hovered a camcorder in front of him, persuading him to move his hands into a claw and hook position which he was told would look 'cool' for the skydiving video.

The door opened and a gush of wind hit his face, thrashing his heartbeat up. He could stop this from happening. He could simply ask to stay on the plane, but then he saw Anna step out of the plane. Pathetic Anna. An eighteen-year-old English girl from Leicester who had taken a shine to Johnny on his two-week tour from Cairns to Sydney. Out she went with her tandem buddy. He had to do this now. How could he not? He couldn't show himself up in front of Anna, the girl who had cried on numerous occasions on the trip. The risks of the jump dawned on him. What if the parachute never came out? *You stupid idiot. You stupid fucking idiot* he thought to himself as he edged closer towards the door.

'You ready?!' asked his tandem partner enthusiastically, a lively outdoorsy type who had different coloured badges sewn around the collar of his jumpsuit.

'Yep,' replied Johnny hesitantly, 'think so.'

He allowed the man to manoeuvre him to the ledge of the door of the plane where he sat with his legs dangling in the air below. He tried not to look down but he couldn't help himself and

11

when he did all he could see were clouds beneath him. He crossed his arms, placing one hand on each shoulder and looked up into the dark blue sky above him. His tandem buddy pushed them both off the side of the plane and Johnny was falling down through the sky with his fear turning into joy in an instant. The cameraman appeared beside them filming Johnny's expressions and within a few seconds there was a jerk up as Johnny was forced upwards into the sky as their parachute opened. The sky fell quiet as their descending speed went down and they could hear every word spoken to each other.

'Pretty neat huh?' asked his tandem buddy

'This is absolutely amazing!'

They floated through the clouds, down towards the landscape of Byron Bay where they could make out the beach, the town and the lighthouse south along the coast. The earth's surface quickly approached and they were soon touching the airfield ground with a thump, where the cameraman, who had landed moments earlier, ran up to film Johnny's reactions.

'How was it?!' asked the cameraman.

'Amazing,' replied Johnny, beaming with excitement. 'Absolutely amazing.'

Johnny gathered his balance, shook the hands of his tandem buddy, and then stumped towards the hangar where he could see other members of the tour group who had come to watch.

'I'll say this now,' said Suzi with an Americanized Austrian accent. 'You are mental. But you did it. Congratulations!'

'Thank you' Johnny said, buzzing from the adrenaline still pumping around his body.

Johnny turned to see Anna crying in the distance.

'Go on, the only thing to cheer your girlfriend would be a hug,' Suzi jested. She had enjoyed mocking Anna's unrequited feelings for him throughout their trip.

'I still can't believe she actually did it. She's not so square after all,' replied Johnny.

'Well guys I hope you all enjoyed that experience,' said Ryan, their forty-something Queenslander tour leader, through the bus microphone as they drove back to their campsite. 'Certainly an experience to share with the grandkids. So we're going to head back to the hostel now and get ready for this evening's events.'

The Moonbeat Travel tour which had taken Johnny and the twenty other members of the group down the coast over the last few weeks had involved a lot of drinking. They had stayed at a number of different hostels and a variety of themed nights had been set up at each one. Having already had a toga party up in the Whitsundays a few nights before, Johnny really wasn't feeling in the mood for dressing up again. Tonight's theme was Plastic Fantastic and everyone had been given three different coloured plastic bags to make costumes out of.

'What are you going dressed up as?' Suzi asked Peter, the fifty-seven-year-old Canadian, the oldest member of the group by quite a few decades.

'I don't think I'll be partaking in this evening's events,' replied Peter.

'Oh come on, you dressed up for the toga party,' said Suzi. 'You should get involved again.'

'Well yes, yes I did, but as I said before this tour really isn't the sort of trip I signed up for.'

They arrived back at the hostel where Johnny walked with Peter to his room, which he was sharing with two other male members of the group; Christoph, an enthusiastic German entrepreneur from Munich, and Darren, a socially awkward type from Cornwall who had been Johnny's roommate for the majority of the trip.

'You're alive! How was the jump?!' Christoph asked Johnny enthusiastically as he entered the room.

13

'It was good. Not as scary as I thought it would be. You should have come.'

'I'll do a lot of things. But throwing myself out of a plane. Not going to happen.'

'Have you decided what you're going as tonight?' Johnny asked Christoph.

'I have. I'm going to go as The Hulk.'

Johnny turned to see Darren lying on the bed texting on his phone.

'Are you coming tonight Darren?' asked Johnny.

'Yeah, think so,' replied Darren in his slow downbeat Cornish accent.

'What are you going to go as?'

'Think I might go as a Teenage Mutant Ninja Turtle.'

'That sounds good,' said Christoph, sounding surprised and impressed by Darren's originality.

'Are you coming tonight Peter?' asked Christoph.

'No, no, not for me,' replied Peter adamantly.

'Oh come on Peter!' said Christoph. 'Why not?'

'I'm just not in the mood really,' replied Peter while folding his clothes neatly on his bed.

'What are you going to go as Johnny?' asked Christoph.

'I'm thinking Batman.'

'I like it!'

They spent the next hour putting their costumes together with Peter finally agreeing to go dressed as an unidentifiable superhero, after been coaxed into it by Christoph.

They arrived at the Captain Cook Hostel in the centre of the town where Suzi quickly appeared with her roommates consisting of Anna, who seemed less teary after her parachuting experience, Lauren, a blunt teacher from Essex, and Gemma, a preppy type junior doctor from Hereford.

'Awesome costumes guys!' remarked Christoph. 'What are you?'

14

'The Teletubbies mate,' said Gemma.

'What are you s'posed to be?' Lauren asked Christoph in her abrupt Essex accent.

'I am The Hulk!' replied Christoph.

'And I'm Batman,' Johnny said pointing to the sign on his chest which he had drawn in black on his yellow bin liner.

'And you?' Lauren asked Peter.

'I am an unidentifiable superhero,' replied Peter timidly.

'And Darren. How about you?'

'I'm a Teenage Mutant Ninja Turtle.'

'Well. Darren's the best dressed,' Lauren remarked before walking off.

'Hey guys,' said Ryan, their tour leader, dressed up in a Tarzan costume. 'They're asking for everyone to head inside'. Ryan had used every themed party on the trip to dress in a way which exposed himself as much as possible, and tonight was no exception.

The group joined other tour organizations in the bar where a rotund Australian woman appeared with a microphone.

'Hi everybody and welcome to Plastic Fantastic! Here we have everyone who wants to be nominated!'

Johnny hastily caught onto the fact that no one else from the group apart from him, Christoph, Suzi and her three roommates were now standing on a stage volunteering to nominate themselves.

'So guys I'm going to come around and ask you individually why you think you should be nominated.'

Johnny turned to Suzi. 'Hang on. I don't want to be nominated. My costume's not even that good.'

'Oh just play along with it,' said Suzi.

'That's OK for you. Your costume's really impressive.'

'Well there's not much you can do now. You're on stage. Suck it up.'

The presenter shot to Christoph who was first in line and shoved a microphone in front of his face.

'So who are you?' asked the presenter.

'I am the Hulk!' replied Christoph.

'And why should you be nominated?'

'Because I'm green, I'm mean and I'm here to be seen!'

There were a few claps came from the audience that didn't quite match his level of enthusiasm.

The presenter moved to Johnny. 'Who are you?'

'I am Batman,' replied Johnny dubiously.

'And why should you be nominated?'

'Because I am the Dark Knight of Byron Bay,' he replied awkwardly.

'Respect!' shouted a lad from the audience boosting Johnny's confidence.

'See. That sounded good,' said Suzi quietly into his ear.

'So who are you guys?' the presenter asked the girls.

'We are the teletubbies!' replied Gemma confidently.

'And why should you be nominated?'

'Well, all we can say is…' she turned to the rest of the group of girls and they all replied, 'Eh-Oh!'

A loud cheer of laughter came from the audience. The presenter moved to the next girl with blonde hair who had a green plastic bag on her head which was cut into leaves; she had an orange bag wrapped around the rest of her body.

'Who are you?' asked the presenter.

'I am a carrot,' replied the girl in a Scandinavian accent.

'And why should you win?'

'Because I am one of your five a day!'

It was obvious the girl was from another tour group as her colleagues were cheering loudly for her. The presenter moved to the next man in line; a sporty type clad in blue plastic bags, with a blue painted face.

'Who are you?' she asked flirtatiously.

16

'I am Papa Smurf!' replied the young lad with a South African accent, receiving the loudest approval in the room.

'Papa Smurf! Papa Smurf!' shouted a group of lads in the corner.

'And why should you win?' asked the presenter.

'Because I'm the best bloody Smurf in the world!'

There was another cheer.

Suzi turned to Johnny. 'Well we're not going to win with that kind of support against us!'

'Where the hell's our tour group?' asked Lauren angrily, trying to seek them out from amongst the audience. 'Where's our fucking support?!'

'I don't think they're really watching,' replied Suzi.

'Well they should be! Our tour leader should be telling everyone to be in here cheering us on, the tosser!'

'You tell them Lauren!' replied Gemma sounding very jolly-hockey-sticks.

'And what are you?' asked the presenter as she got to the last person in the group.

'I am a Box Jellyfish,' replied the skinny girl with an Eastern European accent.

'And why should you win?'

'Because if I don't I will sting the hell out of you!'

More merriment came from the rival group.

'Lets ask our judge. So, who are we keeping?!' said the presenter while she walked towards the bar manager, a chubby Australian man wearing a singlet, putting the microphone to his mouth.

'We want to keep the carrot,' he replied.

'Papa Smurf! Papa Smurf!' shouted the other group in the audience.

'Papa Smurf,' he replied. 'And just because of their originality the Teletubbies!'

A boo came from the rival group.

'Fuck off!' snapped Lauren, riled by the situation.

'Thank you for everyone who nominated themselves but can the ones who weren't mentioned please leave the stage!'

'Tell our leader Ryan to give us some fucking support instead of perving on all the eighteen year olds in the group!' fumed Lauren as Johnny and Christoph walked off.

'Will do.'

Johnny walked towards Ryan who was doing exactly what Lauren had predicted, talking to nineteen-year-old Abbie from Texas.

'Come on guys, the Teletubbies need some support!' impelled Christoph, trying to maneuver the group back into the bar.

'OK, all the people left on stage, you all have to dance as your character!' announced the presenter into the microphone.

Onto the speaker came the track 'Mambo Number Five' by Lou Bega and off went Suzi, Lauren, Anna and Gemma dancing in character as the Teletubbies; jumping up and down with their arms held out at their sides, while carrot swung rigidly from side to side. Next to her was Papa Smurf bopping up and down excitedly, while Box Jellyfish stood smoothly moving her arms in a wave formation as if they were tentacles. The music came to an abrupt halt.

'OK,' said the presenter heading over to the manager at the bar. 'I think we have our winner!'

'Papa Smurf! Papa Smurf! Papa Smurf!' shouted the lively members of the rival tour clan.

'Tele...tubbies! Tele...tubbies!' shouted Christoph, trying to persuade the rest of the group to make some noise, but with little success.

'OK, do we have an answer?!' asked the presenter.

'We do,' replied the Bar Manager. 'The winner is...Papa Smurf!'

Another loud roar came from the other side of the room.

'Oh fuck off!' replied Lauren shooting off with the other three girls in a huff, past Ryan, Johnny, Christoph and the rest of the group.

'Yeah thanks for the support guys, we had no fucking chance up there!' she fumed, giving Ryan a death stare.

Music blasted into the room and disco lights came on as everyone assembled onto the dance floor.

'You want to get a drink?' Suzi asked Johnny.

'Sure.'

They walked to the bar.

'It's weird,' said Suzi searching for a cigarette from her bag.

'What is?'

'The fact we're not going to see each other in a few days.'

'Course we will.'

'Yeah. But like not everyday. I mean who else am I going to make fun out of? Oh, I need more cigarettes.'

'What?' replied Johnny, not hearing her as the music increased in volume.

'I don't have any cigarettes! You want to walk to the store with me?!'

'Yes I might be able to hear you properly there.'

'You sound like an old man.'

'I am.'

They headed up the main street past the other late night bars to a convenience store where they bought cigarettes, then pottered to the beach.

'I think we're pretty lucky with the people we got on this tour,' Suzi remarked while lighting up a cigarette.

'We could have done with a few more blokes though.'

'Yeah, true. With that many girls, it does get bitchy. So were there any girls you liked on the trip?'

'I don't know. Gemma's quite attractive.'

'Yeah. But she's so posh. Her accent is so classical.'

'Any guys you liked?' he asked.

'I'm not telling you that. Maybe,' she remarked, nudging his shoulder.

'Alright. Well come on, spill the beans?'

'I'm not telling you that!'

'Why not?'

'Just. I don't know.'

She paused, then turned to look at him, sipping on her beer. 'Alright. OK. You.'

Johnny looked at her blankly.

'I'm sorry,' said Suzy coyly. 'Now this is really awkward.'

'No. It's not. I just don't really know what to say. I wasn't really expecting that.'

'Do you have a girlfriend?'

'No. No.'

'You do. I knew it.'

'I don't have a girlfriend.'

'I don't believe you!'

'I don't. I really don't. OK. There was a girl.'

'OK.'

'This is going to sound totally fucking crazy'

'What is?'

'I met this girl, her name was Rachel, in the Gili Isles a couple of months ago, before I came here. We sort of had a night together. Nothing really happened. We kissed, we slept together, not slept together, just, were together in the same bed, which was weird, but it felt right, and by the morning she'd gone. Since then, I have not been able to stop thinking about her.'

'Well that's OK.'

'It's insane. I look at my phone everyday hoping that somehow she's got my number. I can't get her out of my head.'

'So what was she like?'

'Really amazing. She was twenty-three.'

'That's young.'

'True. She'd just finished uni. She wanted to design cards.'

'Was she pretty?'

'Yeah. Way above my league.'

'And she just left in the morning?'

'Yep.'

'No note?'

'Nope.'

'Well that's kind of rude.'

'I searched the island for about three days looking for her. Tried to remember people who might have known her but she'd disappeared.'

'Well maybe you'll bump into her somewhere.'

'Come on. Like that's going to happen.'

'Stranger things have happened. I'm trying to make you feel better.'

'Thank you.' Johnny said putting his arm around her. 'This tour would not have been the same without you.'

'I know. More fun than I was expecting. But it's not over yet. We have Sydney to look forward to. Which reminds me you still need to lend me your travel book.'

'I will do.'

'Well let's hope you find this girl one day.'

'Here's hoping.'

'So things aren't awkward between us?' Johnny asked her as he handed her his travel book at the entrance of his room when they got back to the hostel.

'No. I'm so over you. I'll see you in the morning Batman'

'Night night Dipsy.'

'What?'

'It's your Teletubby name.'

'I didn't even know that,' she said laughing.

'And to think you almost won. Appalling.'

'Night.'

It was half an hour later Johnny woke up with his phone vibrating on his bedside table. It was Suzi calling.

'Hello?' he said quietly into the phone, trying not to wake the others.

'You asleep?'

'Yes.'

'I had to wake you. You need to come outside.'

'I'm in bed. What is it?'

'Just get out here.'

Johnny hung up, put on a t-shirt and met her outside.

'What is it?'

Suzy handed him the travel book.

'You might want to turn to the page on Sydney.'

'Why?'

'Stop asking questions. Just do it.'

He took it from her, turned to the page on Sydney, and there it was above the opening paragraph, Rachel's mobile number written in black biro with the brief words '*call me.*'

Sydney, Australia

On the night of discovering Rachel's number Johnny had refrained from texting her. He had waited until the following morning to make contact.

Hi Rachel. It's Johnny here from the Gili Isles. I just found your number in my travel book. Well at least I hope it's the right Rachel. I don't know what you're up too, but I'm heading down to Sydney in a few days. It would be great to meet up if you're around. Johnny,' he wrote.

Rachel replied shortly after. *'Hi Stranger. Sure. I'm living in Sydney now. How about I meet you on Friday at Circular Quay, Wharf 2, say 12 midday? Rach.'*

'Sounds good! See you there. Johnny.'

He woke up early the day of their meeting, got showered and headed down to a coffee shop for a blueberry muffin and a flat white, then browsed through the busy streets. A heatwave had hit the city of Sydney. The sweltering heat had reflected off the tall clean glass skyscrapers in some places melting the tarmac.

When he arrived at Circular Quay, Rachel was standing close to one of the ferry terminals. Her hair looked darker, and from watching her body language, he could tell she was anxious.

'Hey!' she said taking her headphones out of her ears.

'Hello again,' he replied standing awkwardly next to her. 'So you wrote your number in my guide book?'

'I did!' she replied.

'So what do you fancy doing? We can get a drink? I hear the zoo's pretty good. How long have you got?'

'All day.'

'Cool. We have to catch a boat?'

'We can do that.'

'OK then. Zoo it is.'

They walked to the ferry terminal where they paid for separate tickets.

'You want to get a seat in the sun?' he asked.

'Sure.'

They sat down at the front of the boat and waited a few minutes before the vessel moved out into the bay.

'So you're living here now?' asked Johnny.

'I am. In Bondi. Got a job as a waitress.'

'How's that?'

'It's OK. I mean it's a job. It's the first thing I found. I used to work in a bar as a student so it's pretty familiar work.'

'You say it like it's fun. I couldn't think of anything worse. Having to put up with the general public.'

Rachel laughed. 'You get used to it. People can be OK. So how did your trek go?'

'It was good. Felt a bit like a school trip as there was a bit of bickering amongst certain members. But overall, it was pretty decent.'

'When did it finish?'

'Last night. Last location was Sydney.'

'And you started in Cairns, right?'

'Yep.'

'Wow. That's a long way to go. You've seen more of Australia than I have. Nice people?'

'It was diverse.'

'Diverse? That sounds ominous.'

'No, in a good way. A few odd balls.'

'It sounds fun. I'm kind of jealous.'

'You should go on one if you get a chance. It's refreshing just being dumped with a whole load of random people you have to live with for two weeks.'

'I'm too poor at the moment to do anything like that. Maybe in about fifty years when I have money.'

'An OAP trek?'

Rachel laughed. 'Hey, that's sounds pretty amazing.'

'So how long have you been here for?'

'I came down after the Gili Isles. Stayed in a hostel for about a week. I managed to get this job at the bar. I also found the flat through a friend so it's all worked out pretty well.'

'Listen Rachel, I've got to ask you this now, why did you leave your number in my travel book?'

'I don't know. Maybe…. if you ever came to Sydney I wanted you to get in touch.'

'You could have just left your number on the side, or waited until I woke up in the morning before leaving?'

'I know. I'm sorry. It was kind of rude.'

The boat pulled up at the zoo pier where they disembarked and caught the cable car up the hill to the entrance.

'So did you go to Komodo?' asked Rachel.

'I did.'

'Did you see your dragons?'

'I did see my dragons.'

'Were they everything you dreamed of and more?'

'Vicious, but impressive.'

'You do realize you're probably going to see them here, don't you?'

'Hey, nothing like seeing the real thing in its native habitat.'

'So who are you living with now?'

'I have two housemates. All British.'

'OK. What do they do?'

'Angela works in recruitment and the other guy, Ross, works in some boring admin job. We're all in the same situation though. All doing holiday working visas.'

'Maybe I should have done the whole working visa thing.'

'You're not too old. How long are you intending to stay in Sydney for?'

'Not sure yet. I don't really have any plans for the next few weeks.'

'I'm surprised. What happened to Mr Organisation? What with those arrows in your travel book, I thought you had practically every day planned out?'

'Almost every day. So I take it you know all the good sights to see in Sydney?'

'Of course. I know a very good bar where a pleasant waitress serves some very nice drinks.'

'I should come around for a beverage sometime.'

'You should. Then of course there's the Blue Mountains, very pretty, just out of the city, then there's the Hunter Valley.'

Johnny put down his rucksack and got out some sunblock to rub on his face.

'You're being very sensible?' she noted.

'How so?'

'Factor thirty. Don't most of us Brits put on the lowest factor possible?'

'Well I learnt the hard way. First day in Cairns, my nose ended up bleeding it got so burnt.'

'Ouch. The sun here is definitely stronger than back in Europe. So what was Cairns like?'

'It was OK. I mean it's a great base to see all the stuff in the area. We got a boat from there to the Coral Reef, which was easy enough.'

'I'd love to go there. Go diving.'

'You should do it.'

'I will.'

'Then we headed up to Cape Tribulation on another day.'

'Nice beaches?'

'Yeah except you can't go in the sea because of jellyfish and crocodiles.'

'Oh my God that's nuts. The whole wild life here is kind of insane.'

'So have you heard from your family?'

'A few emails here and there. My dad keeps telling me he's coming out for a music gig.'

'Yeah. I remember you mentioning that.'

'I think he's touring as much as he can as things aren't great between him and my mum.'

'I'm sorry to hear that.'

'She's always moaning about him. I think she just feels she's been more of a mother to him than a wife. I mean she's the one who's financed his career practically. Have you heard from your family?'

'I got an email from my sister the other day, complaining about the fact I hadn't paid her enough money for an electricity bill.'

'And your parents?'

'On occasion.'

After a few hours at the zoo, catching up on lost time, they caught the ferry back, sitting in silence as the boat headed back across the bay. It was something Johnny had not expected, from seeing Rachel he felt a feeling of completeness, that he had longed for over the last few months, and as the boat headed back into the quay, he went to kiss her, which she embraced warmly.

'It's funny,' asked Johnny while drinking a beer at a bar they had found by the opera house shortly after the ferry crossing.

'What is?"

'I always knew I was going to see you again. I hope that doesn't sound weird.'

27

'No, it doesn't. Listen, when we're done, you could always come back to the flat if you like?'

'OK,' he said. 'How far is it?'

'It takes about an hour on the bus.'

They walked back into the city to catch the bus from Elizabeth Street which took longer than expected due to the heavy traffic. It's one thing he noticed about Sydney, the congestion always seemed so bad.

Rachel's flat was off the main road of Campbell Parade, close to the beach. A ground floor flat with a small yard at the front.

When they arrived at the entrance Rachel put the key in the door, then stopped and turned to him.

'Do you mind waiting outside for a sec, just so I can clean up?'

'I really don't care about a bit of mess. You should have seen my room in London.'

'I know. I just want to make it nice. If that's OK?'

'Sure. It's your flat.'

She went inside while Johnny waited. She appeared moments later with a worried look on her face.

'Everything OK?'

'No.'

'What's wrong?'

'You have to go,'

'Why?'

'Because my boyfriend's here.'

It took a second for him to take in what she had said. 'I didn't realise you had a boyfriend?'

'I don't know why I didn't tell you. This is really horrible. He wasn't supposed to be here. He was away this week, and now he's here.' There was panic in her eyes.

'Hey,' said a lad around Johnny's age, appearing at the door. He looked like a musician, skinny, attractive in a grubby student sort of way with two flesh plugs, one in each ear.

'Everything alright Rach?' he asked.

'Ross, this is Johnny. He's a friend I met in the Gili Isles. He's in Sydney for a few days.'

'Yeah. First time,' replied Johnny.

'Well you want to come in or stay out here all day?' asked Ross.

'I should head back to the hostel on second thoughts,' replied Johnny.

'You can come in,' said Rachel trying to hold back her emotions.

'No. I'm good. Got plans tonight. But it was good seeing you again Rachel.'

'Well I'll be inside Rach,' said Ross. 'See you later.'

'Bye.' Johnny said. 'I'm going to go.'

'I'm sorry,' Rachel said oozing with guilt.

'You should have told me.'

Johnny looked at her. Humiliated by her actions. He walked away, knowing she was watching him but he did not look back. He arrived at the bus stop, and boarded the next service that arrived. He sat down, went to his phone, scrolled to Rachel's number, and blocking out all emotion, he deleted her name from his contacts.

Bay of Islands, New Zealand

Johnny had been working for the Manta Ray Bay of Islands Overnight Cruise for a month and a half now; a job he had got through Suzi's cousin Eric, who lived in New Zealand. Suzi had given Johnny Eric's number at the end of their Australian trip.

Eric was a laid back surfer who had grown up in Hawaii, and liked to smoke marijuana. He even had a medical card allowing him to grow the drug legally for medical purposes, relating to a highly questionable sporting injury he had got as a child. Aged twenty-nine, Eric was athletically skinny, tall, with a small goatee, and was enthusiastic about practically everything he did in his life.

'Dude, you're gonna love working on this boat!' said Eric greeting Johnny at Auckland airport, before driving him north to the small town of Paihia where the boat was docked. Eric talked for most of the journey, telling Johnny about his life on the Big Island of Hawaii, where he had worked on tourist boats until moving to New Zealand.

The Manta Ray Overnight Cruise was a small company owned by a middle aged New Zealand couple. The boat offered the chance for tourists to spend a night in the middle of the Bay of Islands. It had fifteen beds for guests and six beds for crew. Johnny's job along with Eric and the two other twenty-something year old crew members, Andrew, a sprightly

Glaswegian, and Georgia, a sporty type from Bristol, was to help assist the guests each night with the boat activities such as fishing and snorkeling, as well a cooking and cleaning. The job was busy, the pay was miniscule, but Johnny enjoyed it. While on the boat he had developed a casual relationship with Georgia, who had shown interest shortly after his arrival. Feeling lonely at the time, Johnny had acted on it. Georgia was voluptuous, with short brown hair, and a degree in sports science from Loughborough University. She had swum professionally during her university years, but since graduation, had given up. Johnny felt flattered by the fact she had chosen him out of the other guys in the group; even their boss Dave had a crush on her, which had subsequently caused friction between him and his plump wife, Sue. Johnny had enjoyed the sex, although infrequent due to the close proximity of the crew's living quarters, but would find her endless ways of trying to impress him through her bad jokes and forced sense of humour grating at times.

'Dude if you're not that into her, I'll date her,' Eric had told him, 'Do you know how long it's been since I got laid?'

Johnny had pretended things were good between them but he was finding it hard to hide his true feelings. Georgia was now picking up on this and it was no surprise when she finally handed in her notice. He was thankful in a way, it was an easy reason to break up, but as they prepared for a small goodbye bash one evening, which also coincided with her birthday, Johnny couldn't help feeling guilty that he was the main reason behind her departure.

'Thanks guys,' Georgia said blowing out the candles on her combined birthday-goodbye cake. 'I don't know what to say. I'm so going to miss you crazy bunch!'

All the crew had come to the party except for Sue who didn't like to socialize with the staff after office hours. Not that Johnny and his colleagues were complaining, it made the gathering more relaxing.

'So we just wanted say thank you for being such a star over the last six months Georgia,' said Dave holding a bottle of beer. He looked good for fifty; a healthy tan, an impressive amount of hair and a lean physique. 'It's really been great having you on board. You've conquered Eric in claiming to catch the biggest fish.'

'So not true,' replied Eric.

'You've helped translate Andrew's heavy Scottish accent which has been a godsend for Sue and I.'

'Oh but you're understanding me now though aren't you?' replied Andrew, accentuating his Glaswegian accent.

'Just about,' replied Dave. The group laughed.

The mood quickly changed as Sue suddenly appeared with a bottle of champagne.

'Oh hi love,' replied Dave.

'Just bought you something Georgia,' said Sue coyly handing over the bottle.

'Oh thanks Sue,' said Georgia giving her an obligatory hug. It was obvious that Dave had spoken to his wife about her lack of interaction and had persuaded her to buy a present.

'And I'm pretty sure Johnny's going to miss you,' said Dave. There was silence; it was the first time he had commented on their relationship.

'Of course I am,' replied Johnny. He had to say something in this awkward moment. Georgia smiled at him and they made a toast to Georgia's hard work.

After finishing their drinks, the rest of the crew went to bed leaving Johnny and Georgia sitting on the edge of the boat looking out over the calm surface of the nighttime ocean.

'So what do you think you'll do when you get back to England?' asked Johnny.

'I don't know! Might go into teaching,' she laughed. 'Bit of problem though, I kind of hate kids.'

'Might be a bit of an issue.'

'Look Johnny you don't have to pretend you're madly in love with me. I know you've been less into this than I have.'

'That was honest.'

'It's true though.'

'Look Georgia, I like you, you're a great girl. But I'll be honest, I guess I wasn't really looking for anything serious when I came on board.'

'I wasn't either. Eric told me about your ex. How you were trying to get over her so it's no big issue. I just wished you'd told me about her.'

'She wasn't an ex. How to put this? She was someone I met a couple of times.'

'She obviously meant something to you.'

'I guess. But honestly, I hardly knew her.'

'It's going to be weird not living here anymore. No more rocking floors. I'll be living on stable ground. How fucking weird is that?'

'You won't miss living on a boat. Trust me.'

'Maybe not. But anyway. I hope you find whatever it you're looking for.'

She kissed Johnny on the cheek, and then headed to her room, leaving him to finish his beer.

'Hey dude,' said Eric appearing moments later.

'Hey'

'So did you talk to her?'

'Eavesdropping were we?'

'Course not.'

'Yep. It's all good.'

'You guys are…?'

'Over. Yep. We were a few days ago. Not that we were really anything to start off with.'

'Dude it's going to be so fucking weird with no girl on the boat.'

'We still have Sue.'

'That's so fucking depressing, don't even say that!'

'Do you know if Dave's going to get anyone else to replace Georgia?'

'I think he's been interviewing a few people. Scary thing is I think Andrew's going to leave pretty soon.'

'How do you know that?'

'I don't know. A feeling I get. He's said a few things. I mean, come on, he's been on this boat more than all of us. He must have a whole heap of cash.'

'So Georgia told me you mentioned Rachel.'

'Who?'

'The girl I told you about.'

'Right, was I not meant to have done that? Sorry dude. It was a couple of nights back. We got drunk and she said she felt you weren't that into her so I told her. Hope that's OK?'

'It's fine. Not a big deal anymore.'

'Man, I would have so tried to get with her.'

'I know that.'

'I can't believe you weren't even that into her. Every guy on the boat would have loved to have been in your position. Probably not Andrew.'

'Why did you say that?'

'Dude, the guy is definitely gay.'

'You don't know that.'

'I've got a good gaydar.'

'I see. From personal experience?'

'No way. I like dudes, but not that much.' Eric laughed.

'Dave definitely fancied Georgia.'

'Oh Dave has the hots for every girl who comes on this boat, because he's married to Sue! Who could blame him!'

Eric stood up. He did this when he had a moment of inspiration. 'You want to get one of the kayaks and go out again?!'

'What? No. It's two in the morning.'

'Oh come on! The ocean's so calm. Everyone's asleep.'

'Just relax and stay on the boat Eric.'

'Come on!'

'Keep your voice down. Why do you do this? Make me do the most ridiculous things at the most ridiculous times.'

'You are so easy to convince.'

'Don't I know it.'

They walked to the back of the boat where they quietly went to unload two single man kayaks into the sea. They slipped on their life jackets, smoothly manoeuvered themselves into each kayak, then using their double-sided paddles, steered away from the boat. As Johnny moved his paddle into the sea, he looked down to see the green plankton which glowed in the dark; a spectacle they had shown to their guests earlier that evening.

When they were a good distance from the boat, they pushed the kayaks together and Eric took out a joint from a small waterproof bag.

'Oh so this is why you wanted to go kayaking?' Johnny beamed at Eric's predictability.

'Hell yeah!' Eric laughed at himself. 'Dude I can't smoke on the boat. Imagine if Sue caught me.'

'You know they can probably see the light from the spliff out here.'

'That's why you're going to be in front of me, to block out the light.'

'Loving your tactics.'

Eric took a couple of hits, then handed the spliff to Johnny. Johnny wasn't a big smoker. It was an occasional novelty. It wasn't long before he felt the usual mixture of hunger, giddiness and paranoia.

'Mate, why do you do this to me?' asked Johnny. 'I have the munchies now and there's no bloody food!'

'Which is why I bought supplies!' replied Eric enthusiastically bringing out a large bag of crisps.

Johnny's phone beeped in his pocket.

'Dude, you bought your phone out here!' Eric whooped.

'I didn't actually know I had it,' replied Johnny withdrawing the phone. There was a message from an unknown number which he opened. *'Hi Johnny. Hope you're well. Rachel x.'*

'Shit,' replied Johnny.

'What is it?'

'How fucking weird is this. It's a text from Rachel!'

'Who?'

'Rachel!'

'As in *the* Rachel?'

'Yes!'

'What does it say?'

Eric dropped his joint in the sea.

'Holy shit!' he fumed.

He went to grab it, lost his balance, grabbing Johnny's boat in the process, flipping them both over into the water.

'What the fuck Eric!' squirmed Johnny reaching the surface, swimming around in the sea, trying to turn his kayak back on its side.

'Sorry dude!' Eric said.

'My phone! Fuck!'

'You can't find it?!'

'No. It's in the bloody sea isn't it!'

Johnny ducked down below the surface to try and retrieve it but it was nowhere to be seen.

'Fuck this!' replied Johnny trying to get back in the boat. 'The water's fucking cold. Eric, what the hell!'

'I'm sorry dude. I don't know what happened!' said Eric, stoned, still finding the situation amusing while Johnny got back into his kayak.

'I'm fucking soaked Eric, and stoned!' retorted Johnny grabbing his oar. 'I'm heading back,' he said agitatedly beginning to paddle back to the main boat.

'Dude. It was an accident. Come on!' Eric said, paddling on after him.

They loaded the kayaks back onto the boat, taking their time, due to the lack of concentration affecting both of them, muttering minimal words to each other, before retiring to bed.

Johnny woke the following morning with the sun shining in his face through his cabin window. He walked out on the deck to see the green hills of the Bay of Islands surrounding him in the autumn morning sun. His throat was dry but he felt surprisingly perkier than expected. He walked downstairs where Andrew was preparing the guests' breakfasts.

'Morning mate!' said a buoyant Andrew. 'Stay up late did you last night?'

'You could say that. Lost my phone.'

'Oh no. How did you do that?'

'Got dropped in the sea. Long story.'

'Sounds it.'

Georgia appeared.

'Last breakfast. This is going to be emotional,' remarked Andrew. Georgia smiled and went to pour herself some coffee. She was never very communicative in the morning.

The boat's guests began to appear, including a group of four tanned Danish girls who sat down at one of the tables.

Eric appeared. 'Hey, sorry I'm late,' he said going to get some coffee from Georgia. Dave headed downstairs.

'Morning,' he said.

Andrew began cooking the bacon and the sausages.

'Johnny, Eric, you mind if I have a quick word?' said Dave.

'Sure,' replied Johnny

'In private,' said Dave.

The three of them headed to the back of the boat.

'Look I'm going to be honest with you. You woke Sue and I up last night taking the kayaks out, and well, she saw you smoking.'

Eric was about to reply but Dave quickly stopped him.

'Please don't lie. I found this on the deck by the kayaks this morning,' he replied, showing them a fully rolled up joint. 'You know taking the boats out at night to smoke when there's guests on board is totally against the rules.'

Eric and Johnny were speechless.

'Look you've been great,' said Dave. 'The both of you have, but well, I think what with Georgia heading off, and Andrew handing in his notice last night. We're going to have to ask you to leave in a few weeks.'

'Look Dave, we're really sorry,' replied Eric apologetically.

'Look it's not just the incident. I'll be honest with you. We're suffering pretty badly financially at the moment. I was going to tell you later on but it seems right informing you now. Sue and I, we're going to take a bit of time out. Close down the company. I'm sorry it has to end like this.'

Dave left leaving Johnny and Eric rankled by the news.

'Sorry dude,' said Eric.

'Eric, it's not your fault. I think it was a good excuse to get rid of us.'

They walked back to where breakfast was being prepared.

'Everything OK?' asked Georgia, sensing something was wrong.

'I'll tell you in a bit,' replied Johnny.

'Do you think it's true?' asked Eric. 'About the boat being in financial trouble?'

'I don't know,' added Johnny. 'What are you going to do?'

'Look for other work on a similar boat, if not, I'll head back to Hawaii.'

Later that morning Andrew, Eric and Georgia took the guests out to snorkel in the water, while Johnny remained on the boat using the time to check up on his emails on the boat computer where there was an unread message from Rachel.

SUBJECT: Hello
FROM: Rachel Hortley
<sparkly_rachelhortley@yahoo.com>
TO: Johnny Buxford
<johnny_buxford@hotmail.com>

Hi Johnny,

How are you? I feel rather stupid sending you this after the way I treated you back in Sydney. I don't know if you got my text message. Johnny I just feel so crappy about the way everything ended last time I saw you so I'm just going to be honest. When I met you on the Gili Isles, I was in a relationship. I have been seeing Ross on and off for about five years. I was travelling by myself when I met you with the intention of meeting up with him in Australia as we had both applied for our working holiday visas. I don't know why I didn't say anything. I guess I liked you and I didn't want to ruin that night we had together. I left my number in your travel book because I wanted to give you the option that if you did come to Sydney you would hopefully look me up to see if I was there. I had an amazing day at the zoo. Ross was meant to be away that weekend visiting friends. I had no idea he was going to be there. It's no excuse. I felt awful when you left. Things haven't been good between me and Ross for a while. We argue a lot. Which is why I wanted to tell you, we split up last month. I'm living in Melbourne now which is cool. Still waitressing. Boo! But I feel good. Anyway, my dad is coming to visit me in September. I have no idea where you are, but if you're still in Australia around then, it would be great to meet up. I understand if you don't want anything to do with me. Just let me know.

Rachel x

SUBJECT: RE: Hello
FROM: Johnny Buxford
<johnny_buxford@hotmail.com>
TO: Rachel Hortley
<sparkly_rachelhortley@yahoo.com>

Hi Rachel,

Thanks for the message. I did receive your text last night but somehow managed to drop my phone in the sea. I now have no one's number. I am not in Oz anymore, but got a job on a boat in New Zealand. It's been busy but fun. However, we just got told this morning our jobs are ending so I'm heading off soon. I'm sorry to hear things have finished with you and Ross. I do wish you would have told me you were seeing someone. It hurt when I dropped you off at your flat and he was there. I couldn't say anything and I felt humiliated. It took me a while to get over that. I don't know if I can fly over to Melbourne when your dad comes. Let me know dates nearer the time and we can take it from there.

Johnny

Johnny pondered over why he had replied. He wasn't sure if he had forgiven Rachel for her behaviour in Sydney, but somehow, at the back of his mind, he knew he had to see her again.

Melbourne, Australia

After their dismissal from the boat, Eric returned to Hawaii where he planned to get another job on a tourist boat, while Johnny decided to see the rest of New Zealand. After three months of drinking, doing odd jobs and taking part in a variety of winter sports, Johnny decided to get a plane over to Melbourne to meet Rachel.

With its tall skyscrapers, trams and stylish streets filled with inviting bars and trendy coffee houses he liked what he saw of Melbourne. After dropping of his bags at a cheap hostel he headed down to the Southbank where he stopped for a beer at one of the bars by the river. He grabbed a table where he watched office workers grabbing a quick drink after work enjoying the start of spring. It wasn't long before he realised the time and made a dash over to Flinders Street Station where he caught a tram out to the St Kilda district of the city where he was meeting Rachel at a Subway outlet where she was now working.

When he arrived Rachel was hard at work serving a group of young couples. He admired the way she worked, with an optimistic manner, the sort of girl who would perk you up on a bad day. He had not known how he was going to feel meeting her, but seeing her again, he knew he had made the right decision.

'Just going to change,' Rachel said spotting with a welcoming smile, heading into the back room to change out of her work clothes.

She appeared minutes later wearing a black t-shirt, Ray-Ban sunglasses and jeans.

'That was quick.'

'I'm a quick dresser.'

'Have a good one,' replied her boss from the back of the store.

'So, you're here!' she said excitedly as they headed out onto the street into the evening sun.

'I am. So how's Subway treating you?'

'I continually smell of cheese, but I like it. I'm sorry to hear about your job on the boat.'

'Yeah it was pretty rubbish.'

'Giving you a week's notice, that's pretty poo.'

'Hey, I got to travel.'

'You did. And I want to hear all about it. How was it? I really want to go to New Zealand. You do realize I'm insanely jealous of these trips you keep doing!'

'So, are you missing Sydney?'

'Er….in a way. I mean Melbourne's cool. There's loads of bars here and the food's great. I mean the weather's not as good but it's definitely more liveable and a hell of a lot cheaper. God Sydney was expensive.'

'So what's the plan for tonight?'

'OK. So my dad's arriving around seven-ish. There's a support band on beforehand, so I thought we could go grab some food at the bar, that sound alright?'

'Definitely.'

'They do these amazing burgers. You like burgers, right?'

'Meat is my forte.'

She laughed. 'I never had you down as a veggie.'

They walked off the main road, down a side street to a corner building where the The Crickle Bar was, an indoor themed outback bar, with a stage at the back for live acts.

'So what do you want?' asked Rachel.

'No. I'll get these.'

'Put your wallet away. You've come to visit me. My treat.'

'OK then. I'll have a schooner of lager.'

'Any kind?'

'Surprise me.'

'Deal.'

'I'll go grab a table.'

Johnny found one at the back of the bar near the stage, next to a wall which had a desert landscape painted on it.

Rachel appeared with their drinks shortly after.

'Cheers. Good to see you again,' she said clinking her glass against his and sipping her drink. 'So I firstly want to say I'm sorry. I know I wrote most of the stuff in the email, but I just wanted to say it was totally ridiculous of me to meet up with you, then ask you back to my flat and then not tell you about Ross. I mean he wasn't supposed to be there. Even if he was, I don't know why I did it. I have the tendency to act really stupidly sometimes. I felt so embarrassed over the whole incident. And I know how humiliating it must have been for you.'

'It was. I'm not going to lie. But I'm here now. So let's just move forward.'

A man approached them in his late fifties with a beer belly and a grey ponytail, wearing a black waistcoat over a white t-shirt, blue jeans and an earring in one ear.

'Dad!' Rachel's face lit up with glee as she went to hug him.

'Hello darling,' he said, with a hint of a West Midlands accent.

'So. I want you to meet my friend. This is Johnny.'

'Well hello sir,' he replied going to shake his hand. 'Good of you to come.'

'I'm looking forward to seeing you guys play,' said Johnny.

'If you want to watch a group of old fogies rocking some tunes then you're in for a treat! Now what are you guys having?'

'I think we're good,' said Johnny,

'Nonsense. A couple of more beers?'

'Well OK then,' replied Johnny.

'Thanks Dad,' Rachel said as he walked off to the bar.

Rachel turned to her father's friend, a bald man of similar age wearing a black waistcoat who was standing next to them 'Hey Alan. How are you?'

'All good love,' he replied with a croaky cockney accent. Johnny could tell he wasn't much of a speaker.

The other two members of the band were sat on a table close by. Rachel walked over with Alan to speak to them briefly before returning with her father and their drinks.

'Dad, Mum says you need to email her. She says you've been rubbish staying in contact.'

'Well she's probably right, but you know how it is. We've been busy love.' He quickly changed the subject. 'I heard you and Ross broke up.'

'We did.'

'That's a shame. He liked the band.'

'Can we not talk about it?'

'No. We don't have to.'

'So when are you heading back to the UK?' asked Johnny.

'Well, we've got a few gigs left down here, one more in Adelaide, then we're heading over to The States for a month. So not for a while.'

'Well it must be great having such a good fan base everywhere,' Johnny remarked.

'I'll be honest. We're not as big as we used to be. People move on, they grow up. But I'm telling you, a place like this, ten years ago, we'd have sold out.'

'You're still really popular Dad,' Rachel added.

'We do alright. I keep trying to tell your mum that but she won't have it. She's always seen me as a failure. But I love music. This is what I was put on the Earth to do. She doesn't understand the fact we're more popular in other countries than we are back home.'

'She doesn't think you're a failure.'

'If she'd had her way she'd have wanted me to go into bloody teaching years ago!' He drank from his beer. 'But what the hell, it's lovely to be back here in Melbourne. I love this part of the world and I'm very lucky to be here.'

They sat there talking for half an hour before he left to set up his act with the other band members. When it was their moment on stage, he bought on a guitar and stool which he sat on, while the other members got ready around him.

'Well good evening Melbourne,' he said into his microphone when they were ready to go.

There were a few cheers from the audience.

'We feel very honoured to be playing here tonight and we're always made to feel very welcome when we come here. And, as an added bonus, I've got my beautiful daughter here tonight at the back of the room. I'm a lucky old man. So here we go. We're going to start with one of our early tracks that got us our first few gigs in America.'

Rachel's dad started playing a relaxed piece which impressed Johnny. He was expecting him to sound dated and uninspiring, but instead he had an emotional and original style of music which created a reflective mood in the room which was quickly interrupted by a familiar figure walking towards the bar.

'Shit,' said Rachel.

'What is it?' asked Johnny.

'Ross is here.'

'What? Ross as in?'

'Yes. My ex. He's supposed to be in Sydney.'

She turned back to watch her father, trying her best to ignore the situation.

'I'm going to go speak to him,' she announced.

'Want me to come with you?' asked Johnny.

'No. Don't. Just stay here.'

She walked to the bar while Johnny remained in the audience.

'Hi,' she said approaching Ross who was now standing ready to order a drink by the bar with a friend who she recognized from school.

'Hey. Come to see your dad?' asked Ross.

'I have. I thought you were still in Sydney?'

'I am. I flew down yesterday. Your dad invited me a while ago.'

'You flew down from Sydney to see my dad?'

'Rachel you remember Steve,' he said turning to his friend.

'Sure. You went to Highfields right?'

The friend gave a nod.

'Well he lives in Melbourne,' said Ross. 'I came down to see him for the weekend and thought we'd come see your father play.'

'I see. No other motive?'

'What do you mean?'

'Forget it,' replied Rachel, unconvinced by his answer.

'So are you seeing each other again?' Ross said noticing Johnny in the audience.

'No. We're just friends,' Rachel said, annoyed by the fact she felt she had to justify herself. 'Look if you've come to see my dad then that's fine, but if there's another reason, I think you should go.'

'No other reason.'

'Fine. Well it's nice to see you,' she said giving a civil smile before heading back to Johnny.

'All sorted?' asked Johnny.

'Sure. He says he's here to watch my dad play.'

'You believe him?'

'I'm trying to.'

Rachel's father's first song came to an end and was met with loud applause from the audience.

'Now this second track is a slightly more upbeat song for you. One of our favourites.' He began playing a pacier track which lifted up the energy in the room. Rachel noticed that Ross and his friend had moved closer towards them.

'I'm going to get another drink. You want one?' asked Johnny.

'Sure. Another beer. Just watch out for Ross. OK?'

'What's he going to do?'

'Just watch yourself. He can be erratic at times.'

Johnny meandered through the crowds to the bar where he ordered two more schooners and quickly sensed someone behind him.

'Johnny isn't it?' asked Ross.

'Yes.' Johnny turned to face him. 'Ross right?' Their eyes met. It already felt confrontational but Johnny was determined not to feel intimidated by him.

'Ten dollars fifty,' replied the barman handing him his drinks.

Johnny passed his money over.

'Six years we'd have been going out next weekend,' said Ross standing next to him. 'We met at college you see. She was everything to me. Then she goes off travelling by herself in Indonesia. Comes to live with me in Australia and just something seems different. Then she brings this guy back to the flat, when I'm meant to be out of town. She claims they're just friends. I don't believe her, but you know, I go along with it. It's awkward, he leaves, then we end up arguing a lot after than and then not long after she breaks up with me. Seem familiar?'

'Look I have nothing to do with why your relationship ended. We're just friends, alright mate?' replied Johnny.

'I'm not your mate.'

Ross' friend was now standing close to Johnny.

'Ross. I'm going.' Johnny stepped away from the bar and as he did Ross lifted his foot causing Johnny to trip and fall to the ground. Both beers poured onto the floor and onto people's shoes. Johnny quickly stood up and at that moment he felt a hard painful fist jab into his stomach. He would never admit it but aged twenty-eight it was the first time he'd been punched before. Another punch came which was more painful than the first. All Johnny could think of was how humiliating it was to have people watching him. He felt another jab, this time against his face. He could taste and smell the blood from his lip and all he could do was allow himself to fall to the ground and black out.

He gained consciousness moments later. The room lights were on and there were shadows of people hovering above him. He could sense Rachel next to him.

'He's fine. He's fine, really,' she was telling people.

'Where's he now?' said a local man. 'The guy that hit him. Hell of a punch. They kept going right at him. Bloody kids.'

'Johnny, you OK?' asked Rachel.

He managed to nod as the paramedics arrived to clean up his lip and take him to the hospital to stitch up a cut by his eye. He still had pain in his ribs which he was told was bruising. When they were finished, a policeman arrived to ask if he wanted to press charges, but Johnny declined as he didn't want the hassle of stressing Rachel out.

'You can press charges if you want. I don't mind. He deserves to be punished,' Rachel had told him.

'I've made my mind up. Look good, don't I?'

'You'll look fine in no time. So you're staying at mine tonight.'

'No. I've got the hostel booked.'

'Don't argue with me.'

They got a taxi back to her apartment. A two bed flat above a pizza restaurant in St Kilda.

'So I guess that put an end to your dad's gig?' Johnny remarked.

'I'm sure he'll survive.'

'Where is your dad?'

'He went to track down Ross. I don't know if he got him. I doubt it. I think he saw him in a different light tonight. I always felt like he never believed all the bad stuff I used to say about him. Ross didn't really have much of a father figure growing up and he always looked up to my dad. They both liked music and I think in a way my dad saw him like another son.'

They trotted up the stairs to the flat and entered the living room. Johnny could tell Rachel was living with someone older. The flat was filled with good quality furniture and mature framed worldly artwork.

'Is your housemate in?' asked Johnny.

'Zoe, no, she's away on a school trip in Hobart, so you've got her room. I'm making some tea. You want some?'

'Just water please.'

He sat down on the sofa. He felt relaxed. It was the first time he'd actually sat down in someone's living room in a long time.

The doorbell went. Rachel's body tensed up.

'Should I answer that?' asked Rachel.

'I'm sure it's fine.'

Rachel walked down the stairs while Johnny listened in.

'No luck love.' He heard her father's voice at the door. 'He's obviously done a runner. Where's your friend?'

'He's upstairs.'

'Yeah, we just wanted to make sure everything was OK with the young lad,' said her father appearing at the top of the stairs. 'Alright son. How are you holding up?'

'A bit bruised, but I'll survive.' Johnny replied.

'He needed stitches,' commented Rachel

'Well. I bought you a little something.' He handed him a bottle of whisky. 'Might help ease the pain.'

'Johnny's not pressing charges,' Rachel remarked.

'Well. If you feel that's right.'

'Do you want a drink Dad?'

'No. I've got to be off soon love. We're leaving early in the morning. Sorry I couldn't have been more help. Good thing you broke up with him, behaving like that.'

'He hurt Johnny, he ruined your evening. What an arsehole,' replied Rachel.

Her father went to shake Johnny's hand.

'Thanks for the whisky,' said Johnny.

'Least I can do.'

'I'll take you to the door,' said Rachel accompanying him back down the stairs.

She appeared moments later.

'You OK?' Johnny asked her.

'Sure. I don't know why he bought you whisky. Do you even like whisky?'

'Not particularly. But it's the thought that counts. I like your dad.'

'I wish I saw him more. But anyway.'

'Thank you.'

He got up and walked towards her.

'Oh my God, look at you,' she said examining his bruises, putting her hand to his cheek.

'Despite everything, the painfully bruised ribs, the battered face, I'm pleased we met up tonight,' Johnny said.

'I'm glad.' Rachel went to kiss him, held his arm, and pulled him in the direction of her bedroom door.

Great Ocean Road, Victoria, Australia

'So tell me you've got some good music to play?' Rachel asked Johnny as they headed south west on the M1 motorway out of Melbourne.

'Of course. Got the definitive Great Ocean Road Playlist,' said Johnny.

'Cool. Put it on.'

The track 'Walking on Sunshine' by Katrina and the Waves came on the playlist.

'Oh my god I haven't heard this in ages!' said Rachel.

'Gets us into the mood of things.'

'Damn right,' she replied, jamming the lever into fifth gear which made a loud clunking sound.

'You alright there?'

'Shut up! I'm not used to driving this thing!' She laughed. 'OK so which one of these washes the windscreen?' Rachel asked observing the many switches and buttons surrounding the steering wheel.

'Hang on you might want to close the windows before you…!'

But Rachel had already pressed the lever on the left hand side of the steering wheel, forcing the window cleaning solution to spray half onto the window and half through the sunroof, sprinkling them both in their seats.

'Sorry!' she replied.

'That can be the shower I missed this morning,' Johnny remarked.

Rachel laughed. 'I'm not used to car switches and I haven't driven in about two years and this is the first time I've driven abroad so leave me alone.'

'They do drive on the same side of the road out here, you do know that?'

'I don't find driving that easy. It took me six attempts to pass my test.'

'That's a comforting thought.'

'Alright, how many times did you take to pass?'

'One.'

'Well they say the best drivers pass on their second, don't they?'

'What do they say about people who pass on their sixth?'

Rachel put her hand on the car window washer control. 'Do you want me to press this again?'

'I think you could do with another wash this morning.'

'You're so bloody cheeky! Right mister. Where are these directions?'

Johnny looked at his travel book. 'We're going the right way. We just need to head along this road until we get to Geelong, then head south down to Torquay and I think that's where the road starts.'

'I can't believe we're doing this. This is so cool. So what does the leaflet say?'

'What leaflet?'

'The Great Ocean Road leaflet. The one that Zoe gave you, and I want to know what's good to see.'

He grabbed the leaflet from his rucksack and opened it, displaying a map of the area with pictures of the different sights they could see along the route.

'So you want to hear a bit of history?' asked Johnny.

'Yep.'

'OK,' said Johnny reading from the leaflet. 'So the Great Ocean Road was built by approximately three thousand returned servicemen as a war memorial for the fellow servicemen who had been killed in the First World War. '

'See. I didn't know that.'

'Construction was done by hand, using explosives, picks and shovels, wheelbarrows and some small machinery. It opened in 1932.'

'Cool. So where are we stopping first?'

'Looks like the Split Point Lighthouse might be a good place to start off with, maybe grab a coffee there?'

'Sounds good. How far is that?'

'Couple of hours'

'Perfect.' She looked at the thermometer displayed on the dashboard. 'Oh my God, twenty-five degrees already. By the way we are going swimming in the sea later, right? I hope you bought swimming wear?'

'Of course.'

'Cotton Eye Joe' by Rednex began to play on Johnny's playlist.

'I need to veto this song,' said Rachel.

'Nope.'

'Why not?'

'It's too late.'

'I claim a veto!'

'Vetoes must be done within the first two seconds of the song.'

'That's not fair. I said that within the first two seconds and I didn't know the rules of the games.'

'Tough luck.'

Rachel pressed the windscreen washer control causing spray to come through the sunroof again.

'Ah, how rude!' yelped Johnny.

'Serves you right. Making the rules unfair. Now change the track or you're getting sprinkled again!'

'Alright, you win.'

They arrived at the lighthouse shortly after midday, pulling up into the cramped and busy car park.

'Why is it so packed? It's only a weekday,' said Rachel, stopping the car. 'OK get out.'

'Why?'

'I don't want you to see my parking.'

'Why not?'

'Because it makes me feel self-conscious. Just go. Walk.'

'Well even more reason to help you.'

'No, I'll get embarrassed, just go grab a coffee, and I'll see you up there.'

'Fine,' said Johnny giving in, and walking up the hill to a white colonial style building.

'Successful parking?' Johnny asked as she appeared ten minutes later.

'Of course.' Rachel sat down at the table he had found outside.

'Thanks for the tea.'

'No worries. So you didn't scrape any other cars?'

'No. My parking was fine I'll have you know.' She lay back on her chair and sipped her drink. 'So nice to get out of the city.'

'Your housemate's still cool with me staying right?' asked Johnny.

'Sure. Why shouldn't she be?'

'I haven't really paid rent since I arrived.'

'Well you haven't been working.'

'I've been there a few months now.'

'She's totally cool about stuff like that. But she likes you and she knows it's only temporary. It's all good. Maybe cook for her sometime.'

'Do you really want me to do that? That may be the catalyst for her asking me to leave.'

Rachel laughed. 'OK. Maybe take her out for food sometime.'

After they had finished their drinks they walked up to the lighthouse to find it was closed to the public.

'Oh that's annoying. Hey you know this lighthouse was in that kids' show right? *Round the Twist*,' Johnny said. 'They mentioned it in the leaflet.'

'I used to watch that show so much when I was a kid. And the theme tune was *so* good.'

'Yeah, I remember that,' said Johnny, reciting the tune. 'Have you ever, ever felt like this, when strange things happen. Are you going round the twist?'

'Hey I remember that too! I expect that to be on the car playlist.'

'I think you may just have to put up with my own version instead.'

They walked down some steps to an observation deck which looked out onto the rugged coastline of the Bass Strait.

'OK. Picture time,' said Johnny getting out his camera.

'No. I hate having my photo taken.'

'Why?'

'I look ugly.'

'Come on. Quit your moaning,' he said, moving her into position with the ocean view behind her. 'You ready?' he asked, putting his finger on the camera switch.

Rachel relaxed as he took the photo.

'Nice photo,' Johnny looking back at it.

'Let's see,' she said going to look at it. 'I don't have any boobs.'

'What? Course you do.'

'I don't.'

'The photo's staying. You look amazing as you always do.'

'You want one?' asked Rachel.

'I'll get one later on in the day.'

'Well that's hardly fair!'

'It's my camera.'

The temperature was thirty-five degrees by the time they arrived at Apollo Bay; a small tourist town set an hour's drive further west down the coast. They parked up by the side of the road, got their bags and beach towels from the boot of the car, then headed onto the sand.

'Fuck. It's cold,' said Johnny entering the water in his swimming shorts.

'It's fine once you get in. It's still spring remember,' said Rachel who was already fully immersed in the water enjoying the large waves crashing towards her. Johnny ducked under and his body shook as the coldness embraced him.

'Come here. Warm me up,' he said to Rachel, who swam over and kissed him briefly, before another wave crashed into them.

'Right. I'm heading out. I'm hungry,' remarked Rachel.

'Jam sandwiches. Very primary school,' commented Johnny unwrapping the tinfoil of Rachel's sandwiches, passing them over.

'They're good sandwiches.'

He unwrapped two cheese and ham rolls which Rachel had prepared for him earlier.

'Before you eat. I need more suntan cream on my back,' Rachel said.

'Jesus. You're demanding.'

'I don't want to burn.'

Johnny got out the sun cream from the bag and sprayed her back. 'You've got a very sexy back,' he commented.

Rachel didn't reply, but smiled, cherishing his comment.

After lunch, they lay in the sun, where Johnny turned to Rachel, who was dosing, and picked up a small pebble from the sand and placed it in her belly button.

'Hey!' said Rachel laughing, moving it away.

He placed another pebble in the same place.

'Stop it!'

He ignored her, placing a small pile in her belly button which she left for a while before brushing off.

It was mid afternoon when they reached The Twelve Apostles where they walked briefly around the small visitors centre, then took the path under the road towards the observation deck to take photos of the different rock stacks which stood out on the ocean, a small distance away from the mainland.

They took the steps down to the beach below the cliffs and walked along the sand, which was sheltered from the warm sun.

'Rachel I want to ask you something. If I left Melbourne, to carry on travelling, what would you say about coming with me?'

'That came out of nowhere.'

'This was only going to be a temporary thing. I only planned to see you for a few days and then here we are. Two months later.'

'Why don't you stay in Melbourne?'

'What and stay with your housemate rent free?'

'Get a holiday visa. Work here. You can get a flat.'

'I want to carry on travelling.'

'I forgot. The arrows in the travel book.'

'They've gone slightly off course recently. You remember Eric who I met on the boat in New Zealand?'

'The American guy?'

'Yeah. Well he's back in Hawaii and he said I could visit him if I wanted. I was actually thinking about going after this. You could come with me?'

'*Blue Hawaii*. You know the film with Elvis Presley?'

'I don't think I ever saw that film.'

'My dad was a fan. Ever since I saw that as a kid I always wanted to go there. Always used to watch it on rainy Sunday afternoons.'

'Well now's your chance.'

She smiled at the idea.

'Will you think about it, at least?' he asked.

'Sure,' she said, before walking ahead, dipping her feet into the water and looking out at the warm glow setting on the ocean in the distance.

He knew at times she wasn't one for many words, especially when making decisions.

They sat in silence on the drive back to Melbourne.

'Shit' said Rachel looking at the dashboard. 'We're running out of petrol.'

'How much is left?'

'The light's showing. It's right at the bottom. I didn't even notice it until now. I'm so stupid!'

'Look we might find a petrol station near by.'

'We're in the middle of nowhere Johnny!'

'Let's just keep going at a steady rate, keep it in a higher gear, keep the fuel consumption low.'

They sat on the edge of their seats for the next twenty minutes until the car conked out on a country road.

'This is so not happening!' seethed Rachel.

'Let's just keep calm. We'll sort something out.'

'I'm going to have to phone Zoe and she's going to think I'm a right idiot!'

Johnny retrieved a map attempting to figure out where they were.

'Hey it's me…' said Rachel on her phone to Zoe. 'I've done something stupid. I've run out petrol. I know. Great. I'll give them a call. What's the number?'

Johnny got out a pen from the car and handed it to her and she wrote the down the number on her arm.

'I know this is so stupid. Alright. Thanks. Bye.' She hung up and turned to Johnny. 'OK so she says she's got breakdown cover.'

'Well that's something.'

'How are we going to let them know where we are?'

At that moment a small pickup truck came around the corner which Johnny stood out on the road to flag down.

'Hi there,' said the large leathery skinned woman driving it, wearing a large baggy food stained Minnie Mouse t-shirt, shorts and sandals.

'Sorry to stop you, but we've run out of petrol.'

'You're in luck.'

'What? You've got petrol?'

'Yeah. Good thing I drove by. This is my husband's car, and he always has some in the back.'

'Can we give you some money?' asked Johnny.

'Just give me ten dollars,' she said grabbing the canister off the back. 'This should keep you going until you hit the next gas station. Have you got some paper to use as a filter?'

'Ah…we've got a leaflet.' Rachel got out the Great Ocean Road guide while Johnny went to pull the lever below the driver's seat to open the petrol tank.

'It's open!' replied the woman.

Johnny went to grab the map and folded it so it could be used as a filter, allowing the woman to pour the fuel in.

'Where are you guys heading?' she asked.

'Melbourne. We've just been on the Great Ocean Road.'

'Good day for it.' She emptied the canister into the vehicle. 'There you go. All done.'

'Thank you. You're a lifesaver,' replied Johnny, handing her the cash.

'No worries.'

'Well, good luck,' she said walking back to her truck and driving off.

'What were the chances of that happening?' said Johnny turning to Rachel.

Rachel smiled. 'That was so totally random.' They both got into the car, and put on their seatbelts. Rachel turned on the ignition, then suddenly turned it off.

'What's wrong?' he asked

'I'll do it.'

'Do what?'

'I'll leave Melbourne with you.'

'That came out of nowhere.'

'I know.'

'Are you sure?'

'Yes. I think so. Yes. Why the hell not. Let's carry on following those arrows in your travel book'

He put his hand on her thigh and kissed her. 'You won't regret this,' he said, 'you really won't.'

Hawaii, USA

Johnny looked out onto the light blue tropical ocean as he sat next to Rachel on the small domestic plane taking them from Honolulu to Kona International Airport.

The moment Johnny got off the plane on the Big Island he could tell the geography was different from Oahu. The ground was made up of brown volcanic rock with little in the way of vegetation, giving a desolate and alien feel to the surroundings. The airport itself was much more provincial and Johnny could see why Eric had chosen the Big Island as his home; he liked a quieter life.

Eric was waiting for them by the baggage collection area after they landed.

'Hey!' said Eric, heading over to Johnny to give him a hug.

'Hello mate,' replied Johnny. 'This is Rachel.'

'Nice to meet you,' said Eric going to shake her hand.

'You too,' she replied.

They collected their bags from the baggage reclaim area and headed out into the airport car park to find Eric's dented black open top Jeep.

'It's funny,' said Johnny. 'I always assumed you'd have a 4x4.'

'Well, you know me too well my friend.'

'So how was Waikiki?' asked Eric as he drove off.

'Amazing,' said Johnny. 'I think we're a little bit in love with Hawaii.'

'Hey man. It's a cool place. So what did you guys do there?'

'We had three nights in a hostel. Booked a double room for thirty dollars a night. It was right by the beach. Owned by a Frenchman and his American wife. It was really sociable. I miss it.'

'Well you've got lots to see here too. It's way more chilled than Oahu.'

'So have you got a job on a boat again?'

'Just south of Kona. It's a tourist boat that takes people out diving. Pretty much the same thing we did back in NZ but the tourists go home each day, so it's way less intense.'

'What, you mean to say you don't miss all that cooking and cleaning?'

'Hell no!'

'No moody boss' wife?'

'Nope!' Eric laughed.

'Sounds boring.' Johnny turned to Rachel. 'So our boss in New Zealand had a wife who pretty much got us sacked.'

'Yeah, you told me about that.'

'Speaking of which,' replied Eric, 'the Manta Ray Bay Cruise, like, totally went under. I think Dave and Sue went bankrupt.'

'Well. I guess Dave wasn't bullshitting about the finances being poo. I guess we left at a good time.'

'I think we did dude. So you guys hungry?'

'I could eat. Rachel?'

'Sure, that sounds good.'

'So there's this really great restaurant just up the road from where I live. We can drop off your bags then head down.'

'Sounds good to me,' replied Johnny.

'So I spoke to Suzi,' said Eric.

'Oh right. How is she?'

'Who's Suzi?' asked Rachel.

'Oh. Eric's cousin,' Johnny added. 'She was the one I met on the trek I did from Cairns. In fact, she was the one who got us in touch with each other.'

'Hell yeah,' said Eric.

'I don't think you've mentioned her before,' said Rachel

'Really? I thought I did.' Johnny turned to Eric, changing the subject. 'So is she teaching back in LA now?'

'I think so. She wants to see you. I don't know if you guys plan on going out there at some point?'

'I think we are going to go to California. If I can persuade Rachel.'

'I could be up for that,' replied Rachel.

'I forced her to leave Melbourne.'

'You didn't force me. I said I'd go.'

'So what did you think of Melbourne?' Eric asked Rachel.

'I really liked it. It's more liveable than Sydney, but the weather isn't as nice.'

'I hear there's rivalry between the two cities?'

'Yeah, but they're totally different.'

'So this place is a bit different from Honolulu, right?' asked Eric.

'Yeah, it looks like something out of *Star Trek*, with all the black rock,' said Johnny.

'So the Big Island gets affected a lot by the volcano. This side of the island's really dry and rocky, whereas the other side is really green, has a whole load of rainforest. You guys want to go see the volcano, right?'

'Yeah. Definitely. Don't you have to get a boat to see the crater?' said Johnny.

'Not the way we're going to do it!'

'OK. What does that mean? You got a crazy adventure set up for us Eric?'

'So I know this guy, who basically takes you to the park after hours, when it's really dark, and gets you like insanely close to the crater.'

'Wow. Is that safe?' asked Rachel

'To be honest, probably not, but I spoke to a couple of friends who went there a few weeks ago and they said they had the most amazing experience. I saw their photos, and the lava was like, right in front of the camera.'

'Did it melt the lens?' asked Johnny

'Pretty much!' laughed Eric.

They arrived at Eric's flat which stood at the top of a hill on a small residential street just south on Kona, the largest town on the west side of the island. The flat consisted of a large ground living room covered in surfing pictures, two bedrooms, a dated bathroom and a large patio area.

'So are you pleased you moved back?' asked Johnny.

'Yeah. I think I've found my love for Hawaii again. I got over my island fever.'

He went to open up the door to a small spare room where he had blown up a mattress to make a double bed.

'You guys are in here. So you want to go grab some food?' asked Eric.

'Sounds like a plan,' replied Johnny.

They drove to The Crab Tree restaurant which was situated on the closest bay to Eric's house where they got a table outside with a view of the sun setting on the ocean.

'Wow, cool view,' said Rachel.

'Hey Eric,' said a chirpy blond waitress approaching the table.

'Hey Jamie. So these are my friends from England. Johnny and Rachel.'

'Hey Eric's friends from England,' she said, handing them menus. 'Can I get you guys a drink?

'Sure. I'll have a beer,' said Eric.

'Make that two please,' said Johnny.

'Three,' announced Rachel.

'Sure. A Newcastle?' she asked.

'That would be great. Thanks,' said Eric, giving her a flirtatious smile.

'So Johnny said you got him sacked. Is this true?' Rachel asked Eric.

'What?' replied Johnny, shocked by her bluntness. 'I didn't say that.'

'Yes you did. No offence Eric I just wanted to hear your side of the story.'

'Honestly. I kind of did. Making you smoke in the kayak.'

'Hey I could have said no, and I didn't. It's hard to say no to this guy. He has an infectious way of leading you astray. He's the kid your mother always warned you to stay away from.'

'I merely make life more exciting.'

'Very true.'

They arrived back at the flat later that night feeling tipsy. A girl around Eric's age was waiting outside his front door.

'Hey, what's up?' said Eric said as he got out of the car and walked to the apartment.

'Hey. You know your cellphone's switched off,' she replied.

'Oh fuck,' said Eric. 'You were like, totally coming over tonight. I'm sorry. God, I totally forgot.'

'Ye-ah.'

'I'm sorry. So these are my friends I told you about. Johnny, Rachel, this is Colleen.'

'Hi guys. Shall I come over another night maybe?' Colleen asked Eric.

'No, don't do that. Come in.'

When Johnny and Rachel got into the porch they could see her more clearly. She was a slim, wore glasses and dressed maturely for her age.

'How was school?' asked Eric opening the door.

'Not great. My kids are insane. I'm a teacher, you can probably tell. It's been a crazy day. So you must be the guy Eric worked on the boat with in New Zealand?'

'Yep, that's me,' said Johnny.

'Welcome to Hawaii. Which restaurant did you guys go to?'

'The Crab Tree' replied Eric.

'That's like the best restaurant ever. You like it?' said Colleen.

'Yeah, the seafood was pretty amazing,' said Rachel.

'It's the best. So what are you guys up to while you're here?' replied Colleen.

'They're coming on the boat with me,'

'His crew are totally adorable,' she commented.

'You should come with us?' Eric said.

'Really? OK. I was going to do a whole load of work but you know what, I think that can wait till Sunday. Besides, it's gonna be awesome weather.'

'Isn't the weather awesome most days here?' said Johnny.

'The weather can be cloudy on the Big Island,' said Colleen.

'And then we're going to head to the volcano,' said Eric.

'With that crazy lava guy you know? I take it Eric has told you about him.'

'We got the lowdown,' said Johnny.

'He sounds insane,' said Colleen.

'So I take it you won't be joining us for the volcano adventure?' asked Eric.

'I'm undecided. Ask me tomorrow,' she replied.

The next morning they arrived at the port where the boat Eric worked on was docked. The boat headed south along the coast then pulled into a bay surrounded by lush hills where it anchored.

The guests assembled into a huddle where they were given a safety briefing before they split into teams of divers and snorkelers.

Johnny went with the team of snorkelers, Rachel joined Eric with the divers, while Colleen remained on the boat to sunbathe.

The divers headed out to sea for an eighteen-metre dive by an old shipwreck, while the snorkelers swam to shallower water by the coastline.

'See anything?' asked Colleen after Rachel had returned from her trip.

'Saw a few turtles.'

'So do you dive much?'

'Yeah. When I can. I used to go scuba diving a lot on holidays in Egypt when I was younger.'

'You should come out here and get a job as a diving instructor.'

'That would be amazing.'

'So how long have you and Johnny been dating?'

'A few months.'

'Really? You guys seem like you've been going out forever. How did you meet?'

'In Indonesia.'

'Wow. That's different. I had a friend who went to Bali. That's in Indonesia, right?'

'Yeah.'

'She said it was amazing though she had food poisoning for like a week.'

'Bali Belly. That sucks. We met in the Gili Isles which are pretty close to Bali.'

'I've not heard of them. I need to travel more. I went to England once in February. It was so rainy and cold.'

'Yeah, England in February, probably not the best time to go. How did you and Eric meet?'

'Oh. In a bar. I was drunk. He's so not my type but anyway, it works, in a weird kind of way.'

'Are you from Hawaii originally?'

'No. Iowa. Nothing happens in Iowa. So I went to school in Honolulu, then I got this job over here on Big Island, and it's like a totally different way of life out here, which I love.'

'I can imagine. What's the school you work in like?'

'The high school? Yeah it's small, but good.'

Eric came on board. 'Hey. Think I might have seen a tiger shark.'

'Oh my God, does that not freak you out?' replied Colleen.

'Well, I'm not like a hundred per cent sure,' said Eric. 'It was like way in the distance.'

'So I was saying to Rachel, she should totally get a job out here. She just needs to convince Johnny and we're all set,' said Colleen.

'I don't think Johnny is prepared to settle down anytime soon,' replied Rachel.

The boat left the bay and headed back to the port.

'So I've just spoken to the guy I told you about who's taking us to the volcano tonight and he's totally up for it,' said Eric, finishing a call on his phone back at the apartment. He turned to Colleen. 'Are you coming?'

'When you say we're going to the volcano, what does that mean? Like, how close are we talking?'

'Like, really close. Like as close as the neighbour's yard.'

'It sounds mental, but I'm up for it,' said Johnny joining Eric's side. 'Rachel?'

'OK, I'm in,' replied Rachel.

Johnny looked at Colleen. 'Are you sure we can't convince you?'

'The teacher in me is telling me this is a bad idea, but I don't really want to be the one who misses out on all the fun, so I'm blaming you if anything happens to us.' She gave Eric an authoritative look.

'OK. We're doing this. I'll go phone my cousin, he's out of town but I've got a key so hopefully we can stay at his,' said Eric.

After they got the go ahead from Eric's cousin they packed and left the apartment an hour later driving the two-hour journey to the other side of the island to the small town of Hilo. His cousin's house was a small detached bungalow situated at the top of the hill in the suburbs above the town with an impressive view of the bay.

Their tour guide, Bevin, arrived later that night. He was a middle aged Texan with a strong accent who wore a black t-shirt with the words *I Love Lava'* printed on it.

'Hey dude,' said Eric greeting him at the door. 'Here I am again.'

Bevin laughed, making his slightly emaciated body shake in a peculiar fashion.

'So this is my girlfriend, Colleen,' Eric said.

Bevin smiled nervously.

'And these are my friends Johnny and Rachel from England.'

'Hi,' he said coyly. 'So you guys should bring a hoodie with you, or something to cover you up.'

'OK. I have a raincoat. Will that do?' asked Colleen.

'Yeah, should be OK,' he replied.

'So Eric says you do this a lot, is this true?' asked Colleen.

'Yeah. Every couple of weeks. Weather should be OK tonight. No wind. Good sign.'

Bevin drove them to the Volcano National Park, passing through the entrance, which at this time of night was unmanned, until they came to a dead end where lava had solidified over the road. Bevin parked his rusty Pontiac, got out of the vehicle, walked to the boot of the car to get out four plastic gas masks which he handed to everybody.

'Put these on when we get close to the crater. You never know which way the wind is going to blow and you don't want to breathe in any of the gases that come from the vent. They're poisonous.'

He handed them each a small torch which they used to guide themselves through the dark, while he carried four large battery powered lights which he jabbed into the ground on the top of any hill which they walked past.

'What's that for?' enquired Rachel.

'Pardon me?' replied Bevin. 'I don't understand your accent.'

'What's it for?' Rachel repeated her words slowly.

'Oh. So we don't get lost in the dark. You don't want to lose your way out here as the lava can just come over the hill and roll straight at you.'

'Holy shit. Look at the ground!' said Eric pointing out the cracks in the ground which were lit up below them.

'Oh my God, this is so not safe,' said Colleen panic stricken. 'Is that lava flowing under us?'

'Sure is,' replied Bevin.

'Seriously, this is all good,' Eric said attempting to reassure Colleen who grabbed his hand.

They reached another hill where Bevin put another stick into the ground, then walked down into a small valley where they were surrounded by dead trees. They headed to the top of another hill where they were met by a sight which struck them all by surprise, where the vent of the volcano, which lay at the edge of a cliff by the ocean, was spitting out lava into the sea.

'That is amazing,' said Johnny holding Rachel's hand tightly.

'Now that's impressive,' said Colleen.

'This was so fucking worth it,' replied Eric.

'Anyone want to take a photo?' asked Bevin, taking out an umbrella which he opened up as he walked closer to the vent.

'Isn't that a bit too close Bevin?' replied Colleen.

Eric got out his camera and took a photo of Bevin.

'Eric, sweetie,' said Colleen putting her hand on his shoulder, stopping him walking any further. 'Don't get too close.'

'I won't, but he looks so cool with the umbrella!'

'Shit. I think my shoe's melting!' said Johnny looking at the plastic peeling off from the base of his trainers.

'Oh my God that's nuts,' said Rachel.

'That is Mother Nature, right there,' said Eric, 'and you certainly don't want to mess with it.'

'Eric what are you doing?!' Colleen asked Eric as he lit a spliff from one of cracks in the ground.

'Just using the natural lighter,' tittered Eric.

Colleen turned to look at Bevin doing a little dance with his umbrella in the distance, nodding her head in disbelief.

They all sat down on a nearby rock where Johnny got a whiff of gas from a crack in the ground.

'Jesus!' he said coughing.

'You OK?' replied Rachel.

'Yeah, just got a smell of volcanic gas! That stuff is lethal!'

Bevin returned with his umbrella and went into his rucksack where he got out some uncooked microwave popcorn which he put on a nearby crack in the ground causing the package to quickly increase in size.

'Something tells me you've done this before Bevin?' remarked Colleen.

Bevin smiled. 'Popcorn anyone?' he asked.

'Colleen, you should tell your kids at school about this,' Rachel said.

'I would love to but I'm supposed to be a responsible teacher. I wouldn't want to give them the wrong impression.'

'So the last time we were standing just a few metres away from the vent, we decided to head back and when we looked back at the ground we'd been standing on the entire thing just collapsed right in front of us, falling straight into the ocean. Close call,' said Bevin.

'I really wish you hadn't told us that,' replied Colleen anxiously rising to her feet.

'Honey, it's OK,' assured Eric smoking from his spliff.

'Well no, it isn't. He just told us the ground we're standing on is not stable. I mean look at what we're standing on, there's cracks running everywhere!'

'Anyone?' asked Bevin offering more popcorn.

Colleen grabbed some, gulping it down quickly.

They left half an hour later, passing a young couple who were heading down to the vent.

'How many people actually do this?' asked Rachel.

'What?' replied Bevin.

'She said how many people have done this!' said Colleen loudly as if she was translating to a foreigner.

'Oh a fair few,' replied Bevin. 'There have been cases where people have left their cars at the top. They go down and they never come back.'

'Bevin, I love you dearly but as a tour guide you really don't fill me feel with confidence when you say stuff like that!'

They finally reached the car, where they put the equipment back into the boot, then drove back to Hilo where the dawn was breaking.

'Man that was awesome,' said Eric filling up a glass of water with Johnny back in his cousin's kitchen. 'My throat is so dry.'

'Thanks for organising it mate,' replied Johnny.

'Guys. I'm pooped. Off to bed,' said Rachel who was already in her pyjamas.

'I'll see you in there,' said Johnny.

'So. Rachel seems nice,' commented Eric after she had left the room.

'Yeah. She's great. Despite the fact I spent most of our time New Zealand bitching about her.'

'Hey. I get why. But whatever man. I like her. You guys seem happy.'

'I think we are.'

Johnny and Rachel woke late the next morning to find Eric cooking bacon and eggs in the kitchen.

'Morning,' said Johnny.

'Hey. Sleep OK?'

'Sure did,' said Eric,

'Hey Eric. Could I use the computer? Check my email?' asked Rachel.

'Sure. There's one in the room on the left, should still be on.'

'Thanks.'

'Where's Colleen?' asked Johnny.

'Still in bed.'

Rachel appeared moments later. 'Eric, can I use your phone?' she asked. Her body was shaking.

'Rachel?' asked Johnny.

'I need to phone England,' she replied in a panic.

'I'll grab my cellphone,' said Eric

'It's kind of urgent. I know it'll be expensive,' she replied.

'Not a problem.' Eric took the frying pan off the heat and went to the bedroom to grab it.

'What is it?' Johnny asked Rachel.

'I just got an email from my sister.'

'OK.'

'She was saying my dad's died. I don't know what to do.'

'What?'

'He had a heart attack. I need to find out what happened.'

'Rachel.' Johnny went to hug her.

'Please don't!' she said stopping him. 'I need to speak to my sister.'

'Here you go,' said Eric, passing her the phone.

She headed outside to the yard the front of the house while Johnny sat in the living room waiting for her to return.

'Thanks,' she said, returning the phone to Eric who left the room.

'Come here,' Johnny said.

She let him hug her this time.

'Mum said he came home from the airport. He went up to bed because he said he was tired. She went up to check on him and he was laying down on the floor and he was dead. They think it was a massive heart attack. I never said goodbye, or told him I loved him. I'm never going to see him again.'

'I'm so sorry.'

'I've got to go back. The funeral is going to be next week. I've got to be there.'

'I can come with you.'

'No. It will mess up your plans.'

'I don't care about that.'

'I need to go alone.'

'Are you sure? I can be there.'

She nodded her head.

'I need to book my flight,' she said.

Rachel left the room and Johnny knew that in a few hours the girl he was used to having around would be gone.

Brighton, UK

Rachel was pleased to have her older sister, Becca, with her on the day of her father's funeral. Becca was on maternity leave having had a baby girl with her banker husband. Despite the fact they were in very different stages of their lives, Becca now living in a large detached house in Guildford, the sisters shared a close bond. However, her relationship with her twenty-nine-year-old brother, Mark, felt more distant than ever. Having lost his job in IT a few years earlier, he had moved back to the family home and become depressed; refusing to talk to his friends or even leave the house. He had reverted to the moody teenager she had always remembered him by. Her harsh tempered mother was not helping matters either. The moment she had picked up Rachel up from the airport, she had spoken resentfully about her father.

'We fell out of love a long time ago Rachel,' was a line she had dropped into conversation since her daughter's return. Rachel had gritted her teeth, tried her best to ignore her mother's cantankerous behaviour.

Becca had flipped on the day before the funeral while they were sorting out final arrangements in the kitchen. 'I know you had your difficulties Mother but you can at least respect the fact he was our father and remember him fondly for the funeral!' she had retorted.

Her mother had kept quiet ever since and on the day of the funeral was on her best behaviour.

'I miss him Becca,' Rachel reminisced while they sat in the venue room at the back of a smart local pub in Brighton town centre, where they were holding the wake.

'Me too Rach.'

'He never had any heart problems before, why did it have to happen like this? He was always so active.'

'I don't know. Mum said he didn't really look after himself when he was younger. You know he drank a lot. I'm sure he did plenty of other stuff. Maybe it just caught up with him.'

'She doesn't care. She's pleased he's gone.'

'I think she's taking it harder than you think. You know what she's like, she's a battle-axe.'

Becca's husband, Lawrence, entered with the baby.

'How is she?' asked Becca.

'OK, I think.' Lawrence lifted the baby out of her pram to smell her nappy. 'We're all good. Aren't we darling?'

Rachel could tell Lawrence was a good hands-on dad as well as a loyal husband. There was respect between them, an understanding that both of them were together sharing the responsibility of parenthood; it made them a solid couple.

'You want to go see Mummy?' Lawrence handed the baby to Becca.

'I should probably feed her,' said Becca. 'You guys OK holding the fort while everyone arrives?'

'Sure,' replied Rachel.

'How are you doing?' asked Lawrence.

'I'm OK.'

They turned to see Rachel's brother Mark enter the room to sit down by himself with a pint of beer.

'Are you going to talk to him or shall I?' asked Lawrence.

'I'll go,' replied Rachel.

'So, you think Dad would have liked the service?' Rachel asked, sitting down next to her brother.

'I don't know. He'd have like the fact we were having a few drinks here afterwards.'

'At least Mum is being civil.'

'All I'll say is it's good that they're not together anymore.'

'Why?'

'It was bad. You weren't ever home to witness it. They'd have massive rows every night when they were both at home together.'

'They were always like that.'

'It got worst over the last few years. You were off at uni, and then travelling, so you never saw it. I don't know why they even bothered staying in the same house. Actually, I do, it's because Dad couldn't afford to move out.'

'I'm sorry things haven't been great for you recently.'

'Why do you care?'

'Of course I care. You're my brother.'

'You've been trotting around the globe. You have no idea what's it's been like back here.'

'I know it's been hard Mark.'

'Some days I've woken up and I've thought why do I even bother at all. I reckon Dad's got it best out of all of us.'

'I want you to help me clear out your father's bedroom' insisted Rachel's mother two weeks later on a Monday morning. 'We can take the clothes to a charity shop on The Lanes.'

'Mum don't you think it's a bit quick?'

'Rachel I have got to move on with my life! I spent the last thirty years waiting around for your father and I'm not waiting around any longer!'

'Is Mark going to help?'

'Mark? You'll be lucky. Your brother's nocturnal these days.'

'He's depressed.'

'Yes I know, but at the end of the day, he's the only one who's going to be able break out of this episode.'

78

'Well maybe we need to help him do that.'

Her mother sat down helplessly on her bed. 'What do you think I've been doing? I've tried to set him up for job interviews. Get him out of the house.' She wiped some sweat from her forehead then looked across the room. 'Let's start with his socks,' she said getting up to take out a bottom drawer where she emptied a whole load of them onto the bed. It still amazed Rachel that her parents had still shared the same bedroom.

Rachel spotted a picture on the wall of all five of them at Alton Towers. She remembered it well, a week's holiday where they had all stayed in a caravan in the Peak District when she was eight years old. The countryside had glowed green and there had not been a cloud in the sky. A time when they all seemed happy, a time before she noticed her parents' flaws and the cracks in their relationship.

'What are you looking at?' asked her mother.

'The five of us at Alton Towers.'

Her mother walked over to look at the picture.

'It was a good holiday. I hated the thought of sleeping in that bloody caravan but your father insisted. Funny thing is, I did actually enjoy myself.'

'Wow. You're actually saying you enjoyed something with him.'

Her mother sighed. 'Of course I enjoyed things with him. I married him for God's sake. Had three of his children. He just frustrated me a lot of the time, but there were good moments. Very good moments in fact.'

Her mother sat back on the bed holding two odd pairs of socks in her hands which she she smelt. 'He could never keep the same pair. Always had odd socks on each foot and they always had holes in them.' Her mother smiled. 'Wore some socks for years until they fell off his feet. The truth is I'm sure he felt as frustrated with me as I did with him. I know I was never easy to live with. I never have been. I guess I just never should have married a failed musician.'

'He wasn't a failed musician.'

'Oh Rachel he was.'

'He sold records.'

'He did. But they hardly made any money. I always felt like the breadwinner because I was. Thank God my father was well off. I don't know what we'd have done financially without him. We certainly wouldn't have had this place.'

Mark appeared at the entrance of the door in his pyjama bottoms, wearing a white t-shirt with food stains on it, looking uncomfortable while folding his arms.

'What are you doing?' he asked.

'Just clearing out your father's things,' said their mother. She looked at them both, then suddenly stood up. 'How about we go out for lunch in a bit? After your sister and I have made a start on this. My treat.'

'Go where?' asked Rachel nervously.

'I don't know. Somewhere down by the seafront. We haven't been out in ages, just the three of us.'

Rachel looked at Mark hoping he would decline the offer. She couldn't think of anything worse than an awkward lunch with the two of them.

'I'll go get changed,' he replied, walking off.

Their mother drove them to a fish and chip restaurant on the promenade, a place they had gone to as a treat when they were kids. Rachel was astonished to see it still it existed though the décor hadn't changed much since her childhood. The grand art deco building it once was now looked tired and dated.

'Well I think I might have a glass of wine,' replied their mother, scanning through the menu after they had been seated.

'Slippery slope mother, it's only midday,' Rachel joked.

'It's one glass Rachel, I'm hardly over indulging,' said her mother tetchily. 'What are we all having?'

'Thought I might go for fish and chips,' said Mark sarcastically.

'Well you always used to go for the battered sausage from what I remember?'

'Well I fancy fish.'

Their mother closed her menu and placed it on the table. 'Listen there was a reason why I asked the two of you out today. There's been something I've been meaning to tell you since your father passed away.'

'What is it?' asked Rachel curiously.

'Well, there's no easy way to say this. I've been seeing someone.'

'What?' replied Rachel, trying to take in her mother's words.

'Who?' asked Mark, who seemed unfazed by his mother's revelation.

'No one you know. We've been seeing each other for quite some time actually. I met him on a night course.'

'What sort of night course?' Rachel retorted.

'I was learning Japanese.'

'Japanese? You don't even like the Japanese. You're always saying how cruel they were during the war.'

'Well I find learning the language quite fascinating. Charlie does too.'

'Charlie? I'm assuming that's the person you've been referring to?'

'Yes.'

'And what does Charlie do?'

'He's used to be a teacher, but he's now retired.'

'Did Dad know?'

'Listen Rachel, I know you were very fond of your father.'

'Answer the question!'

'Yes, he did know.'

'And he didn't care?!'

'Fine,' her mother said, folding her hands together while looking at Rachel. 'I wasn't going to tell you this. But I feel you've pushed me into it.'

'Tell me what?!'

'Your father had an affair a year after you were born.'

'No he didn't!' Rachel said, dismissing her mother's revelation.

'He did. The woman lived in Luton. I let him see her for seven years, until it fizzled out.'

'Why are you telling us this?!'

'Because I think it's time we were honest with each other. He knew about Charlie and I knew about his affairs.'

The waiter arrived at the table.

'We're not ready!' Rachel snapped at him.

The waiter scurried off.

'Why did you live together? If you were seeing other people behind each other's back, what was the point in being married?' asked Rachel.

'To be honest with you. I don't know.'

'Because Dad was skint,' replied Mark.

'There were financial complications. I'm not going to lie. But I also think deep down, there was still some sort of love and connection between us.'

'Does Becca know?' asked Rachel.

'Yes,' replied her mother.

'I can't believe you told her and not us!'

'I told her first because I knew she'd understand it more.'

'Well I don't want to meet this Charlie or whatever his name is!'

'Honestly Rachel, you're being incredibly immature. We're all adults here.'

'And I'm being an adult and I'm telling you I don't want to meet him!'

'Do you think this is easy for me telling you this?!' replied her mother vehemently. 'You're going to have to meet at some point.'

Rachel retrieved her mobile and noticed she'd received a text from Johnny. '*Hope things going OK. Thinking of you. Let me know when free to chat x.*'

'Have you got a text message?' asked her mother.

'Yes.'

'From that boy you were seeing?'

'What boy?' asked Mark.

'She met a boy while travelling' added her mother.

'I thought you were still seeing Ross?' he asked

'I broke up with him.'

'Well I didn't know that,' he replied.

'Well maybe if you came out of your room you would know more about these things,' said her mother.

'Fuck off!' replied Mark. 'I'm going for a smoke.' He leaped out of his chair and left through the front door letting a cool breeze in from the seafront.

'That is what I have to deal with,' her mother commented. 'He's twenty-nine and I feel like I'm living with a teenager.'

'I take it you haven't spoken to Ross since you broke up?'

'No. Why?'

'You know he's back in Brighton.'

'No. I didn't know that,' she said, attempting to show minimal interest, though it did surprise her.

'I bumped into his aunt the other day at the funeral. I told her about you two breaking up. She didn't know. I mean I can't say I'm that upset you two were over. He was hardly going places, but this Jonathan sounds nice.'

'His name's Johnny.'

'So what are your plans?'

'How do you mean?'

'I mean do you intend to go back travelling or are you staying in the country?'

'I haven't made up my mind yet. I *did* have plans to go more places with him. It's just all this stuff with Dad. It's put everything on hold.'

After the meal was done they drove back to the family home where Rachel made a hasty escape to her room to phone her sister.

'Hi Rach, just in the middle of something, can I call you back?' she said while being drowned out by baby noises in the background.

'Mum's just told me about her affair,' Rachel said.

There was a moment's pause. 'Well does it really surprise you?' replied Becca.

'What's that supposed to mean?'

'I'm just saying you knew their marriage was hardly a happy one.'

'They were both seeing other people while still being married to each other!' Rachel could hear herself and it made her feel old and judgmental.

'I know.'

'Mum told us about Dad having a mistress in Luton. I know we live in bloody Brighton, but this is freaking me out!'

'Well at least she's opening up about things. See it as a good thing. I wanted her to mention this before, as I thought you guys had a right to know.'

'How can you be so accepting about all this?'

'Because I'm older and I know how hard marriage can be sometimes.'

'Oh great, so you're now going to tell me you're seeing someone.'

'No, I'm not. I'm glad to say Lawrence and I are happy, touch wood.'

'This is so fucked up. Do you think I should carry on travelling?'

'Only you can make that decision Rach. I thought you were going to meet up with that boy you were seeing?'

'I was, but maybe I should stay home, Mum's having an affair, Mark's bloody depressed all the time, I feel like the whole family's falling apart!'

'It was like that before Dad died. From a purely selfish point of view, I would love to have you around, but you're young, maybe you should be back out travelling, seeing more of the world. You didn't want to come back this early anyway. It was only because of Dad that you did.'

Rachel's phone began to beep. She had another call coming through.

'I'll phone you back,' she said going to answer it. 'Hello?'

'Rachel?' replied a cautious male voice.

She knew the voice all too well. 'What do you want Ross?'

'Are you good to talk?' he asked timorously.

'Yeah, I guess so,' she replied, determined to sound standoffish.

'How's things?'

'Not great.'

'I'm sorry to hear about your dad.'

'Thanks.'

'I would have come to the funeral. I had to work.'

'I hear you're back in Brighton?' She regretted it the minute she said this. It showed she cared.

'Yeah. I got a job in a music shop in town.'

'When did you get back from Australia?'

'About a month ago.'

'You got a job pretty fast.'

'Yeah. Are you back for good now?'

'It's complicated. I don't know, is the honest answer.'

'I know you probably don't want to see me, after the way things ended in Melbourne.'

'I really don't want to talk about this now Ross.'

'I just wanted to say I know I acted really out of order punching your friend.'

'What do you want?'

'I wanted to see if you fancied meeting up?'

'I don't think that's a good idea. Do you?'

'I've missed you Rach. God I've missed you. I know how badly I fucked up. I had to call you, to apologise.'

'Well you've said sorry, so…'

'Well just have a think about it, you can text me. I totally get it if you don't want to. But, please, it took a lot for me to call you like this.'

'I don't know.'

'Please.'

'OK. Fine. I'll text you,' she said, lacking the energy to fight anymore.

'It's so good to hear your voice.'

'I'll speak to you soon Ross.' She hung up and stayed in her room for the rest of the evening, contemplating the events of the day.

She didn't know why she had agreed to meet Ross the following morning. They met in a trendy café in the town centre, just up the road from where he worked. The first thing she noticed was how slim he was from the last time she saw him. He had grown a short beard, which made him look older, and as much as she hated it, she liked his rugged appearance. They didn't hug or kiss but acknowledged each other politely.

'Thanks for meeting up. Do you want a coffee or anything?' he asked as she sat down opposite him.

'I hate coffee, you know that. Besides, I'm not thirsty. I take it you're on a lunch break?'

'Yeah.'

'How long do you get?'

'Half an hour. So I know I asked you on the phone but, how are you?'

'Honestly, I'm pretty low.'

'As I mentioned before, I wish I'd come to the funeral.'

'Work wouldn't let you take the time off?'

'Looking back on it, I didn't think I could have actually faced it. I've never been good at funerals. I knew you'd be there. I just didn't think it would be a good idea. How's your mum?'

'I don't know. I think she misses my dad in an odd sort of way, but she's got a weird way of showing it. She's just told me a whole load of stuff which I don't really want to talk about.'

'I saw your brother the other day.'

'Really. You were lucky. He hardly leaves the house these days.'

'He looked kind of lost. He was walking past the shop on his phone. I think he saw me but he didn't acknowledge it.'

'Sounds about right. I wouldn't take it personally. He seems to be in his own world at the moment. So why did you come back from Australia so soon?'

'To be honest, it wasn't the same without you. I moved into another flat in Sydney after we broke up. I had these God awful housemates. Two girls. They were older. They kept blaming me for breaking things and making too much noise. I mean I was hardly in the house. It was awful. Then I lost my job.'

'I'm sorry.'

'That's when I came down to Melbourne. I just needed to get away for a weekend. I knew you might be there seeing your dad for the gig so I went along. I guess when I saw you with Johnny, that's his name, right?'

'Yep.'

'I just got wound up. I was jealous.'

'That's no excuse.'

'I was angry. I know I need to control my anger with things like that. You were right. All the things you said about us when we were living together.'

'Good, I'm pleased you're acknowledging it.'

'Your dad caught up with me, later that night.'

'I didn't know that.'

'He gave me a massive lecture. It worked in a weird way. He told me never to speak to you again. He said I would never be good enough for you.' She could see tears welling up in his eyes. 'But I'm telling you Rach. I've changed. I know I was really moody and hard to live with, but I'm sorting myself out. I really am. So what are you doing? I mean, are you staying here now?'

'For the next few weeks, yes. After that, I don't know.'

'Well what's…?'

'Johnny.'

'Johnny. Right. What's he doing?'

'Well he's travelling, I might carry on and travel more with him.'

'I see,' he said, wiping his eyes.

'Are you OK?' she asked.

'Yeah. I'm fine.'

'Why did you want to meet me Ross?'

'I want you back. I'm a mess without you Rach. I really am. I think about you every day. Now you're back maybe we can try and work things out again?'

'I don't know if I'm back.'

'Well your family will want you here. So will I.'

'Maybe I don't want to be here. Maybe I want to be out there with Johnny.'

'Johnny seemed like a nice guy, but you don't have history like you do with me. We're meant to be together.'

'Look. I've moved on Ross.'

'With him?'

'Yes.'

'He's not here. He didn't come to the funeral.'

'I didn't want him to come. He offered to come with me and I said no, so I left him in Hawaii.'

'Hawaii? You went to Hawaii?'

'Yes.'

'You and me were meant to go there.' He looked down like a disappointed child.

'Look. I'm pleased you're back here and you've got the job, but things aren't going to be like they were before.'

They sat there awkwardly for a moment.

'Listen I should be getting off,' she said, standing up and putting an end to the meeting.

'That's your final answer?'

'Don't make this difficult Ross.'

'Can we hug? One last time.'

She nodded her head. He gave her an intense hug which after a polite amount of time she pulled herself away from.

'Thank you,' he replied.

'Goodbye Ross,' she said leaving him to finish his coffee.

It had started raining heavily by the time she got the bus home and walked up the steep hill to her house on the outskirts of the city. When she headed upstairs past her mother's room, she stopped for a moment. She could hear her mother crying. She felt bad for admitting this but part of her had wanted this moment, a portrayal of emotion from her. She knocked on the door.

'Mum?'

'Yes?'

'You OK?'

'I'm fine.'

'I'll do supper.'

'Thank you.'

Rachel walked into her room and lay down on her bed. She looked around her bedroom. For the first time she noticed how little it had changed since she had left sixth form college. There were still posters of boy bands on the walls, pictures of school friends, mostly male, who she had lost contact with from school; vestiges of her teenage years. She turned to look at an old black and white photo of an American skyscraper on her wall and her thoughts quickly turned to Johnny. He had been so good not pressing her about her plans but she could tell he wanted to know when she was coming back to join him. It seemed like another lifetime, being out there with him. Just so much seemed to have happened over the last few weeks. She got up off the bed and looked out of the window at a rainy view of Brighton, then headed downstairs where her brother was playing computer games on his Xbox.

'Are you in for supper?' she asked him.

'Sure.'

'Chicken OK?'

'Yep. Sounds good'

'So I was thinking, I might stay home for a while. That sound OK with you?'

'Sure. No more travelling?'

'No more travelling,' she replied, with the thought of how she was going to let Johnny know weighing heavily on her mind.

Los Angeles, USA

'So I spoke to my work colleague today,' said Suzi, frying an omelette in her seventies styled kitchen.

'OK,' replied Johnny, holding the TV remote, flicking through the many cable channels American television had to offer, stopping on an episode of *Friends* which he was surprised to find he had not seen.

'And he says he can get you a job, and will pay you cash in hand. So you're off the radar.'

'OK. Where is it?'

'At a small insurance company in Glendale.'

'Sounds good.'

'I mean it'll get you out of the house. Plus, you'll have some money to do day trips with me before your tourist visa runs out.'

'Does he want to meet me or anything?'

'Yeah, his dad said he would be keen on meeting you. So shall l say you're interested?'

'Yes. Definitely. Thanks Suzi.'

'You're welcome. I'll speak to him tomorrow. So you said you were having ham with your omelette, right?'

'Yes please. So if I get this job, you're OK with hanging out with me a bit longer?'

'You kidding? Course I am. If you get the job you can pay a bit towards my bills.'

'Love your honesty sometimes.'

'I know.'

She picked up the omelette with a spatula, placed it onto a plate, sprinkling some grated cheese on top of it. 'OK, it's ready. Though I think it might be burnt.'

'I don't mind burnt. Burnt food is my thing.'

'This is my, what is the word, my carcinogenic cooking?'

'Lovely.'

'You want to eat at the table?'

'Why not. Let's be civilised.'

He turned off the TV, then cleared away her books from the table.

'Don't wait for me. You start,' she said, pouring more omelette mixture into the pan. 'I think it'll be good for you to be busy.'

'How do you mean?'

'Oh come on. You've been miserable since finishing with Rachel, and not doing anything just makes you dwell on it. I know how horrible it is breaking up with someone, I get it.'

'I'm sorry. Thank you for putting up with me.'

'Don't apologise. You're a friend. It's what I'm here for.'

'It can't be much fun for you,' replied Johnny. 'I know I've got to move on. It's silly but a part of me still thinks she's going to email me back and tell me she's changed her mind.'

'I think you need to just focus on the future. This job will help with that.'

'I know, keep me busy, that's the key.'

Suzi sat down next to him with her food.

'So what do you want to do tonight?' asked Johnny.

'We've been invited over to Nicola's house party, remember?'

'Oh, shit sorry, I forgot.'

'You're coming right?'

'I do want to, but I also feel like a night in.'

'It's not going to be anything crazy. You can meet my LA friends. I think you'll like them. Come on. What else are you going to do? Watch another episode of *Friends*?'

'I like *Friends.*'

'I've more or less got you a job. You're coming Johnny.'

'Alright. You win. I'll go.' He often found Suzi rather frightening in arguments and he wasn't willing to have one with her tonight.

They left the house shortly after 8.00pm. Suzi had taken time getting ready and Johnny had been quietly surprised by how glamorous and attractive she could look when she made the effort.

Nicola's place was a bungalow at the end of a quiet hilly leafy road, a short walk from Suzi's house which felt pleasant after a warm January day; part of the winter heatwave they were currently experiencing. Nicola was a perky alternatively dressed girl with short hair, a lip piercing, and several tattoos; evidence of what Suzi referred to as her wild days where she almost failed her undergraduate degree. Now, aged thirty, she had cleaned up her act and got herself into medical school.

'Hey!' she said giving Suzi a hug.

'We bought wine.'

'Cool. Thank you. I love wine.'

'So this is my friend Johnny.'

'Hey. Nice to meet you. Come in. Will's here. The others are on their way.'

The apartment was tidy, with a large living room and an old fashioned kitchen, and a small balcony which overlooked the distant suburbs of Pasadena.

'Nice flat,' said Johnny.

'Thanks.'

'Is it yours?'

'No. No way. I'm a student. I'm poor. I rent it with my friend Will, who is this guy.' A slim laid back twenty-something male with curly blonde hair appeared at the door.

'Hey,' slurred Will. 'Listen I'm going to crash.'

'What? You're not going to be here for the party?' said Nicola.

'Yeah I'm not feeling so great, think I'm coming down with something and I've got an early start tomorrow.'

'OK. Hope you feel better. We'll keep it down,' replied Nicola, sounding understanding, but disappointed.

'Don't worry. I'll be all drugged up on painkillers. They'll knock me out.' Will shut his door.

'So what are we all drinking?' asked Nicola as the doorbell went.

'I'll get it!' said Suzi.

'So I have beer or wine,' said Nicola opening up her large fully stocked American fridge.

'Beer sounds good,' replied Johnny.

She opened up a bottle of Mexican beer and handed it to him. 'So Suzi said you went to Hawaii?'

'I did.'

'How was it?'

'Amazing. I went to see Suzi's cousin, Eric.'

'Right. I forgot she had a cousin over there. That's handy. I want to go there.'

'Well I'm sure Eric would put you up.'

Suzi gave her work colleague, Dan, a hug at the door. Johnny recognised him from photos on her fridge door. He was around Suzi's age, and from comparing past photos, had put on weight.

'Dan this is my friend Johnny,' Suzi said.

'Nice to meet you,' replied Dan in a slow articulate arrogant voice. He shook Johnny's hand firmly.

'Dan teaches Asian Studies,' added Suzi.

'Well Asian Political Studies to be more precise,' replied Dan.

'I have snacks,' announced Nicola putting bowls of nuts and crisps on the coffee table. 'Dan, you want a beer?'

'I do.'

'Suzi?'

'Sure.'

94

Nicola handed them drinks and they all sat down. There was a quietness in the room, which, due to the lack of music playing, dulled the atmosphere. Nicola's phone rang and she left the room.

'So what do you think of Southern California?' Dan quizzed Johnny.

'Yeah. I like it. I love the weather.'

'A vast improvement from what you guys get in the UK, right?'

'You could say that. So do you live near here?'

'I do. Just down the road. I live in Alhambra. But I'm from New York.'

Nicola entered the room.

'So that was Katie,' Nicola said. 'Her sister's broken up with her boyfriend and she's taken it really badly, so it doesn't look like she's going to make it tonight.'

'You say that like it's a bad thing?' replied Dan.

'Hey, come on,' said Nicola abruptly, 'she's my friend.'

'So what do you do for work in the UK Jonathan?' Dan asked Johnny quickly evading the situation.

'It's Johnny actually,' he corrected him. 'I used to work in insurance.'

'Oh really. Did you like that line of work?'

'Not really. I'm hoping for a bit of a career change when I get back.'

'I think you should go into teaching,' said Suzi.

'Really. Why do you say that?' asked Johnny.

'I don't know. I think you'd be good at it. You're patient. You're not boring. I think kids would relate to you.'

'OK. I'll bear that in mind,' said Johnny, liking the fact Suzi had obviously thought about this.

'Well it's just a thought,' replied Suzi.

'So how's school?' Dan said, turning to Nicola.

'Yeah. It's OK. Competitive. But I got some results yesterday which shows I'm fairly high up in my class.'

'Hey, that's good,' said Suzi.

'I got some pretty good news myself yesterday,' announced Dan, attempting to take centre stage.

The more Dan spoke, the more Johnny disliked him.

'Really. What?' asked Suzi.

'So it looks like the paper I wrote on Hong Kong's relationship with Mainland China is going to be published.'

'Wow congratulations,' said Suzi who seemed to be the only person in the room making an effort towards him. 'You worked so hard for that.'

Did she like this guy? Johnny thought. Her body language and efforts to engage with him gave off this impression.

The evening carried on at the same tempo. Dan endlessly talking about himself, Suzi being the only one to show an interest, and Nicola feeling frustrated by the lack of people who had come to her party. After a couple of hours, Johnny decided he'd languished in this situation long enough.

'Listen I might head back if you don't mind?' Johnny said to Suzi while Dan and Nicola were bickering across from them.

'OK,' replied Suzi. 'I thought we'd have stayed a bit longer.'

'It doesn't mean you have to come with me. I can head back alone. I'm just pretty tired. I'm also old and boring.'

'You're not old and it's only 10.30pm.'

'I'm sorry, I know I'm being rubbish.'

'You're going?' said Nicola catching the conversation.

'Yeah. I'm usually more exciting than this,' replied Johnny, trying to justify his actions.

'He is. I spent two weeks getting drunk with him in Australia,' said Suzi. 'Tonight, you are lame.'

'I am. I admit it,' he said standing up and facing Nicola and Dan. 'But it was really nice to meet you all.'

'You too,' replied Dan, shaking his hand.

'I'm sorry hardly anyone turned up,' said Nicola. 'I'm obviously not as popular as I used to be.'

'I doubt that's true,' said Johnny.

'Shall I take the key and you just ring the doorbell when you get back?' he asked Suzi.

'Yeah. Just don't fall asleep.'

'Won't do.'

Nicola showed him to the door, and when it was closed behind him, a sigh of relief crossed his face.

Johnny walked down the hill, back into the suburbs towards Suzi's house, around the outskirts of the college where she worked. He had spent some time walking around the campus; with it's well kept gardens and Spanish style buildings it was not surprising it had been used in a number of different films and TV series.

He sauntered left down a suburban road past a college fraternity house with large Greek lettering on the front of it, where a party was taking place. Two attractive girls in their early twenties were standing at the front of the house watching him.

'Hey,' said the taller one with blonde her and impressive legs.

Johnny smiled.

'Do you smoke?' she asked.

'Sorry. No.'

'Wait. Your accent. Where you from?'

'England.'

'You go to school here?'

'No.'

'I recognise you.'

'I have a friend who teaches at the college.'

'No way. What's her name?'

'Suzi Ley.'

'Oh my God like I totally know her! I did this class last semester with her on contested territory in North America. She's German, right?'

'Austrian.'

'Right. So you guys live together?'

'Sort of. Temporarily. I'm staying with her for a few weeks.'

'Are you guys dating or what?'

'No. She's not my girlfriend. We're just friends.'

'So where you going?'

'I was just heading back.'

'You should totally hang out with us.'

'That'll be OK right?' she asked her friend

'I guess,' replied her shorter friend with a shrug.

'I wasn't really feeling it tonight to be honest. That's why I was heading back actually.'

'Like you seriously won't regret it,' she said flirtatiously in a confident manner which he found very appealing in American women.

'Alright, why not,' said Johnny, succumbing to her charms.

The girl grabbed his hand and took him into the house with her friend where the party was rammed full of younger students, who were drinking out of red plastic cups.

'You wanna beer?' she asked him.

'Sure. So you live here?'

'I do. What's your name?'

'Johnny.'

'Cute name. British Johnny. I like it.'

'And yours?'

'Ashley.'

'Nice to meet you Ashley.'

'Can I just have your accent? Can you just give it to me right now?'

He smiled. Ashley had managed to lose her friend and it was just the two of them, walking upstairs to one of the larger bedrooms which was full of drunken students dancing to R&B. Ashley grabbed some shots of multicoloured vodka from a tray, held by a buff male student wearing shorts and an open Hawaiian shirt.

'You ready to down it?' she asked

'OK.'

They knocked back their shots. He could feel the alcohol entering his system. He had not realised how much he had drunk at Nicola's. He looked at his phone to see he'd received a text from Suzi. *'Get home OK?'* it read. He didn't reply.

Ashley's friend appeared with some more beers, whispered in her ear, then left looking frustrated. Ashley passed Johnny a beer. The Black Eyed Peas came on and Ashley turned her back to him, then danced amorously against him.

'So why don't you have a girlfriend British Johnny?'

'I did have.'

'What happened?'

'She went back to England and then dumped me. Some bad family stuff happened.'

'Too bad!' she said, taking his hand, leading him up another flight of stairs where she got a key hidden within a bookshelf in the hallway and then went to a bedroom door which had several locks on it. She entered the sparsely furnished room and shot to a drawer where she got out some coke wrapped up in cling film, hidden under some clothes. She lined it up with a credit card on a bedside table, rolled up a dollar note and snorted it.

'You want some?' she asked.

'No I'm alright.'

'You can just put some on some on your gums. It'll relax you. I'm telling you. Don't knock it until you've tried it right?'

'I don't know.'

'Give me your hand.'

She poured a small amount into his hand, maneuvered his fingers to pick some up, then rubbed it onto his gums.

'If you want some more just tell me,' she replied provocatively.

She looked at him and then suddenly went to kiss him. They moved towards the bed when there was suddenly a knock on the door.

'Yeah?' she shouted angrily. There was no reply so she went to open it, and spoke to a guy behind the door.

'Lets go,' she said, grabbing Johnny's hand, taking him out, back downstairs into the room where the music was playing where they periodically drunkenly kissed, her tongue aggressively moving around in his mouth.

The next moments were a blur with Johnny returning back to the bedroom where Ashley convinced him to take more coke to snort up his nose. They headed to the garden where there was a large bouncy castle which Ashley walked onto, then tripped over on. She laughed as Johnny grabbed her hand and they began jumping on the castle together.

'I'm fucking loving this!' said Johnny dancing next to Ashley. He was feeling high very high by now.

'What?!' she replied.

'I said I am fucking loving this!'

'Well I'm fucking loving this too!'

Ashley jumped up again, throwing herself against the castle walls, while Johnny turned to his phone to notice Suzi was calling him.

'Hello?!' Johnny said shouting down the phone. 'I can't hear you! I'm at a house party! And guess what? I'm with one of your pupils!'

'Who are you talking to?' asked Ashley.

'Suzi! Suzy Ley!'

'She should totally hang out with us!'

'There's a bouncy castle here and everything!' Johnny screamed down the phone. He couldn't hear what she was saying as there was loud music now playing in the yard but Suzi had hung up. Johnny put the phone back in his pocket and turned to Ashley causing them to bang their heads together. Although it felt painful at first, they both ended up laughing, then fell to the soft floor. Johnny could see his phone lighting up in his pocket, it was Suzi phoning again.

100

'You hung up on me!' he said into the phone standing up. 'What?! I can't hear you.' He could make out Suzi was asking for the address of where he was. 'I'll text you the address. I'm hanging up because I can't hear you!'

He did as he had said then attempted to text her the address.

'Wait, where the hell am I?' he asked Ashley who went to kiss him again.

'I've got to tell Suzi where I am. The address.'

'You're on the corner off…' Ashley's face suddenly went white and she moved to the edge of the bouncy castle where she vomited.

'Is she OK?' asked Johnny, slurring his words, noticing her friend coming to her aid.

He maneuvered himself off the castle, trying to gain his balance when he saw Suzi suddenly walking towards him from the back of the house.

'Suzi!' said Johnny going to hug her enthusiastically.

'No. I am not in the mood,' replied Suzi irritably, pushing him away. 'I hope you have not lost my keys?'

'What? No.' He smiled and dug into his pockets, taking them out to dangle in front of her smugly.

'Let's go.'

'Hang on!'

Johnny turned to witness Ashley vomit again. Her friend looked fiercely at him as he moved towards them. He followed Suzi into the house instead.

'How did you find me?' he asked her.

'You texted me the address.'

'Did I?'

'Well you wrote the words bouncy castle. Thankfully, I spotted it from the street.'

She turned to see familiar faces giving her funny looks.

'Oh my God all my students are here. Why did you bring me here?'

'I need some water.'

'Wait till we get home!'

He ignored her and walked into the kitchen to pour himself some water from the tap.

'Hey, aren't you?' said an awkward looking student hovering close by.

'Hello. Yes. I teach you,' said Suzi moving Johnny out of the house. 'We're going.'

'You're pissed off with me?' said Johnny as they left the front door.

'Yes I am. You left my friend's house for a student party. I think it is kind of rude. You didn't even warn me you weren't back in the house. I was knocking on my front door for half an hour waiting for you to wake up!'

'I wasn't expecting to get sidetracked.' He tripped on a step but managed to gain his balance.

'Oh my God, how much did you drink?'

'Quite a lot. I had a lot at Nicola's. Then this girl made me do shots, and I snorted coke.'

'You snorted coke?'

'Well, I rubbed some on my gums and then put a bit up my nose. It just feels like I'm really drunk.'

'Let's go Johnny,' she said storming in front of him.

'Don't be annoyed with me,' he said following her.

'Why not?!'

'OK. I'm sorry, but to be honest, your friend Nicola's cool, but it was hardly the most exciting bash in the world. And that other guy...'

'Dan?'

'Yeah. He's kind of a dick.'

'Hey don't be rude about my friend.'

'He has a very high opinion of himself. Why are you defending him, do you fancy him?'

'What, no, I don't fancy him, he's a friend.'

'You want to go grab some food?'

'You can grab some when we get back in my house.'

'Or we could go to the taco truck!' his face lit up by the thought of this. 'Yeah, let's get tacos!'

'No. I don't want to go to the taco truck Johnny. I'm tired.'

'Please I need some food. It'll sober me up!'

'It's miles away.'

'What? It's about a mile down the road!'

'This is LA. A mile is a long way.'

'I really need some dirty food to sober me up. I'll get to bed and my head will be spinning!'

'I'm not going to win this.'

'Is that a yes?!'

'Fine, we'll go to the taco truck if it shuts you up!'

They headed down to the end of the road where they ordered cheese enchiladas, then walked back to the house.

'I don't want to go back, just yet,' replied Johnny.

'Johnny, we've ordered food like you wanted. Let's just go back home.'

'What's the hill above you called?'

'Mount Arthur. Why?'

'Let's go there.'

'Why do you want to walk up there now?'

'Because I still have tons of energy. There'll be a great view. It'll be totally worth it. Come on!' He grabbed her hand.

'I'm eating my food. Why do I always give into you like this?!' she said giving into his drunken enthusiasm.

They walked up through the quiet college grounds, passing the odd student heading back to their dorm, up the steps to the top of the campus where they sat down on the dry soil of Mount Arthur and looked out at the impressive view over the greater LA area which shone in the night.

'I love that view,' Johnny remarked.

'It's not too bad.'

'I'm sorry about tonight.'

'It's OK. It was nice seeing you have fun for a change.'

Johnny turned to look at her and suddenly went to kiss her. Suzy flinched.

'Oh my God Johnny what are you doing?!' she said quickly standing up.

'I'm just. I don't know.'

'You like me as a friend. And you're drunk, or high. Whatever you are, we're friends, OK?! I do not want to be some rebound girl!'

'You're not a rebound girl.' He ducked his head shamefully as he suddenly began to sober up. 'I'm sorry.'

'Just don't do it again.' She sat back down, brushing away some dirt on her shoulders.

'I won't. I'm sorry.'

'I said it's fine!'

'We should head back.'

'I think that's best.'

They walked back down the hill in silence, keeping a suitable distance from each other, and as Johnny began to sober up even more, he felt increasingly embarrassed about what he had done.

'I'll see you in the morning. Drink some water,' Suzi insisted before she retired to her bed.

Johnny did as she requested, downed a glass of water from the tap, filled up another pint, and took it to his room. He quickly undressed, throwing his clothes all over the floor. He was about to turn off the bedside light when the thought suddenly dawned on him. He got up, went into his jeans pocket and got out his phone. He had done what he had sworn not to do after he had spoken to her last and she had ended their relationship. He had texted Rachel at some point during the night, a brief message which read, *I am drunk and I miss you. Johnny x.*

Los Angeles, USA and Rosarito, Mexico

Johnny arrived at LAX Airport mid-afternoon feeling smug as he had successfully made his way through the confusing LA freeway system using a hired car. It was the start of spring break and Suzi had left earlier that morning to attend a work conference in Florida. Knowing he was going to be alone for the week, Johnny had contacted his sister to ask if she wanted to visit him. 'I am very busy with work,' she had told him on the phone, playing tough to get. 'It'll be very hard to just take time off like that and very expensive.' She had messaged him a week later, asking for dates, then followed it up with a confirmation email of her imminent arrival. Johnny had gone online shortly after this, managing to get a good deal on a hotel for two nights in the small Mexican resort of Rosarito.

He arrived in the arrivals area moments before his sister, Claudia, appeared. She was wheeling a trolley holding an expensive designer suitcase; it was obvious she was making the most out of her recent promotion.

'Hey!' he said going to give her a hug. 'How was the flight?'

'I went business. Plenty of room. No screaming kids,' she boasted.

'Alright money bags. How did you afford that?'

'I have air miles. *Had* I might add. Where are you parked?'

'Not far. So I need to tell you something.'

'What have you done?'

'Nothing bad. I may have invited someone else to come Mexico with us.'

'Who is this someone?'

'No one you know. A girl.'

'Why haven't you consulted me about this?'

'Well I only found out she was coming a couple of days ago.'

'Who is she?'

'She's called Rachel, and well, we went out briefly.'

'Oh great. So I've flown half way around the world to spend time with you and an awkward ex. That's money well spent.'

'Look her dad died. That's sort of why we broke up and they got some money in his will to bury his ashes in the Grand Canyon. Her family has all been over here doing that and she had a few days before she went home and she asked me if I wanted to meet up. This is the only time I could see her. I thought this would be OK.'

'I'm not sharing a room with her.'

'I've booked two rooms. But it does mean we have to wait around here a bit longer for her flight to arrive.'

'Fine,' she said, handing over her trolley. 'I'll go get a coffee.'

He got a text from Rachel. *Just landed. Still in Terminal 2? x*

Yep. Here now. See you in a bit, he replied.

The first thing he noticed when he met Rachel was how casual she acted around him, as if they had never broken up at all.

'Good to see you,' he remarked.

'Hey stranger.'

He gave her a stilted hug.

'So this is my sister.' Johnny said trying to glaze off the awkwardness between them. 'Claudia, this is Rachel.'

'Hey Claudia.'

'Nice to meet you.'

'So let's head to the car,' said Johnny. 'Anyone want a hand with their bags?'

Claudia handed her suitcase over with a cheeky smile.

'So how was the Grand Canyon?' Johnny quizzed Rachel.

'It was OK.'

'Sorry to hear about your dad,' said Claudia.

'That's OK.'

'Where's the rest of your family?' asked Johnny.

'They're all flying back today.'

'By the way, I might be a little tipsy. I had a few drinks on the plane,' said Rachel.

Claudia shot a subtle disapproving look at Johnny and he knew comments like this were not going to go down well.

'I'm sure my driving will sober you up,' jested Johnny.

They drove south out of Los Angeles towards San Diego on the 405.

'God it's just so nice to get out of LA for a few days,' Johnny remarked.

'Get you sounding all Californian,' said Claudia.

'Well I have been here a while. So I should also probably warn you both that it's spring break and I think the resort where we are going is probably going to be full of a whole load of drunken American college kids.'

'Sounds like fun,' said Rachel.

'Could we have not chosen somewhere less studenty?' asked Claudia.

'Let's just see what it's like when we get there.'

'So where do you live Claudia?' asked Rachel.

'London.'

'Right. I forgot you guys used to live together.'

'We did. Before he gave up his room to go travelling.'

'So who have you been staying with in LA?' asked Rachel, coaxing information out of him.

'Suzi,' replied Johnny.

'She's the Austrian girl, right? Eric's cousin.'

'That's the one.'

'You must have been staying with her a while, right?'

'Yeah. She managed to get me a job for a few months. Cash in hand.'

'Isn't that illegal?' Claudia interrupted.

'Well technically, yes. But it's all done under the radar.'

'So when did you and Johnny last see each other?' Claudia asked Rachel.

'About four months ago,' replied Rachel.

'And you've been back in England since then?'

'Yep. Back in Brighton.'

'How's that been?'

'Pretty depressing to be honest. My family are having quite a few issues at the moment.'

'Your dad must have really wanted his ashes to be scattered out here if he paid for all of you to come here,' said Johnny.

'I think he did. He was probably worried Mum would pour them down the kitchen sink if he didn't.'

'Would she do that?' asked Claudia, taken back by her comment.

'They had a complicated relationship,' replied Rachel.

The hotel in Rosarito was a small and dilapidated establishment, dwarfed by a modern tacky hotel next door which was playing loud music for its college guests.

'OK, so there are two rooms,' said Johnny handing out keys in the lobby after he had checked them in. 'I don't know if Rachel you want to go in one. Claudia and I can go in the other?'

'Sure,' said Rachel taking it.

'I'm sure Rachel can survive by herself,' remarked Claudia.

'Be nice,' said Johnny, after Rachel had headed to the lift.

'I am being nice,'

'Do you not like her?'

'She seems fine. A bit young, a bit immature, but I'm sure we'll survive.'

That evening they went for food down the road at a small Mexican restaurant the hotel receptionist had recommended.

'So have you managed to get a job since you moved back to Brighton?' Claudia asked Rachel while they looked through their colourful menus.

'Not yet. I inherited a bit of cash off my dad so that should keep me going for a while.'

'What do you want to do?' asked Claudia.

'Rachel wants to design greeting cards,' Johnny informed her.

'That's very niche,' said Claudia.

'What do you do?' asked Rachel.

'I'm a solicitor.'

'Wow, impressive.'

'What you want to do sounds a lot more interesting,' replied Claudia. Johnny was pleased she was starting to make an effort. 'Can you order me chicken fajitas and a coke?' she said turning to Johnny.

'Where you off?' he asked.

'The ladies.'

'Why did you put me in the room by myself?' asked Rachel, once Claudia had left.

'I thought that would be better. Less awkward. We're not going out.'

'I know that.'

'I mean, we broke up. You broke up with me, via email which I didn't think was the nicest way to do it, but still.'

'Are you *seeing* that Suzi girl?'

'What? No. We're friends.'

'If you didn't want me to come on holiday with your sister then you should have told me.'

'When did I say I didn't want you to come? Look can we just try and enjoy this trip.'

Claudia returned to the table shortly after.

'That was quick,' said Johnny.

'Someone was already in there. Did the waiter come?' said Claudia.

'Nope,' replied Johnny.

'Everything OK?' asked Claudia, sensing the tension between them.

'Fine,' said Johnny.

They sat there awkwardly throughout the rest of the meal until the bill was paid.

'Are we going somewhere else for a drink?' asked Rachel.

'You guys can. I'm off to bed. Have you got the key?' replied Claudia.

Johnny felt for it in his pocket. 'Yep.'

'Good,' said Claudia, grabbing it. 'I'll see you guys tomorrow.'

When Claudia had left, Johnny and Rachel walked to a beach bar, down the road, which was full of college students.

'What do you want?' asked Rachel as they pushed their way through the crowd of exposed body parts.

'I'll have a beer.'

She disappeared amongst the crowd while Johnny found a spare spot to wait for her. Through a gap in the rabble he noticed Rachel was now talking to a student of similar age, at the bar.

'Who's the guy?' Johnny asked when Rachel approached the table with their drinks.

'I don't know. He just sounded American and drunk. Got your eye on anyone?' she said, quickly changing the subject.

'I'm not really looking,'

Rachel started to laugh as she made eye contact with the student.

'What's he doing?' asked Johnny.

'Nothing.'

'Well he's obviously doing something otherwise you wouldn't be laughing.'

'Nothing. Just drink your beer.'

Johnny quickly finished his bottle. 'You want another drink?' he asked.

'Sure. Vodka lemonade. I'll see you on floor,' she said, walking off, disappearing into the crowds.

Johnny walked to the bar, ordered and collected their drinks, then headed back to the same spot. Half an hour later, Rachel had still not returned. Losing his patience, Johnny got up, scurried through the crowds, where he found Rachel dancing alluringly with the student she had been flirting with earlier. He tapped her on the shoulder.

'I'm going,' he said. 'There's your drink.'

Rachel quickly followed him out of the bar.

'Wait. You can't just go off!' she retorted.

'You seem like your making friends.'

'I was having fun. Can you please wait for me because I don't know the way back to the hotel!'

'Well I'm going back now.'

'Fine! Well I don't really have a choice then do I?!' Rachel fumed.

'I guess not!'

She followed on behind him.

The next day after they had eaten breakfast the three of them walked down to the beach to sunbathe. Rachel kept her sunbed noticeably apart from Johnny and his sister.

'Everything alright between you two?' asked Claudia, pausing on her book, pressing him for answers, after Rachel had left her sunbed to walk alone along the beach.

'It's not great,' replied Johnny.

'Why did you invite her if it was going to be weird like this?'

'Honestly. I don't know.'

'What are we doing after this?' inquired Rachel after they had finished their meal at the bland hotel restaurant on their second evening.

'We can go for a couple of drinks,' replied Claudia. 'I'm actually rather in the mood to have a few cocktails.'

Johnny felt uncomfortable by his sister's unexpected burst of playfulness but he was willing to go along with it.

They entered another bar nearby which was also full of students dressed in beachwear, drinking around a swimming pool. There was a Mexican man with a microphone on a stage by the pool, next to a large collection of young attractive men and women.

'What do you want?!' shouted the Mexican man into the microphone.

'Tits!' shouted the group of jocks.

The Mexican edged towards the girls and said down his microphone, 'What do you want?!'

'Dicks!' shouted the girls.

'What do you want?!' he said again to the group of boys.

'Tits!' they replied even louder.

'What do you want?' he said enthusiastically to the girls again.

'Dicks!'

Claudia looked on in horror.

'Enjoying yourself?' Johnny asked his sister.

'This place is foul,' replied Claudia cuttingly.

'Are you now ready for naked bungee jump?!' replied the Mexican presenter. There was a loud cheer.

Johnny looked up to see a naked girl strapped into a harness standing at the top of tower above them.

'One. Two!' said the Mexican man.

The crowd joined in. 'Three!'

They all faced up to view the naked girl tumble off the edge of the tower, attached to the bungee rope which stretched down with her weight as she fell, dipping the top of her head into the swimming pool, while the crowd cheered with joy.

Johnny turned to see Rachel talking to the student she had chatted up the night before.

'Someone's up for a good time,' Claudia jested. 'And you thought bringing your ex-girlfriend wasn't going to be awkward.'

'Fuck off Claudia,' replied Johnny.

'I'm just saying.'

Rachel headed over with the student.

'Hey. This is Phil,' she said.

'Hi,' said Johnny instantly dismissing him. 'I think Claudia wants to go somewhere quieter.'

'Good luck finding somewhere quieter around here,' replied Rachel.

'I take it you're not coming?' he asked.

'I'm good,' Rachel said, touching Phil's back.

'You OK finding your way back this time?' asked Johnny.

'Yes. I'll be fine.'

'OK. Well text me when you get back?'

Rachel didn't reply, she smiled insincerely, then turned her back to him.

'You think she's going to be OK?' Johnny asked his sister as they walked out of the bar, unsure as to why he still cared.

'Well she obviously wants to stay out so I don't think you really have a choice,' replied Claudia.

It was 2.30am when Johnny got the call on his mobile.

'Johnny,' said a distressed Rachel down the other line. 'You've got to help me. You've got to come pick me up.'

'Where are you?'

'At a hotel.'

'What's it called?'

'The Motel Blue Moon.'

'Just stay there.'

He didn't bother waking Claudia who was fast asleep. He got dressed, left the room and managed to get a taxi from the hotel reception. He was surprised by how far Rachel had ended up from the resort. When he arrived, she was sitting on a bench, outside of a neglected motel, below a half-lit neon sign.

'You OK? What happened?' asked Johnny while getting out of the taxi to sit down next to her. Her eyeliner was smudged and her eyes were red.

'I came back to a house party out here with that guy I was taking to. He seemed really nice. When we got there they all started drinking and doing loads of other stuff. He kissed me and then he was getting really full on. I told him I wasn't in the mood and he got really angry with me. He wouldn't let me go, so I pushed him away and just left the building. The next thing I know I was walking down this country road. I had no idea where I was. I saw this place and the guy at the motel let me call you.'

He opened the taxi door for her, helped her in and sat down next to her.

'I was really freaking out being alone out there. I thought some drug baron was going to come and kidnap me. We are in Mexico after all,' she remarked.

Johnny turned to the driver. 'No offence.'

The driver grunted disapprovingly.

'Any chance we could head back please?' asked Johnny.

The driver turned on the ignition. As they were on the road, Rachel fell asleep on Johnny.

'You got your key?' he asked as he approached her hotel room door.

She sleepily went through her purse. 'Yes, thank you,' she said going to kiss him on the cheek.

'You OK?' he asked.

'Sure,' she replied closing her door behind him.

Rachel did not appear for breakfast the next morning. After Johnny and Claudia had packed their bags, they met Rachel at reception and walked to the car and made their way north, back

114

over the border, to LAX airport where Rachel was getting a flight back to Heathrow that evening.

'You OK waiting here?' he asked Claudia after he pulled up outside the terminal building.

'Sure. Have a safe flight Rachel.'

'Thanks,' she replied.

Their goodbye had been more civil than Johnny had expected.

'I'll take it,' insisted Rachel when Johnny got her bag from the boot of his car.

They headed into the building to find her desk.

'Well. You should probably head off. I don't want you getting overcharged for the hired car,' she said.

'I'll be fine. Listen Rachel. I don't think we should see each other again,' replied Johnny.

'Why did I know that was coming.'

'I think it's for the best. Don't you?'

Rachel looked down, and fumbled with her suitcase label, then looked up at him and nodded in agreement. 'Well. Goodbye then, it was nice knowing you,' she replied, giving him a brief smile, then walking off to join the queue. It seemed uneventful considering what was happening.

'Goodbye Rachel,' he replied, quietly to himself before leaving the building, feeling perplexed by their sudden parting.

New York City, USA

Johnny grabbed his shabby rucksack, flung it over of his shoulders then went to pick up Suzi's smart weekend suitcase

They entered a plain 1960s building, taking an escalator up into the trendy boutique hotel Suzi had booked them into. They arrived in the spacious lobby which had several large plants growing up exposed brick on all four walls and an impressive glass roof.

'So, a room together?' asked the girl behind the desk

'No, separate,' replied Suzi bluntly.

'Are you happy to have rooms next to one another?' the girl asked.

'Yeah, that be great,' replied Johnny.

After a quick check in, they caught the lift to the thirteenth floor to find their smart but small rooms, with dark blue walls, dark wooden flooring and chic mahogany furniture.

'Good find,' remarked Johnny, drinking from his Mojito while they sat at the hotel's rooftop bar, enjoying the unusually warm spring sunshine and looking out at a view of the Hudson River and the Upper West Side.

'Well I'm pleased you approve,' Suzi said.

'Even my trusty travel book recommends it,' he said lifting up the book up which was starting to look tired and warn out.

116

Suzi tittered. 'You love that book way too much. So, what do you want to do?'

'There's a few ideas,' he said looking through the pages on New York. 'Maybe we should head to Central Park.'

'Sure, we can do that.' She gave an indifferent shrug.

'You don't sound so keen? We can just hang out here. See the sights tomorrow?'

'No, let's do stuff today. You're only here for a few days, before you leave me for England,' Suzi winced, then looked at her phone.

'Still thinking about Robert?'

'Yes. I'm ashamed to say it,' she replied. 'I just keep thinking if he wants to finish with me, he should just tell me, and not leave me hanging like this. I don't know why I'm getting so worked up about this.'

'Well sometimes people have that effect on one another.'

'I don't like feeling this way. Like I'm not in control. It's not even been three months.'

'Hey, nothing wrong with admitting you're a control freak.'

'Well, yes. I know I am,' Suzi smiled. 'You're right, I think we should go to Central Park. I could do with a walk.'

They walked towards Columbus Square where they entered the park.

'So, you remember much from when you were last here?' Suzi asked

'Sure. We came here as kids when I was about eight. Don't remember much, except my mum being obsessed with going to Macy's,' replied Johnny.

'Oh, that's sweet.'

'You've been here right?' asked Johnny.

'Yeah, with my dad,' replied Suzi.

'You don't mention him much?'

'No. I know. It makes me sad. He loved this place though. He was rude about a lot of cities in America, but not here.'

'So how come you chose to live in LA?'

'I got a job there and I liked the idea of the weather always being good.'

'Well it's pretty good here at the moment'

'It gets cold here in winter. Trust me. In LA you can sunbathe in January. Where else can you do that?'

'Well you can sunbathe in England in January, but I doubt you'd get much of a suntan.'

'The sun never comes out in England, even in summer.'

'You're very rude about my home country.'

'The fog islanders. That's what my dad used to call the British.'

'A pretty accurate description.'

They sat on a bench at the side of a busy walk way and watched joggers, tourists and workers going about their busy lives.

'So, have you enjoyed your time in The States?' asked Suzi.

'Every moment.'

'I wish you could have stayed longer.'

'Me too. But we'll stay in touch.'

'Damn right we will. So, what's next?' she asked as he read from his book.

'Staten Island Ferry?'

'How far?'

'Well it's in Lower Manhattan, so we'll have to catch the subway.'

'And what does the travel book tell us about the ferry?'

'It calls it the best free attraction in the city.'

'I see.'

'A 5.2 mile journey between Lower Manhattan and the Staten Island district, offering breathtaking views of the city. An unmissable adventure it says, and free.'

'I'm sold.'

They caught the subway down to the ferry station where they got on board the next boat with a scattering of tourists.

'I always thought the Statue of Liberty seems so small in real life. In the films they make it look so big,' Suzi commented as she lent on a greasy rail as the boat sailed out of the harbour.

'Everything looks bigger in the movies,' replied Johnny.

They took photos of the Manhattan skyline in the distance, then walked downstairs as the ferry arrived at Staten Island where Suzi's phone rang as they left the vessel.

'I gotta take this,' she said walking off.

Johnny strolled towards the terminal store to look at tacky merchandise, sporadically looking over to see Suzi who was deep in conversation. After he had bought a hand sized Statue of Liberty, he turned to see Suzi ending her conversation with tears in her eyes.

'He just broke up with me,' replied Suzi.

'I'm sorry.'

'Some stupid nonsense about not being in the right frame of mind to be dating. Who says that clichéd crap?! I'm annoyed at myself for getting so worked up about it. I hate him. Fucking dick head.'

'I love it when you swear in your German accent,' joked Johnny, trying to make her feel better.

'It's not a German accent, it's Austrian,' she said alternating between tears and laughter.

'Let's go walk this off,' Johnny said aiding her out of the port building.

They walked aimlessly around the suburban streets of Staten Island, with Johnny trying his best to salvage the situation. He'd always been the guy the girls spoke to at university after breaking up with boyfriends. The one to give the male perspective but he knew very little about this guy. It was clear he had messed Suzi around and that annoyed him.

They spotted the ferry coming back into port and decided to return to Manhattan.

'Any word from Rachel?' asked Suzi, taking a sip of her cool beer in a bar close to Wall Street, trying to move the conversation onto Johnny.

'Nope. Not since Mexico. And from the way she acted last time I think it will probably be the last. Don't ever go on holiday with an ex.'

'Well there isn't much chance of that happening. I'm going to be alone the rest of my life.'

'As if.'

'But I'm OK with that. I like my company.'

'You don't know what's around the corner.'

'How about we get some food here?' asked Suzi.

'We're booked into that snazzy restaurant at the hotel, remember?'

'What?'

'I told you about this. My treat as you booked everything and did all the hard work.'

'I love you right now.'

They returned to their hotel to get dressed for the night and met in the downstairs hotel bar at 7.30pm. Suzi appeared wearing an exquisite black dress, and Johnny a blue shirt with smart casual grey trousers. They were both impressed by the efforts they had made. A waiter showed them to their table where they ordered an expensive bottle of red wine.

It was just before they were about to order food, when Suzi asked what they had planned to do the following day, when a feeling of panic took hold of Johnny's face.

'Hang on, I didn't bring the travel book back with me when we got back to the hotel. You don't think I left it somewhere, do you?' he said.

'Possibly, or it could be in the hotel room?'

'Shit,' Johnny said, standing up with his heart pumping inside his chest.

'I'm sorry. I'm going to have to check my room.'

He left Suzi, then strode out of the restaurant towards the lift which took him back to his room, where he willed his way through his items, searching every nook and cranny, but his travel book was nowhere to be found.

'Any luck?' asked Suzi, trying to show an interest when he returned to the table.

'No. I'm sorry, I'm going to have to go back to the bar.'

'What! Now?! Johnny, it's a travel book. You can just buy a new one.'

'This makes no sense but I have to find it.'

'This is insane. We've just sat down in the restaurant!'

'I'm sorry.'

He dashed out of the room, heading out of the hotel to catch the subway south to the bar they had gone to earlier, which was full of business types drinking after work.

'Hi, sorry, I think I left a travel book here,' flapped Johnny, asking the first waitress he could find.

'OK. Let me check if anything got left here,' replied the small wiry middle-aged woman.

Johnny turned to see a group of young men in their twenties drinking in the spot he'd sat before.

'No book here,' said the waitress returning.

Johnny looked at the group of lads and walked over.

'Hey guys.'

'Hey,' said the alpha male of the group. He had thick black hair which gave off a cocksure demeanour.

'I was sat here earlier,' said Johnny. 'I think I might have left my travel book.'

'Oh. OK. You mean, this one?' he said, lifting it up.

121

'That would be the one. Cheers,' Johnny heaved a sigh of relief, then went to grab it.

'Woah woah woah,' he replied, withholding the book. 'How do I know it's yours?'

'Come on Zac, hand the guy his book,' said his friend.

'Well, it's got my handwriting in it,' Johnny remarked.

'OK,' he said flicking through it. 'Well how do I know it's your handwriting? That could be anyone's writing.'

'Give the guy his book,' said his friend, irked by his cockiness.

'OK, fine. I'll prove it. Chapter on Sydney, above the opening paragraph, there is a girl's name written on there with a number,' said Johnny.

'OK. So now we're onto something,' he said sourcing out the page. 'What name is it?' he said testing him.

'Rachel. Her name is Rachel.'

'Come on man. Just give the guy his book back,' riled another member of the group.

The guy looked straight into Johnny's eyes, attempting to figure him out. 'This girl meant something to you,' he asked.

'Yes. At one point. She did,' Johnny answered wistfully.

'She's all yours,' he replied, handing over the book.

'Thank you,' Johnny held the book tightly to his chest, then darted straight to the door.

When he arrived back at the restaurant, Suzi had gone, so he made his way up to her room and knocked on the door, where she answered moments later.

'I'm sorry,' Johnny said propping open the door, stopping Suzi from closing it.

'I waited there almost an hour.'

'I know.'

'I needed you today after breaking up with Robert. You said we were going to have a nice night and you just walked out on me, leaving me there in the restaurant alone to go get some silly little travel book! Ok, I get it. it has history. But it's a shitty way to treat me!'

'I'm sorry, but I don't know why, I just had to find it. I know it's bonkers.'

'Yes, it is.'

Johnny suddenly went to kiss her. Suzi pushed him away.

'Why did you just do that?!' she snapped.

'I don't know. It just felt like the right thing to do'.

Suzi looked back at him. 'You totally confuse me Johnny. What do you want from me?'

Johnny went to kiss her again, and against all logic, she did not resist his advances.

Brighton, UK

A hung-over Rachel lay in her bed as a draught swept towards her from a crack in the old crumbling sash window next to her. Although it was mid-spring, winter had made an abrupt return and the small electric heater in the high ceilinged room was making little difference. Rachel's throat felt unbearably dry as she turned to find her cup of water empty. She noticed a brown sweater lying on the floor which gave off a smell of cigarettes, left by the lad who had been in her bed earlier. She couldn't remember his name. He seemed more of a man the more she recalled.

She looked up at the unappealing ceiling above her with its patches of peeled paint and damp stains. She was sharing the room with her old school friend, Sam, who had allowed Rachel to move in, rent free, until she got herself sorted. It had seemed like the only option after the ferocious argument she'd had with her mother which had ended with her leaving the family home.

Sam had only left the night before to visit her boyfriend. In this time, Rachel had managed to spill wine on the carpet, unload the contents of her bag and most of the clothes from Sam's cupboard all over the floor. Her friend would not be impressed by the state of her room.

Rachel forced herself out of bed. Her balance was disjointed, but she managed to control it. She grabbed her father's dressing gown, then walked downstairs where Sam's housemate, Jovita, a short-tempered Latvian girl, was making tea in the kitchen.

'Morning,' said Rachel attempting to make an effort.

'Afternoon,' she replied waspishly. 'I heard you come in last night.'

'Yeah, sorry. I may have been loud.'

'The guy you bought home was louder.'

Rachel didn't reply.

'So how long do you stay here?' Jovita asked abruptly.

'Hopefully not too long.'

'There's some post for you in the hallway,' she said leaving the room.

Rachel had felt guilty for putting their house address on her mail, but it had seemed like a temporary solution.

She walked back upstairs to look at her phone. She'd got a text from her sister. *Please phone Mum. She's worried about you x'* Rachel put down her phone and turned to look at the time on Sam's alarm clock. It was not long before she was meeting her new friend, Vanessa, for another night of drinking. She didn't dare think about how much she had spent over the last few weeks, or wonder how much of her father's small inheritance she'd drank her way through.

She forced herself to have a shower which made her feel refreshed for the night ahead. She would feel even better once she'd had another drink. She went to Sam's cupboard where she found a red sequin dress. Sam wouldn't mind her borrowing it. After all, none of Rachel's clothes were clean anyway. Justifying her actions, she grabbed it from the hanger and remorselessly slipped it on. She turned on the radio which was playing dance music, then went to grab a bottle of vodka. She poured it into the glass by her bed. It warmed her throat and numbed the anxiety she'd been feeling. She grabbed a pair of Sam's high heels and slipped them on. Vanessa hadn't liked the casual shoes she had worn the last time they went out.

125

Her phone rang, it was the taxi driver waiting outside. She grabbed her jacket and left the house.

'You again,' jested the taxi man.

Rachel smiled.

'You snooze you lose, right?' replied Rachel.

'Don't know where you get the energy from love. You're young, I'll give you that. Same address?'

'Yep.'

Vanessa's house was a ten-minute drive towards Hove in a new build estate.

Vanessa was looking as glamorous as ever when she answered the door. Large gold dangly earrings, an impressive tan and a perfect body. She went to kiss Rachel on the cheek.

'The taxi driver remembered me, thinks I go out too much,' Rachel remarked.

'Nothing wrong with that. I would have got Jason to pick you up but he's up north playing football' said Vanessa.

Rachel entered the house which looked like a showroom. Vanessa, who worked in accounts, had moved in there recently with her estate agent boyfriend. The whole house was full of pictures of the two of them in love heart picture frames.

Vanessa grabbed the Prosecco in her smart black and white kitchen and poured it into some new sparkly glasses.

'Jason's dad got us these glasses as a housewarming present. But Jason's trying to stay off it for a while. Cheers.'

They both took a sip.

'This Prosecco is lovely. Always quite fancied Jason's dad,' Vanessa remarked.

'How old is he?'

'I don't know. Fortyish. He's quite hot. I quite like an older man. So, thought we'd stay here for a few, then head to All Bar One, then go onto Ronny's.'

'Ronny's again?'

'It's good music.'

126

They moved to the beige carpeted living room which was fitted with fairy lights and more pictures of their perfect relationship.

'Feels like ages since I've been out without my Jason,' said Vanessa.

'Why is Jason not drinking?'

'Trying to be good. Says he's losing his six-pack.'

She looked back at Rachel. 'You need to get yourself a boyfriend Rachel.'

'I will one day. For now, I'm fine.'

Rachel was starting to feel fuddled by the alcohol when she caught another taxi to the centre of Brighton with Vanessa.

When the taxi pulled up on the other side of the road from All Bar One, Rachel tottered out of the vehicle, stepping out into the road, narrowly missing a bus which was heading her way.

'For fuck's sake Rachel, that was well close!' fumed Vanessa.

'I'm fine.'

'You gave me a bloody heart attack! You've got to watch yourself! Can you imagine what may have happened?!'

'Sorry. It's OK.'

'Need a drink after that.'

They walked across the road then headed into the busy bar. They could hear whistles from a group of older lads in smart shoes and plain prime coloured shirts, which they both ignored.

Vanessa walked confidently to the bar. Her height and looks always meant she got served quicker.

Rachel felt a nudge on the shoulder. She turned to see her brother-in-law who she was surprised to see out.

'Hello,' he said awkwardly.

'Oh. Hi Lawrence,' replied Rachel. 'Is Becca here?'

'No. At home. Let me off for the night. Mate's stag do drinks.'

'I see.'

'Your sister's been worried about you. She says you never reply to her texts.'

'I'm fine. Living with a friend.'

'Saw your mum the other day. She's worried too.'

'I'm fine. Honestly.'

'Look I know it's not my business but can I tell them I saw you?'

She knew he would do anyway. 'OK, fine,' she replied. 'Not that my mum really cares.'

'I know she's tricky, but she does care about you in her own weird way.'

'Have a good night,' said Rachel, making it clear she wanted to end their conversation.

'You too.'

She barged through the crowds to find Vanessa who was talking to an inebriated middle-aged man at the bar. She looked at her phone to see Sam calling.

'Hey' Rachel said picking up.

'Where are you Rachel?' said an irritated voice.

'Just in a bar.'

'Well I've just got back to my room.'

'You're back tonight? I thought you were coming back on Sunday?'

'Rachel, my room is disgusting!'

'Oh, sorry.'

'I thought I was doing you a favour, giving you a place to stay.'

'You were.'

'And this is how you repay me? There are wine stains on the carpet, you've emptied half my cupboard on the floor, this is *so* not cool.'

'Who are you talking too?' asked Vanessa approaching.

'Just a friend,' replied Rachel, putting her hand over her mobile so Sam couldn't hear.

Vanessa grabbed the phone. 'She'll call you back', said Vanessa loudly down the phone laughing.

Rachel took the phone back off her.

'Ignore that, it's just a friend. Look, I know I'm messy. I'll clean out the room in the morning. OK?'

'You'll be hungover. You already sound drunk Rachel. I'm sorry. Look, this isn't going to work. You're a friend, but I can't have you treat my stuff like this, I think you need to find some other accommodation.'

'You're kicking me out?!'

'Yes. I feel really horrible about what's going on with you and your mum, but my housemates are getting really annoyed about the whole living situation.'

'Your housemate, Jovita, is a bitch!' snapped Rachel.

'They've already pointed out you've been sending letters to our address.'

'I had nowhere else to send them!'

'You need to clear your stuff out tomorrow Rachel.'

'Where am I supposed to go?'

'I don't know. But I've done my fair share of helping you out, you don't appreciate people Rachel, you never have!'

'That's not true!'

'And how are you affording to be going out all the time when you say you have no money?!'

Rachel didn't have an answer for that. 'Fine! Well some fucking friend you are!' she replied tersely, ending the call.

'She's throwing me out!' Rachel said, turning to Vanessa.

'Who is?'

'Sam, my friend I've been sharing a room with! You haven't got a spare room have you?'

'Oh babe, we do have the spare room, but we're doing it up. Decorators coming in on Monday. Otherwise, I'd totally take you in.' She quickly changed the subject. 'Now come on, get another one of these down to you.'

She passed her another shot.

'Fuck it. I'm going just going to get drunk. Really fucking drunk!' Rachel decided.

Vanessa ordered another round, before they headed to a club where Vanessa had managed to get them on the VIP list.

The club was in an old restored church, where there was a dance floor on different levels. The two girls stuck to a group of men in their late thirties who bragged about their impressive salaries. It was on the fourth round of drinks Rachel's balance got the best of her. She turned to Vanessa who now had her lips stuck on a member of the group. She was too drunk to be surprised by this. She knew she needed to get home as every time she closed her eyes the room spun around violently. She grabbed hold of a handlebar and made her way down to a lower level of the building, close to the bar. She could sense people moving away from her as she sat down on some purple suede seats next to a table full of half empty glasses.

'Rachel?' uttered a familiar voice.

She opened her eyes. It was Ross.

'We need to get you some water. Who are you here with?!' he asked worryingly.

She did not answer him. All she could do was vomit onto her dress, and hope that somehow she could escape the lights and voices surrounding her.

York, UK

'Are you going to be warm enough in that?' fussed Johnny's mother passing her son in from the front garden with the family Labrador.

'I'm twenty-nine years old Mum, I think I know how warm I'm going to be.'

'You're looking very smart,' his mother said, remarking on his old sixth form college suit he was wearing.

'It's a temp job.'

'Don't undersell yourself. Now what time's your friend arriving?'

'I'm meeting her at the station. We'll grab some food and then head back afterwards.'

'Oh, so you won't be home for supper?'

'No. I told you we were going to go out. You haven't got stuff in have you?'

'Well, yes, I was going to make a shepherd's pie.'

'Mum. I told you we were going to be out!'

'It's fine.'

'Why do you do this? I tell you something and you don't listen. We'll have to come back now or I'll feel guilty.'

'No, no, you go have a good time. It'll keep for another night.'

His father appeared.

'Clive have you turned the heating on in the spare room for Johnny's friend?' she squawked.

'Yes Pamela. Johnny can you tell your mother to stop fretting!'

'I am not fretting. I am merely asking.'

'Can you guys stop rowing,' said Johnny trying to curb their bickering. 'I'm off.'

'Right, well what time will you be home?' asked his mother.

'He's a grown boy.' His father sighed. 'He'll be home when he's home.'

'See you guys later,' Johnny said, walking away.

Johnny had been back in the UK three months now. He had managed to get a short-term admin job in the office of a bank in an industrial park on the edge of York City Centre. It felt strange to be living back with parents. He hadn't lived with them since before university. The dynamic in the house made him feel like a teenager again. Living with them required certain considerations, informing them if he would be home for supper, and warning them if he had friends staying over, but the fact he didn't pay rent made up for it.

His data entry job at the bank was dull but the people he was working with were friendly and it got him out of the house. His colleagues mainly consisted of York University graduates, who, like him, were temping. His boss, Sean, an unshaven ex-teacher in his late thirties was easy to get on with and created a relaxed environment for them to work in.

'Sorry guys but we've got a company meeting,' announced Sean as Johnny and the rest of the team arrived at their desks that morning.

Johnny and his colleagues were corralled to the other side of the office floor.

'Morning everyone,' said the well-presented mid-forties skinny regional manager, who wore large grasshopper glasses and had a slight nervous twitch whenever she spoke.

132

'I just wanted to meet you all so you knew who I was. I'm Angela. I hope you've all settled in nicely. I know I'm biased but it's a lovely company to work for and there really are a lot of opportunities here. We do have actually have some full-time vacancies popping up very soon at our sister company next door which deals more with the insurance side of things. You might have seen the advert for that company on TV with the nodding horse. We also have nice rewards like our temp of the month, which results in a lucky person getting a small prize and their picture on the company website. That's really everything. I hope you all have a good day and thank you very much.'

There was a small clap from the floor.

'I'm properly going to go one for one of those positions,' said Aatika with her strong hybrid Yorkshire Pakistani accent. Aatika, who was nineteen, had arrived at the office as a temp a month earlier with her younger cousin, Jude, who she enjoyed bossing around.

'How about you Johnny?' asked Aatika as they walked back to their desks. 'You going to go full time here?'

'Probably not. I still want to head back to London at some point.'

'I could never live in London man. Too many people and it's well expensive. My husband wanted me to go to London but I told him I'd leave him.'

'Shut up Aatika,' replied Jude. 'You'd never leave your husband.'

'She's right you know, I wouldn't. You got a girlfriend Johnny?'

'Not right now, no.'

'Why's that?'

'Well I've been travelling. It's hard to meet people when you're always on the move.'

'So, who's this friend you've got coming to stay tonight?'

'Suzi's a mate I stayed with in LA.'

'Oh man, I'd love to go to America.'

133

'You should go.'

'Only country I go to is Pakistan. Never been anywhere else. Saying that if I went to America I'd probably eat too much food, get fat and me husband would leave me.'

Jude chortled at her older cousin's comment.

'What you laughing at Jude?' Aatika smoldered.

'Nothing. Laughing at you. You're funny,' replied Jude.

'So, are you guys actually related?' asked Johnny.

'Yeah man,' replied Aatika. 'I wouldn't call her me younger cousin for nothing would I? She'd be lost without me. She got this job because of me.'

'I got this job off me own back!' Jude snapped back at her cousin. 'You didn't do nothing for me!'

'Shut up Jude. I do *so* much for you!'

'You're so bossy Aatika,' said Johnny intervening.

'I am. I know. That's what my husband tells me,' replied Aatika gleefully.

Kate, a feisty York University graduate from Reading sat down having got a coffee from the machine.

'Where have you been Kate?' asked Aatika.

'Grabbing a coffee, what's it to you?' replied Kate.

'I'm only asking.' Johnny could tell Aatika was scared of Kate.

'Are we a tad hungover?' Johnny asked noticing Kate's languid face.

'Don't. I was working in the hotel last night and it was one of the guy's leaving drinks. I didn't get back 'til 3.00am. I'm knackered.'

'Jesus. How do you manage to keep up with two jobs? Do you actually get any time off?'

'Well I'm not going to pay the rent on the crap money you get here. So, how long's this Austrian friend of yours staying for?'

'A week.'

'Where you going to take her?'

'Probably just show her the sights of York.'

Johnny left work and walked down to York Station where he was meeting Suzi off the 5.30pm train from Manchester Airport. She welcomed him with a tight hug in the station concourse.

'I cannot understand what people say in this country,' said Suzi, handing over one of her bags for Johnny to carry. 'They speak so fast and their accent is so classical. American English is way much easier to understand.'

'Nice to see you too.'

Suzi tittered. 'You OK?'

'I'm good. Pleased to be seeing my favourite Austrian.'

They sauntered out of the station and walked back into the city centre.

'Are you going to tell me what happened, deciding to completely uproot your perfectly amazing LA lifestyle for Austria?' he asked.

'Let's go get a drink.'

They walked towards a pub overlooking the River Ouse.

'So, it all happened very quickly,' said Suzi placing her pint of pale ale on the table with deliberation. 'I got an email from my old boss in Vienna. He told me they were looking for someone and asked if I was interested, so I told him I was. Then I had a Skype interview, which I thought didn't go that well. Saying that I never can tell how well interviews go. Anyway, I got it, and they offered me a salary. It was less than I was getting in the US, so I said I wouldn't return unless they gave me a pay rise. They agreed, I didn't have much time to think about it, so in the end I just decided to, break the bullet, is that the phrase?'

'Bite the bullet.'

She laughed. 'Right. So now I have three weeks off before I start my new life back in Vienna!'

'Wow.'

'It's kind of crazy.'

'Aren't you going to miss LA?'

'Yeah, of course I'll miss it, but I can go back.'

'This is mad. Not that long ago we were in New York and now you're here, and you're moving back to Europe.'

'I know.'

'You want to grab some food?' Johnny said grabbing a menu from the table next to them.

'Sure. What's good?'

'I highly recommend the pies.'

'So how is it being back home with your parents?'

'It's temporary. As I frequently remind myself. But it's fine. Mum just stresses all the time about silly things and my dad basically potters around gardening.'

'And the new job?'

'It's fine. Pay is crap but it gives me time to look for jobs back in London.'

'Really. You're really going to move back?'

'Ah-huh. That's the plan. I mean York's fine, but not where I want to be. I know it so well, it's boring.'

'You should come live in Austria.'

'Yeah, big downside, I don't speak German.'

'So? Unlike you lazy British people, we make the effort to speak other languages. Most young people speak English. You'd be fine.'

Johnny smiled. 'So, have you decided what you're having?'

'I'll go for the ham and mushroom pie, I think,' she said looking at the menu.

'Very decisive, good choice.'

Johnny walked to the bar to order.

'So, are you looking forward to seeing the sights of Yorkshire? God's own county as it's known by many,' he said, placing down their pints on the table.

'Of course. You've got vacation days?'

'Listen to you sounding all American with your vacation days. We call it annual leave here.'

'Whatever.'

'I've got Friday off, but that's it. It's not paid, as I'm temping.'

'That's OK. I'll be tourist. Alone by myself on the other days.'

'But on Friday we can drive off somewhere. Maybe head to the coast if the weather's nice.'

'Which it won't be. This is England.'

'Shut it you.'

'This looks surprisingly good,' Suzi said observing the pies that had arrived at their table later on. She prodded her fork into the middle of the pastry centre, letting out a creamy sauce which slowly flowed onto her plate.

'This just proves this ridiculous stereotype of English food being bad as nonsense!' said Johnny.

Suzi took a bite from her meal. 'This is really good.'

'Hey, I grew up here. I should know where to take the tourists, right?'

'True,' she said mumbling with food in her mouth.

When they had finished their food they walked to another pub where Johnny bought more drinks to the table.

'So, are we going to talk about what happened?' he said broaching the subject they had both ignored

'What do you want to say about it?' she replied.

'I don't know. If you feel it's changed things, I want to know. I don't want it to be awkward.'

'It's not going to be awkward. It was just weird, one minute you're looking for that damn travel book, because I'm assuming it reminded you of Rachel, and the next thing, you're kissing me.'

'Rachel doesn't mean anything to me. She's moved on. I've moved on.'

'I had got over you, you know that? Since you rejected me in Australia.'

'I didn't reject you.'

'Oh. Come on. You did.'

'Alright. Maybe I did, but you rejected me when I kissed you after that party in LA.'

'Rightly so. You were drunk, or high, or whatever you were.'

'Look, I know you're going through a massive transition at the moment, but this could work, you, me, being on the same continent.'

'Yeah. The same continent. Vienna is still a good three-hour flight away.'

'It's better than you being in America.'

'True. OK, I'll give you that.'

'Look we don't have to discuss this now.'

'No. I'm pleased you bought it up. It clears the air.'

After they had finished another round of drinks they walked along the narrow cobbled streets towards York Minster which was fully lit up displaying its majesty in the clear nighttime sky.

'I am liking York, it's sort of pretty,' noted Suzi. 'So how far is your house from here?'

'A twenty-minute walk.'

'What? We are walking? I've had a long day. What happened to driving?'

'No.'

'You forget I've been living in LA. What is this walking?'

'Yeah it's a weird thing us Europeans do.'

'I do not like the sound of this.'

'Well you're back in Europe now so it's time to get used to it.'

Johnny suddenly had the urge to hold Suzi's hand.

'You don't mind me doing that?' he asked.

'No. I don't mind. I'm a little drunk.'

He went to kiss her briefly. They kept their hands locked and walked over a bridge where they looked down at the river flowing quickly below them. Johnny turned to Suzi, who put her hand to his mouth as he edged his lips towards her again.

'No,' she said

'What is it?'

'Before you do this, before we carry on with whatever direction this thing is going, you have to promise me that everything that has gone on with Rachel is over.'

There was a pause as Johnny thought about this. 'Everything that has gone on with Rachel is no more,' he replied.

'Well OK then. I believe you,' she said going to kiss him, and as they walked back to Johnny's parent's house that night, Suzi held Johnny's hand tighter than she had held anyone else's before.

London, UK

'Hello Tremor Productions,' muttered Rachel holding the work phone, trying to pronounce her words audibly, hiding the fact she was still drunk from getting in from a club a couple of hours earlier. 'Sorry? Your name? I can't hear your name?!'

Sahara, her colleague, a young trendy type of similar age, handed Rachel a coffee at the reception desk. She sat down on a chair opposite which collapsed from under her, causing her to fall to the ground. They both fell into a fit of hysterics.

'Hello? Hello?!' said Rachel, trying to hold in her laughter but there was no reply as the person she was talking to had hung up. 'Fucking arse hole! They hung up on me! Arse wipe!' she jeered, putting down the phone turning to Sahara who was attempting to put the chair back together.

'That was hilarious,' said Rachel watching her friend unsuccessfully achieve her goal.

'Shows how cheap the furniture is in this place. I'm still pissed Rach.'

Martha, the company accountant, an abrupt humourless woman appeared at the top of the stairs. 'Someone seems very giddy this morning,' she said in a deep corporate voice.

'My chair broke,' replied Sahara.

'Right, well you better let George know so he can get a new one. By the way I'm expecting a very important phone call from

America. Make sure it's put through,' she demanded before marching back up the stairs.

'She's a right miserable cow,' commented Sahara.

'I just think she needs to get laid,' replied Rachel.

'Yeah. Laid by a lezzer.'

'Is she a lesbian?'

'Probably. She acts like one. What man would want to fuck her?'

'Maybe she's more chilled out when she's not working.'

'Yeah, right.'

'I see glimpses of stuff which makes me think she's actually alright if you got to know her.' Rachel winced and put her hand to her mouth.

'You OK?' asked Sahara as Rachel's face turned white.

'Can you man reception?' said Rachel. 'Think I'm going to be sick.'

'No, you are not!' said Sahara, seeking humour from the situation.

'I am,' said Rachel rushing to the toilet door.

'Such a lightweight!' Sahara called out while taking over her seat at reception.

After closing the toilet door Rachel hovered above the toilet sink then threw up. She lifted her head to look in the mirror then faced the sink to vomit down it again. Rachel looked back at her herself in the mirror. She did not like the unattractive pallor of the face staring back at her. She had gained more weight around her neck and her skin looked blotchy. She knew her endless drinking sessions were beginning to catch up with her. She couldn't remember the last time she had a night in, exercised, or cooked a healthy meal. Her life consisted of trendy Soho bars and cheap takeaways, a lifestyle which seemed to come with her job as a production assistant. If this was what the world of advertising was about, she was unsure how long she could keep up with it.

'Thanks,' said Rachel taking over reception.

'Feeling better?' asked Sahara.

'Think so,' she said attempting to rally herself. Her mobile phone beeped. She'd received a text from Ross.

'What time did you get home last night?' it read.

'Not 'till five,' she replied.

'Who are you texting?' asked Sahara.

'Ross.'

'You're not going to tell him, are you?'

'What? Why would I do that?'

'I don't know. I was worried you were feeling guilty. He was fit Rach. I'd cheat on a boyfriend for someone like that.'

'Why did we drink so much?'

'Because we're young and beautiful. It's what we should be doing at our age. I'm going upstairs to see if they've run out of milk before they start complaining. You want me to get you some Paracetamol, might make you feel better?'

'Yeah. Would you?'

'Course.'

'How can you not feel hungover?'

'Good genes,' bragged Sahara, heading upstairs, passing Martha who was on her way back down.

'Has someone been sick?' asked Martha, sniffing the office air.

'I don't know,' replied Rachel, glossing over the fact there was an unsightly smell coming from the toilet.

'Well it smells very peculiar,' Martha noted while heading to the photocopier room next to reception.

Rachel had got another text from Ross.

'What time are you coming back?'

'When I'm done at work. Why?'

'Missing you x''

Rachel didn't reply. She was finding it harder to reply to these messages of affection. Five months had passed since they had moved to London and Ross had still failed to find employment.

The stress of this had put a lot of strain on their relationship and Rachel was questioning her reasons for getting back together with him.

'*How's the job hunt going?*' she texted.

'*Not,*' he replied.

'*Have you contacted the temp agency Sahara told me about?*' She hated henpecking him but felt it necessary now. There was no reply for a while so she texted him again. '*??*'

The internal office phone rang.

'Rach?'

She instantly recognized the toned down Liverpudlian accent.

'It's Naomi,' replied her boss 'Can youse come up for a minute?'

'Sure.'

She could tell by her tone it was important.

'Put the phone on divert to Barbara,' said Naomi.

'Will do,' replied Rachel worryingly.

She did as Naomi requested and walked upstairs to the third floor heading past Sahara.

'The cows upstairs want more milk. I'll see you later.'

It was an in-joke between them; referring to the bossy personal assistants as cows due to the amount of milk they would get through on a daily basis.

'I've got to see Naomi,' said Rachel.

'What about?'

'I don't know.'

Rachel arrived on the third floor where she saw Naomi's assistant, Barbara, trying to look important while she sat at her computer. She turned to give her a disapproving look, then nudged her head towards Naomi's office, signaling her to enter. Rachel disliked Barbara, ever since she had arrived at the company, Barbara had berated her at every opportunity.

Rachel knocked on Naomi's half-open door.

'Hi Rach,' replied Naomi sat in the office.

'Shall I close the door?' asked Rachel.

'Yeah. Thanks.'

Naomi was looking particularly glamorous today, clad in tight blue jeans and a revealing black top. She looked good for her age, which Rachel guessed was around fifty. She had a healthy tan, a slim physique and a fashionable dress sense. No kids but a husband who lived in Kent whom she seldom spoke about. She liked Naomi, they had got on well at her interview, but there was something about her, and element of ruthlessness, which made Rachel feel she could never trust her.

'Listen Rach. I'm going to be honest with you. I know you guys went out last night with the guys from post production.'

'Sahara and I went out for a few drinks. Sure.'

'I know it was more than a few. You don't need to lie to me. I get it. Going out, is like, part of the job. When I got into advertising, I was out every goddamn night of the week, coming in all hours, getting pissed with clients, you name it. But coming in drunk, laughing down the phone at someone who actually was very important, and like, swearing at them, is totally not acceptable.'

'I'm sorry.'

'How much sleep did youse get last night?'

'A bit.'

'Well that's really not good Rachel. I need you and Sahara to be on the ball when you come in here, alright?'

'I'm sorry.'

'Well this is an official warning. Now I want you to go home, get some sleep and come in tomorrow fresh as a daisy. Am I making me-self clear?'

'Yes,' she replied obediently.

'I'll be telling Sahara to go home too and Barbara can take the calls from reception.'

'I'm sorry to let you down.'

'I'll see you tomorrow,' replied Naomi dismissing her apology.

Rachel headed downstairs to pick up her bag from behind the reception desk.

'Has America called for me yet?' asked Martha.

'I'm not sure. The phones are being diverted to Barbara.'

'Well does she know that I'm getting a call from The States?!'

'No, I didn't tell her. I'm sorry. I'll do it now.'

'I'll do it!' she said impatiently. 'I take it you're going home?'

'Yes. Naomi wants me to.'

'Probably best. We've all done it,' she said with a hint of kindness in her tone, melting her icy front. Rachel was unsure how to handle this sudden change in temperament. Rachel let out a brief smile then left the office, making her way through the busy streets of Soho, towards Tottenham Court Road.

'What are you doing back?' asked Ross when Rachel entered their poky top floor flat in Borough, half an hour later. He was watching *This Morning* in his pyjamas holding his guitar.

'I got sent home,' Rachel replied, tearing off some paint peeling off the living room wall.

'Why, are you sick?' he asked.

'Hungover. Naomi found out I'd been sick in the toilet and sent me home.'

'You stay over at Sahara's last night?'

'Yeah, I texted you.'

'You said you were staying at a mate's. Not whose flat it was.'

'Well yes, I stayed at Sahara's in Hackney.'

Rachel went to open the window as she could still smell the marijuana he had been smoking that morning, drifting into the room.

'Ross can you please open the window after you smoke.'

'Sorry.'

'Or at least smoke out of the window. And how are you affording to buy it when you're unemployed?'

'Thanks for reminding me.'

'You didn't reply to my text about the temping agency?'

'Yeah. Sorry. I'll phone them.'

'Will you?'

'Yes!'

'Today?'

'OK.'

'I'm going to head to bed. Please don't play your guitar,' she implored, before walking off to close their bedroom door. She went to plug her phone in at the wall and noticed she had got a text from Sahara.

Naomi sent me home as well. Feel like I'm back at school!'

'I know. Me too. But will be nice to get some sleep though!'

'Yep. Bloody good night babe!'

She slipped on comfier clothes, slipped under her warm duvet, and instantly fell asleep.

Rachel woke up several hours later to the sound of rain, hitting the skylight above her. There was something depressing about London rain, its dankness differed it from rain in other places, and made her long to be in a warm exotic location.

It was dark outside and the flat felt unusually cold. She went to turn her bedside light on but there was no power shown by the blank screen on her alarm clock.

'Ross?!' she shouted but he did not answer.

She jumped out of bed and dashed into the living room where she found him asleep on the sofa. She tested the light switch at the entrance to the room but it wasn't working.

'Ross?!'

He flinched at the sound her voice.

'Yeah?!' he mumbled hastily.

'You didn't top up the electricity meter like I told you too!'

'Oh, right. Sorry, I forgot.'

'Where's the meter card?'

'I don't know.'

'I gave it to you the other day.'

'Well it must be in the same place where you gave it to me.'

'You're really pissing me off! I ask you to do one thing and you can't even do that!'

'I'm sorry, I said I forgot.'

'Well maybe if you stopped smoking so much, you might get some memory cells back!'

She found the top-up card on the bookshelf then flounced out of the living room to get changed in the bedroom.

'Alright, so you're pissed off with me, I'll go change it now,' Johnny remarked, getting up from the sofa to face her.

'I'll do it,' she replied vehemently.

She walked out of the bedroom, almost losing her balance as she put her shoes on in the corridor, then stomped angrily down the stairs, slamming the flat door shut and heading out into the nighttime air.

She arrived at a local petrol station five minutes later.

'You got fuel?' asked the young Turkish man serving.

'No. I just need to top this up,' she said handing over the tatty plastic meter card.

'How much?'

'Thirty pounds.'

He dipped the card into a yellow machine which looked like something from the 1980s.

She left the petrol station and walked to a cash point close by to retrieve some more money. She walked off the main road, taking a longer route to avoid the rush hour crowds. The rain got heavier as she headed down a dimly lit street. It was very sudden when it happened. A large force hitting her back, then the feeling of a hand knocking her down, banging her head against the pavement. She could feel the cold tarmac pressing against her ear.

'Don't fucking move!' said a youthful but intimidating male voice with an ethnic London accent above her. She didn't want to see his face. He grabbed her bag and in an instant he was gone. She lay there on the pavement as a black woman, with a Nigerian accent, ran over.

'You OK my love. I see what happened,' she said

A despondent Rachel grabbed her hand and the woman helped her up.

'I will phone the police,' the woman said, trying not to panic, dialing the mobile phone in her hands. 'You safe now my love.'

Rachel was out of breath, in shock, and all she could do was cling onto this total stranger, hug her, and cry.

Vienna, Austria

'What are you doing? I'm going to be late!' shouted Suzi waiting for Johnny at the bottom of the communal stairs in their modern apartment building.

'Alright. I'm coming!' said Johnny closing the door, nipping down the stairs to join her.

'Jesus, it's cold,' Johnny whined while putting on his gloves in the dark early morning air.

'Hello, it's November.'

'It feels like winter happened overnight. Yesterday it was autumn and now I'm freezing my bollocks off.'

They walked slowly across the ice outside the front door, then tottered towards Suzi's tatty white Volkswagen Golf in the car park, where Suzi went to press down her keylock. It failed to unlock it.

'Can you get the anti-freeze? It's in the trunk,' she asked as she manually opened the door which took some force to open, due to the frost which had glued it shut.

'You mean the boot?'

'You know what I mean and I prefer the American saying!'

Johnny sprayed the cold half empty can over the windows, then got inside the vehicle to wait for the frost to liquidise. Suzi turned on the ignition, blasted on the heating, then placed her fingers on the chilly driving wheel. They set off, driving through the small village of Leopoldsdorf where they were now living, across flat farmland towards Vienna.

'So, what are you going to do in Vienna?' asked Suzi.

'I'm off to see the sights of the city.'

'I'm jealous.'

'I have been looking for work you know.'

'You don't need to tell me that, I know you have.'

'I don't want you to think I'm just sitting around, living off your wage.'

'I don't think that Johnny.'

'The fact I don't speak German hardly helps.'

'Some companies do speak English you know?'

'I know. But I want to make the effort to learn the language.'

'Well you've got the classes. It will improve over time. You know this move was never going to be easy. So where am I dropping you off?'

'Reumannplatz. That OK?'

'Sure.'

'You getting the metro in?'

'Yep. How's your day looking?'

'OK. Though I have my class where none of the students speak.'

She parked up at the side of the road next to the entrance to the metro station.

'You got a map?' she asked him.

'I have my travel book. Going to look like a proper tourist.'

'OK. Enjoy,' she said going to kiss him.

'You too. Enjoy those rowdy students.'

'It'll be a riot.'

It was daylight by the time he got the train into the centre and walked up to street level from Stephansplatz Metro station. St Stephen's Cathedral stood directly above the station, dwarfing the streets surrounding it in a crisp shadow from the morning sunlight. He walked to a café close by to order a coffee and a croissant where he sat by a window to people watch, but instead, began to think about how much his life had changed since leaving the UK.

His decision to move to Vienna had happened so fast, only a few weeks after Suzi's visit to York. After starting the new job, she had phoned Johnny and told him how difficult she had found the move back to her home country. Notably, the loneliness she felt due to the fact that most of her friends now had partners, were married, and having children. She had joked about the idea of him moving out there. He had not taken the idea seriously, until suddenly, the notion of moving back to London didn't seem that tempting anymore. After a few weeks of deliberating Johnny had phoned Suzi, and after a long conversation, had agreed on an arrival date.

They had quickly found a flat, and so far, living together had gone smoothly. There had been no serious arguments, just occasional playful bickering. They had also agreed to officially call themselves boyfriend and girlfriend. Suzi had got drunk one night and told him she was calling him this at work. Johnny was happy to go along with this, despite part of him knowing he did not feel completely committed to their relationship. He was attracted to Suzi, but he knew deep down, something was missing. Whenever he had these moments of doubt, he remembered what a work colleague had told him once; if your partner ticked two out of three things that you were looking for in a relationship then they were worth keeping. Suzi was worth keeping.

'Darf es noch etwas sein?' asked the waiter, interrupting his thoughts.

'Wie bitte?' he replied in a strong English accent.

'Would you like something else?' repeated the waiter.

'Nein, danke.'

He looked at his phone to see a text from Suzi.

151

'Just asked a student to leave my class. They hate me x.'
'What happened? x.'
'Didn't do the reading. This is the fourth time! Maybe I'm too harsh x.'
'Lazy fucker x.'

He finished his drink, left the café and walked towards the museum district of the city where he wandered aimlessly around the museum of modern art.

He strolled down towards the river, passing by a Christmas market which was being constructed. Suzi had told him how much she was looking forward to visiting the markets in the coming weeks; she loved the idea of drinking warm alcoholic drinks out of mugs on cold wintry nights.

He sat down on a bench where he began to think about Rachel. He wondered what she was doing. Different thoughts played on his mind. Did she think about him? What would she think about him now living in Austria? Would their paths ever cross again?

By lunchtime he was walking towards the old funfair at the Vienna Prater when Suzi phoned him.

'Where are you?' she asked, hearing fairground organ music playing in the background.

'Right now, walking towards the Ferris wheel.'

'You going to go on it?'

'We can come back one evening and do it together. What's up?'

'You want to grab some food tonight? I might be able to leave work early. I need to talk to you about something.'

'Everything OK?'

'Yeah. So how about I meet you back at the flat after work and we drive to that pizza place you like?'

'Yey! The one with the model planes dangling from the ceiling?'

'Yeah,' she laughed. 'That's the one.'

'So, what did you want to talk about?' asked Johnny after they had sat down at their table later that evening.

'Here we have it.' She tapped her fingernails nervously on the wooden table surface, then looked into his eyes. 'I've been offered another teaching job.'

'OK.'

'In Hong Kong.'

'What?!'

'I know.'

'That's…far away.'

'I applied for it ages ago when I was looking at moving from LA, before I even came out here. I even had an interview but they kept telling me they weren't sure if there was a position. I forgot about it and then they got back to me at lunchtime today. They said they liked me and they offered me the position. I mean I never thought I would get it and now I have to make this ridiculous decision.'

'What's it doing?'

'It's teaching. And it's also an advisory role which I've wanted to do for a while.'

'Wow. Hong Kong.'

'This is so crazy, I know.'

'I mean do you want to live in Hong Kong?'

'Yeah. I went there when I was young. I visited last year with work, it's great. So yeah, I do.'

'But you just moved back to Vienna. That's why I moved here, right?'

'Oh Johnny, I know. But Hong Kong would be so different, so exciting. I mean whenever will I get a chance like this?' He could see this new life brewing inside her.

'You said you liked having seasons again. I doubt there'll be many seasons in Hong Kong. I mean it's subtropical, right?'

'I know, this doesn't make any sense. Doing this and now doing something else. Don't get me wrong, I like being in Vienna, but truth be told it feels exactly the same way it did the day I left. You think I'm a crazy girl, right?'

'Maybe, a little bit. Look I've never been to Hong Kong, so I can't really comment. When do they need an answer by?'

'End of the week.'

'Not long.'

'If I did decide to take it, would you come with me?'

Johnny looked down at his menu which had all the pizza options written in German. 'Possibly. I mean the fact they speak English out there will help.'

'Look we don't need to decide tonight. We just enjoy our meal, and somehow, over the next few days, I will come to some sort of decision and we can take it from there.'

'No need to make any rash decisions just yet,' replied Johnny.

They drove home in silence that night with thoughts buzzing around in their heads. Over the next few days they didn't mention the job offer again. It was the elephant in the room. It felt like an exciting opportunity for Suzi but Johnny had just uprooted his life to Austria. Was he really prepared to do it all over again?

How are you? I miss you,' his sister texted him early on the day of the decision while Johnny was cleaning the bathroom.

He phoned her straight back.

'Hey!' she said answering the phone. He could hear London traffic in the background.

'Are you free to talk?' he asked.

'Yeah, fine, just walking to work. How's Vienna?'

'Cold, but nice.'

'You fluent yet?'

'Oh absolutely. My German is Wunderbar.'

'How's Suzi?'

'She's good. Working a lot. She's just been offered another job in fact.'

'Another one?'

'Yep, but this time in Hong Kong.'

'Oh. In Hong Kong? Right. I see,' she replied diplomatically.

'Yeah, it's sort of why I was phoning. She's making the decision today and I think she's going to take it.'

'OK. How do you feel about that?'

'Well she asked me if I wanted to go with her.'

'Well I guess you would do, right?'

'I don't know. I seem to move around a lot. A bit too much I think.'

'But you also seem to like Suzi. You guys are getting on OK?'

'Yeah.'

'Well then I think your decision is made. You wouldn't have to learn German. Just learn Mandarin or whatever Chinese they speak over there. In fact, there's a whole loads of expats out there so you can just speak English. It would be a pretty amazing opportunity. What would you do job wise?'

'I guess I'd go back into insurance, despite hating the thought of that right now.'

'Most people hate their jobs Johnny.'

'Do they? Or is that just a London thing?'

'Oh, bus is here. Let me know what you decide.'

'Will do.'

'Bye Johnny.'

'Talk to you soon.'

Suzi arrived home late that evening.

'Hope you're hungry. There's loads of food,' Johnny announced from the kitchen.

'It smells good.'

'I got some wine as well. You want a glass?'

'Sure.'

He plated the food and brought it over to the table.

'So, I've made my decision,' said Suzi looking decisive.

'OK,' he said playfully trying to play down the intensity of the moment.

'I told them I'm going to take it.'

'OK.'

He poured them both a glass of red wine.

'I will hand in my notice at work tomorrow and I guess the question is, are you going to come with me?'

Johnny began to eat his pasta. Suzi looked down moving her finger around the edges of her wine glass that had not been topped up as much as she'd have liked.

'Yes,' Johnny replied.

'Yes?' Suzi said with recoiling excitement appearing in her eyes.

'Yes. This is crazy, mental, the idea of moving again but I think I'm prepared to do this.'

'Really?'

'Yes.'

'I've been dreading what you were going to say all day. This is going to work Johnny. I will make it work. I promise you that. Thank you!'

And at that moment all Suzi could do was jump up in elation, almost tipping over her glass of wine, and kiss the boy sitting in front of her.

.

London, UK

It was mid-morning when Rachel woke up. She had given up setting her alarm. Sleep was a way of getting through the day. She could hear Ross dawdling in the other room playing on his guitar. He had been smoking again. She had refrained herself from asking him to stop as it would only lead to another argument and there had been so many over the last few months. The last one had ended with Ross moving into the spare room. It was obvious now, she was no longer in love with him. There were many reasons why she hadn't finished their relationship. She seemed to lack friends these days, and the notion of moving into a flat share with strangers seemed risky and unappealing. She didn't want to move back home with her mother and watch her gloat at her situation with her needling remarks. There was always her sister's place, but it would hardly be ideal moving in with a baby. The only other option was finding a place of her own to rent, but having been out of work for the last three months, this was outside of her financial capabilities.

She pulled herself out of bed, slipped on her dressing gown and dragged her feet to the kitchen. The room was filled with dirty dishes that hadn't been washed for weeks. She had given up taking care of the space she lived in. She had always been untidy and she was the first to admit this, but up until now, she had relied on other people who had nudged her about her messy habits. Ross had been one of those people but his lack of respect showed another aspect of how their relationship was broken.

She looked down at her phone to see a message from an unknown number; she had been looking forward to this text for some time. She opened it.

'Drink tonight? Pete x,' it read.

She had met Pete briefly a few weeks beforehand at a local coffee shop in Borough Market. He was a slim attractive city type who she assumed was in his thirties. She had caught his eye the moment he had entered the shop. He had approached her while she'd been sat down job-hunting on her laptop, placing a ripped up piece of newspaper on her table with the words, *'Hello pretty girl.'* He had written his number below and the flirtatious messages had carried on ever since.

'Drink sounds good. Where do you want to meet?' she replied.

'Angel. Meet by tube. 7.30pm.' She liked the way his texts were succinct.

'You're on. See you then.'

Ross entered the room.

'I think I might I have a job interview,' he muttered while adding another dirty dish to the pile by the sink.

'For what?' she asked.

'A temp job.'

'Well that's something,' she said, feeling surprisingly happy for him.

'I phoned that temp agency you told me about. It's just a data entry at a company near Holborn. It's something at least.'

Her phone beeped. She would wait until she got to her bedroom to read it.

'Maybe you should phone the agency as well?' Ross advised.

'Maybe I will. I just want to hear back about a few applications for more permanent roles first.'

'Listen Rachel, I know the last few weeks haven't exactly been fun but when we both get back into work, I'm taking you out for a nice meal so we can get things back on track.'

She couldn't think of anything worse, an evening of stiff conversation with him but she attempted to show some gratitude. 'Well let's hope we both find something soon,' she replied.

She began to walk to her bedroom.

'Rach?'

'Yep,' she said, turning back to him in the corridor.

'I do care about this relationship. You do know that?'

'I know,' she replied, giving a forced smile then closing the door in front of him. She lay on the bed. She hated this situation. She resented the fact Ross clearly saw there was hope for them.

She attempted to look at more jobs on her laptop but spent the rest of the day procrastinating and thinking about her date with Pete.

'So, my sister just texted me,' she informed Ross midafternoon. 'She's in London for a meeting and she wants to take me out. She's offered to pay for everything. You don't mind? I'll probably be home late.'

'No. It'll be good for you. Get you out of the flat.'

'Great.'

This all seemed too easy. Did he not suspect for a second what was going on? It made him seem so unobservant for someone she was supposed to be going out with. She glanced at her phone to see another message from Pete.

'Bring on tonight.'

'Working hard I see?'

'Thoughts of you are highly distracting.'

'I will see you later.'

She returned to her room where she had three tops laid out on the bed. She had never been this indecisive before. She chose the middle stripy blue and white one.

'So I'm off,' she said to Ross.

'You look amazing,' he replied.

'Thanks,' she replied humbly.

'Say hi to your sister for me.'

'Will do.'

Her journey to Central London was filled with mixed feelings of nervousness and excitement. There were several young professionals waiting outside Angel tube station when she got there. She wondered if they were all there to meet their dates for the evening. She worried about not recognising Pete. After all, she had only met him for a few minutes before.

Pete appeared from the tube moments later looking dapper in an expensive dark suit; his jawline was more chiseled than she remembered and his stubble had grown.

'Hello,' he said with a hint of an Essex accent. 'Recognised me then?'

'Of course.'

'Where do you fancy?'

'I don't really know the area.'

'Good thing I do.'

He oozed confidence, sexy fun confidence and Rachel was determined to enjoy her night with him.

They walked to an upmarket cocktail bar on Upper Street.

'So, why don't you tell me a little bit about yourself,' he asked while they waited for their pricey drinks which Pete insisted on paying for.

'What do you want to know?'

'Were you a good girl at school?'

'Yes. Were you a good boy at school?'

'Absolutely not.'

She laughed flirtatiously. 'So, do you work in the City?' she asked.

'I do. Financial consultant. You?'

'I used to work in advertising. I'm sort of in between jobs at the moment.'

'Well, good thing I'm paying for the drinks.'

'What?' she asked, unsure if he was trying to be offensive.

'I'm joking. I'm sure something will turn up.'

'I hope so.'

'You live with housemates?'

'No, by myself.' It scared her how easily she could lie these days.

'That must be getting expensive. How old are you?'

'I'm twenty-five.'

'You got rich parents?'

'I've got a few savings. Nothing crazy. My dad died and left me a bit of money.'

'My condolences.'

'You live by yourself?'

'I do. Not far from here.'

'I bet you own. All you bankers. On silly money, right?'

'I do. And the money is good, I can't complain.'

'Your own little bachelor pad?'

'You could call it that.'

It didn't take them long to finish their drinks before they went onto the next bar.

She got a text from Ross. *'Hope you're having fun with your sister x.'*

She didn't reply. She slipped her phone back in her handbag and turned to see Pete approaching with shots.

'On a school night?' she asked as he sat down next to her.

'Fuck it. Why not.'

They downed their drinks then caught each other's eye. Claiming his moment, Pete went in to kiss her. She felt his sharp bristles rub against her.

161

'You're very sexy, you know that Rachel?' he said kissing her neck. 'Young and naughty, just how I like them.'

'You're not so bad yourself,' she said lifting her head up closing her eyes, enjoying his lips on her.

Ten minutes later they were in his flat. A stylish modern flat with laminate flooring, black minimalist furniture and large windows with an impressive view of St Paul's Cathedral. It didn't take long before they were taking off each other's clothes, skin on skin, hair on skin, the sex lasting most of the night; lustful aggressive sex.

They were awoken early by his alarm the following morning. Rachel looked at her mobile lying by an empty glass on the bedside table. It had been on silent all night and she had received numerous missed calls from Ross.

'You want a shower?' asked Pete as he entered the room topless wearing only a towel.

'Sure.'

His bathroom was spotless and clinical. It felt like it belonged in a smart hotel room. She still felt drunk as she stood in the shower as the powerful force of the water from the showerhead repeatedly stabbed at her skin. She began to think about what she would say to Ross. She would lie and tell him that she had stayed overnight at a friend of her sister's who he did not know.

Pete walked her back to the tube, kissed her briefly on the cheek, then darted towards a taxi.

She got back to the flat half an hour late where Ross was sitting in the living room reading a music magazine. There was something different about it. It felt tidy and smelt of cleaning products and she noticed he had cleaned the pile of dirty dishes in the kitchen.

'Good night was it?' asked Ross.

'Sorry I didn't tell you I was staying over.'

'I tried phoning you. There was no answer so I rang your sister.'
Rachel's heartbeat fluttered inside her chest.

'She said she didn't know anything about your night out,' he added.

Rachel sat down opposite him and took off her shoes.

'So, who did you go out with?' he asked.

'I....'

'And don't fucking lie to me,' he said tightly. She had never seen him this angry before and it frightened her.

'OK,' she said. 'I went on a date with a guy. I had a really good time and I slept with him because I don't love you anymore.'

He looked straight at her and with calm emotion that cut straight through her. 'You bitch,' he replied.

He stared at her for a second then shut his laptop, got up and walked to the spare bedroom where he slammed the door shut. The flat shook for a second. Rachel sat there in silence. Numb. Her heartbeat still racing. She took a deep breath, stood up, then walked to the bathroom where she wet her face by the sink and wiped away the remaining makeup left on her face from the night before.

London, UK

Johnny followed his sister out of her Kentish Town basement flat, both wearing colourful reflective running gear that glowed in the morning fog. They dashed across the high street, jogging north onto Hampstead Heath, to the top of Parliament Hill where the fog was disappearing to show a bright clear day.

'Missed this did you?' asked his sister, taking a swig of her water.

'I did.'

'So, who are you meeting at the South Bank?'

They sat down on a park bench which overlooked the city.

'Just a friend,' he replied.

'Alright. Secretive.'

'It's Rachel if you must no.'

'As in your ex? Mexico Rachel?'

'Yes.'

Claudia frowned. 'Does Suzi know?'

'No. We're only meeting as friends.'

'If James was meeting an ex, I would want to know.'

'Can you stop judging me.'

'I'm not judging,' she denied lifting her hands up and jogging away.

'No. Clearly not,' he replied, running on after her.

As Johnny got dressed that morning he reflected on what his sister had said. He did feel guilty for not telling Suzi, but what was the point in complicating matters? He was meeting Rachel in a purely platonic way.

He met Rachel in Central London around lunchtime. She looked like a young Londoner now, trendy, well put together with sunglasses, but with messy hair.

'Hey stranger' Rachel said. 'Long time no see.'

He kissed her amiably on the cheek. 'Good to see you.'

'What do you want to do? I mean have you eaten? We can grab some food?' her words flowed out uncontrollably, a sign that she was nervous.

'Food sounds good.'

'Shall we head along the river? It's a nice day.'

'Good plan.'

They walked south over Embankment Bridge.

'All ready for your move half way across the world?' she asked.

'Attempting to be.'

'Things seem to be going well with you and Suzi?'

He was pleased she'd bought this up.

'They are. It's all been a bit crazy, I won't deny it. First of all, deciding to move to Vienna, and now Hong Kong.'

'You like to travel around a lot don't you?'

'I do. My itinerant lifestyle. I'm not complaining. What is it some philosopher once said. I saw it written in an airport advert once. 'The world is a book, and those who don't travel, only read the one page'.'

'Very philosophical.'

'Or maybe I just like to pretend to be on holiday all the time.'

Rachel smiled. 'It could just be that.'

'So where are you living now?' asked Johnny.

'I moved to Stoke Newington.'

'Nice area.'

'It's a house share. It's all good.'

'I'm sorry about Ross.'

'Thanks. It was so horrible Johnny. I mean it hadn't been good for a while but it got so much worse and I treated him so badly. It's good that I'm not in a relationship with him anymore.'

'Where is he now?'

'I think he moved back to Brighton. I don't think London really agreed with him. I hope he's happier. Despite everything, I do care about him in a weird sort of way.'

They headed down the steps past Royal Festival Hall and walked to the book market stalls under Waterloo Bridge.

'So how's things on the job front?' asked Johnny. 'I know you said you were having some difficulty.'

'I finally got something,' she replied, flicking through a second hand romance novel. 'It's with a marketing company.'

'Sounds promising.'

'It's mostly doing boring admin stuff but it gets me out of the house. It's definitely an improvement from working in advertising.'

'You said that didn't end so well.'

'It did not. I was out drinking all the time and this girl I was working with turned out to be a real bitch. I don't really want to talk about it. A dark time in my life.'

'How's your family doing?'

'My sister's all good, busy with my niece. My brother finally has a job.'

'That's an improvement from the last time you spoke about him. What's he doing?'

'He's working for a printing company in Hove. I think he likes it.'

'And your mum?'

'She's happy I think. I'm supposed to be meeting her next week. My sister forced me into it. I haven't seen her in a while. We had a big argument.'

'What about?'

'Her being a massive cow all the time.' She smiled. 'It's more complicated than that, obviously. I've actually been seeing a counselor about a whole load of stuff to do with my dad and my relationship with my mum.'

'OK. Is it helping?'

'I think so.'

'Is your mum still seeing the teacher guy?'

'As far as I'm aware.'

'I take it you still haven't met him yet?'

'No.' There was a pause. 'And your family?' she asked.

'They're good. My sister's just bought a flat.'

'Very grown up.'

'She's also started seeing someone.'

'Do you approve?'

'Yeah. He's a nice guy actually. A bit older. Late thirties. Sensible but they seem to like each other.'

'I don't think your sister really liked me much.'

'Why do you say that?'

'The way I was in Mexico. I was a kind of a dick. I'm sorry about that.'

'You were... different.'

'Full marks on the diplomatic reply.'

'You were having a hard time with losing your dad. I get it.'

'I'm starting to see that. Did you tell Suzi you were meeting me today?'

'No. I didn't actually,' his face showed a hint of shame.

'Do you think she'd like the fact we were meeting up?'

'I don't know is the honest answer.'

She could tell he didn't want to delve any deeper into the matter. 'So what jobs are you looking for in Hong Kong?' she asked.

'I'm thinking of going back into insurance.'

'Oh my God, really?'

'Hey, it's good money in Hong Kong. If you get in with a good company.'

'Yeah, but you hated insurance, right?'

'It's better than busking on the streets.'

'You've changed your tune. I thought your year of travelling was supposed to inspire you, help you choose something new. So corporate Johnny is making a return?'

'He very well may be.'

'I've never been to Hong Kong. Hey, if you're still there in a couple of years maybe I should come visit? Or would that be weird?'

'Maybe. Lets just see if I'm still there in a few years.'

'Deal. So I'm sort of seeing someone.'

'OK.'

'It's sort of casual.'

'Who is he?'

'He's called Pete. He works in the city, he's a bit of lad, and well, basically, the sex is good.'

'Fair enough,' he said smiling, unsure how to handle her honesty.

'You don't mind me telling you that?' she asked.

'It's kind of odd but I'm sort of intrigued.'

'So yeah, there's loads of chemistry but I don't think he really wants a relationship and right now it kind of suits me.'

'How did you guys meet?'

'Randomly. In a coffee shop.'

'I take this was after you broke up with Ross?'

'About a week after. Maybe two.' She was lying and Johnny could tell. 'OK. There might have been a sort of overlap. God. I really can't lie in front of you! I slept with him and I came clean to Ross. He shouted at me and moved out straight away. It was horrible. I ended up having to give up the flat and move back in with my sister. I'm a bad person.'

'I can see why that could be messy.'

'I don't normally do that. Cheat on someone like that.'

'You cheated on Ross with me.'

'That was different.'

'Was it?'

'Maybe not. I don't know.'

It began to rain.

'Let's go grab some lunch,' Johnny suggested.

They found a pub close by.

'So, do you think Suzi is the one?' asked Rachel after they'd grabbed a table by the window.

'That's quite a question. Jesus. I don't know.'

It's something Johnny had never thought about before and it worried him. He still felt he was at an age when dating someone didn't involve having to ask questions about whether you saw yourself with that person for the rest of your life. 'It feels good for now,' he replied. 'I must like her if I'm moving to Hong Kong with her.'

'True. It's commitment. I was going to ask you something else. I've forgotten. How's Eric? Is he still in Hawaii?'

'That's funny, I was just thinking about Hawaii the other day. Truth be told, I haven't really been in touch with him recently. I can be a bit crap staying in touch with people.'

'You can't be as bad as me. I'm awful. I wonder if he's still with that girl?'

'Colleen.'

'I totally forgot her name!' Rachel laughed. 'She was kind of insane and so totally different from him.'

'I know. Properly like chalk and cheese. I guess I might see him in Hong Kong if he comes to visit. He is still Suzi's cousin so I hope so. He was a good guy.'

'Course. I totally forgot they were related. It's so weird how you meet people just like that. Just think if you'd never gone travelling you'd never have met these guys, Suzi, Eric, *me.*'

169

'That's true, without the Gili Isles I would never have met you.'

There was silence as they both reflected on their first night together.

'Wouldn't mind being there now, Gili Meno,' Rachel said ruefully looking out of the window at the ominous clouds hanging over the Thames. 'Maybe I should move there. That would be nice.'

'And do what?'

'I don't know, maybe become a diving instructor.'

'Well there's nothing to stop you.'

'I do still feel like I need to get a career going. I see all these friends from university all making good money now and here's me in my crappy low paid role and I feel jealous.'

'Well there's no rush, we are living longer.'

'I'm pleased we did this. I felt like Mexico ended on a sour note and I wanted to make sure things were OK between us.'

'Me too.'

'I'm sorry about the way things ended at the airport.'

'Well we're here now. We might not have been.'

'Very true.'

They spoke for a few more hours reflecting over their times together until Johnny looked at his phone realising it was time to head back.

They left the pub where it was now raining heavily.

'I didn't bring an umbrella!' said Rachel.

'Use this,' he said taking off his Barbour jacket and using it as a cover for the both of them as they ran through Borough Market up the steps and across the road to London Bridge tube station.

'Well. This is me,' he said at the entrance to the tube. 'Where you heading?'

'Bus-sing it.'

'OK,' he said going to hug her. As he broke away they both looked at each other, and caught by a rush of adrenalin, they kissed.

'Sorry,' he replied, breaking the embrace. 'I shouldn't.'

'I know.'

'It was just seeing you. It was just nice seeing you.'

She moved his hand and placed it on her cheek.

'I've got to go Rach.'

'I know. I know.'

She looked at him, nodded her head, and let him go, and in an instant, he had disappeared amongst the crowds.

Hong Kong, China

'I wish you'd have let me buy you that shirt,' said Suzi whilst sitting next to Johnny on the top deck of the tram as it moved along the rickety tracks of the King's Road.

'I think you've spent enough money on clothes as it is.'

The tram jammed to a halt at their stop.

'You have to tell me to stop spending so much. It's an addiction,' replied Suzi.

'You clearly weren't up for that debate in those clothes shops!'

She went to hold his hand as they crossed the road from the station. 'See, this is what our Saturdays should always be like. Shopping in the morning. Casually getting the tram back to our luxury apartment,' she said.

They entered the reception area of a tall lean building and took the lift up to their fifteenth floor apartment. Johnny had been reluctant to take the flat because of the high rent, but the view from the window looking out across the bay to Kowloon had sold it to him. It was the first apartment they'd seen that didn't look out onto a wall or an air conditioning unit.

'Who's cooking tonight?' asked Suzi cutting off the price tags from the clothes she had bought while Johnny lolled on the sofa watching BBC World News on the TV that had come with the apartment.

'I can.'

'Or we can go out. It's Saturday night. We could go for some noodles?'

'Tempting, but it's more money.'

'Look stop going on about money. I'm on a good salary. I want to enjoy spending time with you. You can take me out when you get that job which you will be getting.'

He knew his constant budgeting concerns were starting to annoy Suzi and she was right. She was on a generous enough salary to comfortably support the both of them.

'Alright. Noodles it is,' Johnny agreed.

That night they headed to a large shopping centre in Causeway Bay to a dodgy looking Noodle restaurant which had got rave reviews from one of Suzi's work colleagues.

'You seem restless. What's wrong? Are you thinking about the interview?' asked Suzi noticing him fidgeting with his chopsticks.

'I just wish they'd let me know.'

'These things take time. Also, it's your first interview. Listen how about we get the tram up to Victoria Peak tomorrow?'

'I thought we were waiting for your mum to come out before we did that?'

'My mum tells me she's coming to visit me all the time. You know how many times she visited me in LA?'

'I don't know.'

'None. In *seven* years.'

'She used to live in LA. She didn't like it.'

'So. That's no excuse. I'm her daughter.'

'Fine. We'll go,' he yielded.

'Can you stop just saying fine, like I'm nagging you into everything and you just end up agreeing with me because it's easier that way.'

'I'm not.'

'Yes, you are, and you always go high pitched with your voice when you're not telling the truth.'

'Look, I do want to go to Victoria Peak and I am happy going tomorrow. I just wanted to make the point that if we do all the sights now, we'll just end up having to do them all again when your mum comes out to visit us.'

'OK. Fine. If she comes out, which I doubt she will, we'll do it all again, and I will pay for it. How does that sound?'

'You probably will be paying for everything because I still won't have a job.'

Suzi laughed. Johnny playfully nipped the skin of her arm with his chopsticks.

'Don't nip me,'

'Come here,' he said going to kiss her lips.

Johnny awoke late that night because the air conditioning had stopped working making the room unpleasantly humid. It had been breaking down consistently since they had moved in, and despite making numerous phone calls to the estate agent, no one had been over to fix it. He dragged himself out of bed in his boxers and walked to the kitchen to grab a torch from under the sink and attempted to fiddle with the unit. He touched random buttons but they had no effect. He slid open the balcony doors where he sat on one of their uncomfortable seats to cool down and watch the lights of Kowloon glow in the distance across the water. It still didn't feel real living there. It was so different from anywhere he had lived before. Everything so tightly crammed together, but not in a way it felt unpleasant and claustrophobic; it still felt exotic and exciting. He traipsed back into the living room to grab his laptop from the kitchen table, conscious not to wake Suzi. He returned to the balcony where he logged on and opened up his email to compose a message.

SUBJECT: Greetings from HK!
FROM: Johnny Buxford

<johnny_buxford@hotmail.com>
TO: Rachel Hortley
<sparkly_rachelhortley@yahoo.com>

Hey Rachel,

How's life?! All settled now here in Hong Kong. Jobless but feels like a holiday. Good seeing you in London :)

 Johnny

He was about to read through what he had written when he noticed Suzi walking towards him from the kitchen.

'Hey,' she said.

'Couldn't sleep. Air conditioning off again,' Johnny said, quickly minimising the email window.

'I wished they'd fix it,' she replied, rubbing her eyes, sitting down next to him.

'Any news?' she asked.

'What?'

'On your email.'

'Oh, I was just browsing.'

There was a sudden jolt in the kitchen followed by the sound of the air conditioning unit springing back into life.

Johnny shot out of his chair and dashed to the kitchen to investigate the situation more closely. 'I think we may be back in business,' he said.

Suzi followed him in. 'I am loving this machine. When it works,' she replied.

'How can you love it? It tortures you every day with its failure to blow out cold air.'

175

Suzi closed the balcony door in an attempt to trap the colder air. 'I'm just going to appreciate the rare times it does work.'

'It'll be off in a minute.'

'Well I'm going back to bed, before it decides to die on us again. Its love is short lived. You coming?'

He turned to see his laptop on the balcony.

'Sure,' he replied, grabbing the laptop, putting it back in the kitchen, then returning back to the bedroom with her.

They left early the next morning to catch the tram up to Victoria Peak. When they arrived at the top they browsed through the different tourist shops, then stopped to take photos off the city and the different bays in the distance.

'We made the right decision coming here, right?' asked Suzi wistfully as they headed along one of the walking trails later that afternoon.

'Course we did.'

'I wouldn't have come here without you. I want you to know that.'

Johnny didn't reply to her comment. At that moment he realised Suzi has become too dependent on him. It scared him.

The next morning Suzi left for work early at 6.00am while Johnny stayed in bed. He had set his alarm for 7.30am and had made a point of trying to get up at this time each morning. He knew he functioned better when unemployed if he had a routine. He put on his running gear and headed out of the apartment to go on his usual route around the local area along the harbour.

When he returned to the flat, he noticed he'd received a voicemail on his phone. It was from the manager who had interviewed him for the insurance job he had applied for.

'Hi Jonathan, this is Matthew Li from Keedle Hammond.' The man spoke fluent English with a mild Hong Kong accent. 'I'm just phoning about your interview the other day. If you could please call me back on 8102 4464. Thank you.'

Johnny dialed his number.

'Hi Matthew. It's Jonathan. Or Johnny as most people call me. You just left a voicemail on my phone.'

'Oh, hi Johnny. How are you?'

'Very well thank you. You?'

'Good. Yes. So, we would like to offer you the position as Underwriting Assistant.'

'Really? OK. Great. Thank you,' he said quietly scrunching his fist, shaking it with a feeling of sheer delight.

'So, you would like to accept this position?'

'Yes. Yes, I would. Very much.'

'Great. Well someone from HR will call you to speak to you about a starting date and sort out a contract. Your salary details are as discussed in the interview but HR will give you more information about the other benefits of the position.'

'That's great news. Thank you so much.'

'They will also discuss a start date and we will see you then.'

'Perfect. I'll see you then.'

The minute Johnny hung up he got a call from Suzi.

'Hey!' said a buoyant Johnny

'Hey,' replied Suzi. 'Did I leave my keys in the flat? They should be in my top drawer. They've got a baseball key ring attached to them.'

He went to look at the drawer on her bedside table.

'Yep, yes you did.'

'Thank God. Phew. I was worried I'd left them on the train. Are you going to be home tonight to let me in?'

'Sure. Can be. Hey good news. I got the job.'

'What? Are you serious?!'

'They just called me!'

'Oh Johnny, I'm so happy for you! This is such good news! See I told you! I knew you would get it!'

177

'I know, I can finally start paying for things.'

'So proud of you. We are meant to be here, you know that? I'll bring some champagne tonight. We can celebrate!'

'On a school night?'

'*Yeah*, on a school night!'

'Well who am I to argue.'

'Love you! See you tonight!'

Johnny sat down on the sofa with a feeling of relief. The restlessness and anxiety he had felt over the last weeks suddenly leaving his body. He turned to see his laptop on the kitchen table. He picked it up and went out on the balcony to sit down with it. He saw the email message window he had minimised the other night at the bottom of the screen, below a desktop photo of himself and Suzi. He brought up the computer window and looked at the message he had failed to send. He amended *'jobless'* in the email to *'got a job,'* then moved his cursor to the recipient bar and typed in Rachel's name. He read through what he had written, then paused for a moment, closing his eyes, blocking out any guilt he felt at that time. He slowly opened them, moved his fingers along the touchpad, then hastily pressed down on the send button

Paris, France

It felt mature going on a romantic weekend to Paris Rachel thought as she watched Pete sleeping across from her on their Eurostar train. His invitation two weeks earlier in a Central London pub after work had taken her by surprise. He had been honest about his reasons behind the invite. A friend had been forced to cancel his trip after a family death and had offered the trip to Pete at a discounted rate. Nonetheless, it was still an invitation, and, in her eyes, it showed signs of commitment. It was something he had not shown before. Everything leading up to this point had been so casual, so last minute. Dates being arranged by text on the same afternoon they took place which she would inevitably drop everything for. Despite dating Pete for some time now it was odd that he still felt like a stranger. She knew nothing about his life really. She liked the elements of mystery surrounding him but what made her uneasy was the fact she didn't know where she stood with him. Was she his girlfriend? Or just a girl he liked to slip into bed on occasion? She saw a future with Pete and as she walked from the Eurostar carriage after its arrival at Gare Du Nord station, she decided that this weekend she was going to find out how he viewed their relationship.

The hotel where they were staying was a short taxi ride from the station. It was plusher than she had expected. A boutique hotel in a period building that had been recently renovated to create a modern quirky feel. Their room was spacious, with Parisian vintage furniture, dark grey carpet, white walls, except for a feature wall decorated with fancy jungle themed wallpaper.

Rachel placed down her luggage and walked into the bathroom like a child on the first day of her holiday, turning on the light to show a large Jacuzzi style bath and an impressive washbasin.

'This place is amazing,' she said, returning to the main room.

'It'll do,' replied Pete in his usual jokey tone.

She lay on the king size bed. 'Let's just stay here forever.'

He lay down next to her. 'So what are we doing tonight?' he asked unbuttoning her new white shirt which she had bought especially for the trip.

Rachel sat up and covered herself up. 'I think we should go and explore,' she said, standing up purposefully.

'Someone's in a hurry,' remarked Pete.

'I've never been to Paris before.'

'You've travelled half way round the world, but you've never been to Paris?'

'I'm going to change my top.'

'I like your shirt.'

'It feels too corporate.'

She changed into a white summer dress and they left the cool air-conditioned hotel and made their way towards the Bastille area of the city. The streets were full of tourists and locals sat outside the different cafés and bars, enjoying the muggy summer weather. Pete tracked down a restaurant he remembered from his last visit where they found a spare table looking out onto the road. He ordered two glasses of wine in French, his Essex accent making it sound less sophisticated than Rachel would have liked.

'Thanks for asking me what I wanted,' Rachel said.

'That's what you normally have. What else did you want, a Carlsberg?' he replied.

'It would have been nice to be asked. That's all I'm saying.'

She didn't know why she was making a deal out of this. She had let him order wine before.

Pete took out his Blackberry and checked his emails.

'Anything exciting happening?' she asked.

'Not especially.'

'I thought you said you were going to try and ignore your emails this weekend?'

'All good,' he said, slotting the device back into his pocket and smiling at her.

The waiter returned to the table and poured wine into Pete's glass for him to taste. He swished the small amount of wine around in the bottom of his glass then drank it slowly.

'Très bien,' he replied, allowing the waiter to fill their glasses.

'I never liked that custom,' Rachel commented after the waiter had left.

'What custom?'

'When the waiter pours the wine for you to taste.'

'Why not? I don't want to order any old shite.'

'It just feels a bit humiliating for the waiter.'

Pete spotted a chip on the rim of his wine glass which he touched with his finger.

'Why don't I know anything about your family?' asked Rachel suddenly.

'Well that came out of nowhere. I don't know much about yours.'

'You know I have a sister and a brother. That my dad died.'

'Well I don't have any siblings. Only child.'

'And your parents?'

'Mum died when I was twenty-five, and my dad's in a nursing home, and honestly, he's a prick. Don't really see him much.'

'Why not?'

'They divorced when I was young. He had some other woman on the go. He left. Had another family. Why do you want to know all this?'

181

'You just seem guarded. Like you don't want me to know anything about you.'

'Well maybe I don't,' he replied. It shocked her how blunt he could be sometimes.

'Right, so I obviously don't mean that much to you?' Rachel remarked.

'I don't understand why you've bought this up now? Here we are in Paris and you're spoiling it.'

'We've been seeing each other a while now right. Yes, we're in Paris, you invited me here, which is great, but I can't stop wondering where I am with you. Are we in a relationship?'

'This is casual. I don't want you to think this is anything more than that.'

'Wow. That was honest.'

'Well, did you want me to lie to you?'

His Blackberry pinged and he removed it from his pocket.

'Can you please not look at that,' she insisted.

'I'm going to take a quick phone call and I'll be back.'

'Fine. Do what you want,' she replied passive-aggressively as he walked away leaving his wallet on the table. She put it in her bag for safekeeping and carried on drinking her wine.

'I'm sorry your husband wanted to set up a tab, I will need a card,' said the waiter in English, assuming she didn't speak a word of French.

'He's not my husband.'

She was going to pay from her own card but took out Pete's wallet instead. It was the first thing she spotted when she opened it, there in one of the compartments, a small picture of two little boys, aged around six and three. She closed the wallet, incredulously handing over the card to the waiter.

Pete arrived back at the table.

'The waiter came by and asked for a card for the tab. You left your wallet so I gave him yours.'

'You got the wallet?'

She handed it back to him. 'Why is there a picture of two little boys in it?'

'Are there?'

'Yes.'

'OK. Do you really want me to answer that?'

'Why wouldn't you answer that?' she replied, wondering what a weird thing it was to say.

'Right. Well. They're my kids.'

Rachel smiled in disbelief, trying to grasp what she had just heard. 'Wow. You have kids?'

'I have kids. I also have a wife,' he said, staring at her confidently.

There was a delay in Rachel's response. 'I see. And you didn't think about telling me this?'

They sat there in silence for a moment.

'I think we're done here,' Rachel said, getting up.

'Rachel. Come on.'

'I can't believe you've lied to me!'

'You never asked.'

'It's humiliating, you're an arsehole!' She stood up, left him at the table, then stormed back to the hotel room where she started to pack away her things away.

Pete arrived back shortly after.

'What are you doing?' he asked.

'I'm going back to London.'

'Rachel. Come on. We just got here. Rachel!' He grabbed hold of her arm. She slapped his hand and he moved it away.

'Fuck off Pete!'

'Look this was never going to be anything serious. You must have known that?'

She forced more items into her bag.

'I'm sorry I never told you the truth. OK. I just thought it would complicate things,' he said.

'And to think I was beginning to like you. I cannot believe this. I am such an idiot.'

'Can you stop packing so we can please just talk about this?'

'You have a family Pete. Two kids. A wife. How could you treat them like this? Do you not care?!'

'OK! You're right, it's not a nice thing to do, but I don't love my wife and things have been pretty awful for years!

'That does not justify to go and sleep with someone else and not inform them about the situation! You are still married! Where are they, your family?'

'Canterbury.'

'Nice big house?'

'Yeah. It's nice.'

'How old are the boys?'

'Jake is six, and Harry is four.'

'Fuck, said Rachel sitting down. 'And how old are you? Are you really thirty-six or did you lie about that?'

'I'm forty-two.'

'I take it I'm not the only girl you've cheated with?'

'There was a girl at work I saw before I met you. Yes.'

'Were you seeing both of us at the same time?'

'No. Look you don't know my wife. You don't know what she's like.'

'Does she sleep around?'

'I doubt it.'

'Does she know about me?'

'No, look….'

She tried to zip up her suitcase but it jammed.

'Let me help you,' said Pete trying to intervene.

'I'm doing it myself!' She zipped it shut and shot towards the door.

'There won't be any trains at this time of night. You know that?'

'I'll wait for the first one at the station. If not. I'll hitchhike.'

'That'll be safe.'

184

'Better option than staying with you!'

'Look.' He said grabbing the handle of the door preventing her from leaving. 'Just stay here tonight. OK. I'll sleep on the floor.'

'No!' she said trying to open the door.

'Rachel, sit down!' he shouted.

Unsure why, she did as he said.

'Look just stay here tonight. If you really want to leave, you can go in the morning. Trying to get home tonight, it's ludicrous,' he said.

'You're right. It is, so you can sleep on the floor, but you will not stop me from leaving this room and going for a walk to clear my head. When I get back you will not talk to me, you will not look at me, you will stay there on the floor and not say a bloody word!'

She put her bag down against the wall and left the hotel room. The reception of the hotel was still busy when she got down there. A man dressed in a tuxedo was playing on the piano and there were a number of guests milling about drinking at the lobby bar. She left the building and began to walk in the humid air which was already causing her to sweat on her back.

She had the urge to talk to someone, to tell them about what had happened, how betrayed and awful she felt. She was a mistress, a home wrecker, or had at least been deceived into being one. The truth was her options of people to talk to were limited. After all, only a handful of people knew about their relationship. She thought about phoning her sister, telling her about Pete, but even that filled her with dread. Her sister would look at her differently. She already thought her life was a mess. What would she think of her now, sleeping with a married man? She couldn't bare this. It was at moments like this that Rachel realised how hard it was having no female friends. A best friend to console with her in times of need. But girls never seemed to warm to her, they always seemed threatened by her in a way she didn't understand and she could never fully trust them because of this.

She walked for hours through the city with no bearing of where she was going. It got quieter the further she headed into the suburbs. It was only when the sky began to get lighter she noticed how long she had been walking for. She would have to get a taxi back but she noticed she had left her wallet in the hotel room. There was a large building across the road, half a McDonalds, and the other half a club. She crossed the road to see if she could talk to a bouncer about getting a taxi when she spotted a skinny boy with curly dark hair in his mid-twenties standing by a smart SUV.

'T'as du feu?' he asked

'Anglais.' she replied.

'Ah. English. You have a lighter?'

'No. Sorry. Do you know if I can order a taxi here? I need to get back to my hotel. I have no idea where it is.'

'Which hotel?'

'The Abiatic.'

'I know.'

'Is there a taxi I can get?'

'OK. I wait for my friend and we drive you there?'

'I should probably get a taxi.'

'It will be hard to get a taxi now.'

'I don't know you.'

'You don't know me. No.' He smiled. There was something non-threatening about him which assured her.

'OK, I don't have my wallet, but I can get you money when I get back to my hotel?' she replied.

'You don't have to pay. I go not too far from your hotel when I drive home.'

His friend arrived who looked the same age and equally as innocuous.

'So, we go,' he said, prompting her to get into the back of his car which she imagined he had borrowed from his rich parents who lived in a big house in the Parisian suburbs.

As they drove back, the two boys talked energetically in French about their night, girls they had chatted to, Rachel assumed. All the time Rachel sat there, she prayed that Pete would be asleep when she got back to the hotel room or at least he would pretend to be.

Half an hour later they arrived at the lobby entrance.

'Thanks so much,' said Rachel.

'It is OK,' replied the young man driving.

'Have a good night.'

She closed the car door and entered the hotel. It always surprised Rachel how you could bump into strangers who would show random acts of kindness, especially in Paris. She always thought the French were supposed to be so hostile and rude to the English.

Pete was lying on the floor using pillows he'd taken from the sofa and a duvet which she assumed he must have got from the wardrobe. She went into the bathroom to change, closing the door slowly. She didn't know why she was making an effort to be quiet around him. She knew he was awake and he didn't deserve any courtesy after the way he had behaved.

The next morning it went as she had planned. She woke up early, got changed, packed her last few things and was about to leave the room when Pete sat up to talk to her.

'You're off then?' he asked. She did her best to ignore him. 'Rachel. Just look at me.'

She turned to stare at him blankly.

'I'm sorry,' he replied, with an element of remorse in his words.

Rachel grabbed her suitcase, headed to the door, and left the room with no reply. It was the last time she would ever see Pete Barclay.

Hong Kong, China

Johnny and Suzi sat with their new set of friends as the horses were released from their pens for the fifth race of the night. It was a weekly event at the Happy Valley Racecourse, where expats and tourists assembled for drinking, eating and gambling every Wednesday night. Johnny had chosen to bet on the horse Flash Hero because the name had stood out in the betting leaflet. Suzi had gambled on Able Warrior because a work colleague had dated its owner. As the race came to an end, neither horse won.

'Oh well,' said Suzi turning to Johnny. 'Are you going to bet on the next race?'

'I'm good,' replied Johnny

'Cheer up.'

'I'm sorry. I'm just tired.'

It surprised Johnny how drained he could be after a long and mundane day in the office. It hadn't even been a busy one. It rarely was in his new job and Johnny was beginning to question why he had gone back into the world of insurance. He was aware his new position was going to be a junior one, but he had been shocked by the sheer lack of responsibility he had been given. He had made subtle hints to his manager about increasing his workload but there had been little response. At the age of thirty, he had realised how much he resented being bored at work. At least being busy made the day go quicker. What made it worst was the lack of interaction between his team members who

189

barely spoke to each other; each one silently glued to their computer screen. His attempts at conversation would always be brought to an abrupt halt by one-word answers. The only sociable member of his team was his manager, who had been given a promotion recently and was rarely in the office. Younger teams in the office surrounded him who seemed to be having the time of their lives, endlessly laughing, enjoying their work, highlighting the despondency of his situation.

'Thinking about work?' asked Suzi.

'What's there to think about? I don't do anything all day.'

'OK,' replied Suzi getting aggravated by his grumpiness. 'I won't ask you again.'

'I'm going to get another beer. You want one?'

'Hello? I have to teach tomorrow.'

Suzi's friend, Chloe, sat down between them. She had a habit of doing this.

'Oh my God, there are so many fucking wankers here,' replied Chloe in a strong aggressive Kentish accent. She held a pint of beer with her big arms and broad swimmer's shoulders which didn't seem to fit with the rest of her lean body. 'Where do they all come from?!'

'England mostly,' replied Suzi.

'Wish they'd fly home!' snapped Chloe.

'Johnny was going to get a drink. Do you want one?' Suzi asked her.

'No, I'll be pissed,' said Chloe.

Johnny headed off. He could only handle Chloe in small doses and he still didn't understand why Suzi liked spending so much time with her. She had met Chloe through work and ever since Johnny had been introduced to her he'd found her possessive over his girlfriend. It was obvious Chloe viewed Johnny as a threat to their friendship.

'Alright mate!' said an inebriated stumpy British preppy type, clad in pink shorts and a blue and white stripy shirt, greeting Johnny while he queued at the bar.

'Oh. Hi,' Johnny said. He recognised him from work but it was the first time they had spoken. 'How's it going?'

'Oh mate. I fucking love this place. Happy Valley, gets me through the week every time mate. You win anything?'

'Nope.'

'You placed a bet, right?'

'Flash Hero.'

'Flash Hero. Oh mate. Bad choice.'

'OK. Who did you bet on?'

'Golden Eagle. Every time matey.'

'Did he win?'

'No he did not!' he said laughing drunkenly patting him on the shoulder. 'Well it was great seeing you. We should go out for a drink, after work soon mate.'

'Yeah. Sounds good.'

'What's your name again matey?'

'Oh, Johnny.'

'Mate, Lewis. To DBH Insurance!' he said giving Johnny a high five which he felt obliged to reciprocate.

'Laters.'

'So, Chloe was thinking of going to Stanley this weekend?' said Suzi as he arrived back with his beer

'Oh right,' replied Johnny attempting to sound engaged.

'You want to come?' asked Suzi.

'Sure, why not.'

Johnny knew this was not going to go down well with Chloe. She disliked it when he intervened on their girl time. It was no surprise that Chloe refused to mention the trip any more.

'You don't like Chloe much do you?' Suzi asked Johnny later that night in their apartment kitchen.

191

'I just find her aggressive, and honestly, a bit possessive over you.'

'Why don't you try and be a bit friendlier with her?'

'Well she clearly doesn't like me so what's the point?'

'How do you know she doesn't like you?'

'Come on, when I told her I was going to go to Stanley with you guys she looked like she was going to punch me in the face.'

'You're imagining things.'

'She gets physically aggressive when she's angry, you've told me yourself.'

'Yeah. When she's drunk. Oh, I don't know why I mentioned it. I'm not surprised you don't like her. You don't like any of my friends.'

'What's that supposed to mean?'

'You hated most of my friends in LA.'

'The girl whose party we went to in LA was alright.'

'Nicola. One friend you like.'

'I liked your friends in Austria.'

'You hardly spoke to them.'

'Because they didn't speak English. I'm sure there's some of my friends you don't like.'

'I've hardly met any of your friends!'

'Well I'm sorry but you're right, I don't like Chloe, and I really don't understand what you see in her.'

Johnny sat down on the sofa and turned on the television.

'Fine. I'm going to bed,' said Suzi.

'I'm watching TV so I'll see you in there.'

'Keep the volume down!'

'Whatever.'

As Johnny watched the television thoughts reared up in his mind of how things had turned sour over the last three months. What had started out as small disagreements had turned into catty arguments. Suzi had recently gained more responsibility in her new teaching job which meant longer hours, and as a result, there never seemed to be any time for just the two of them. Whenever they did go out Suzi would inevitably invite her work colleagues, which of course would include Chloe. It felt as if she was consciously choosing not to spend time alone with him.

Johnny turned off the TV and went to grab his laptop to look at his emails. He noticed a recent reply from Rachel. Their email conversations had become more frequent over the last few weeks.

SUBJECT:RE: Brit Abroad
FROM: Johnny Buxford
<johnny_buxford@hotmail.com>
TO: Rachel Hortley
<sparkly_rachelhortley@yahoo.com>

Hey Johnny,

I'm sorry things aren't great between you and Suzi. I've never been one to offer good relationship advice. I guess you just have to work at it and understand that you're always going to go through hard times. Life generally makes people act in weird ways, especially when there's stuff going on. Remember me? I was a complete nightmare after my dad died! Her job in HK also sounds stressful so maybe it has something to do with that? Also, speak to her. Sometimes it's the best thing and if you're both honest and you know how each other is feeling, you might start to appreciate each other a bit more. Take her out for a meal and talk about it. However, this Chloe girl seems like a right nutter, get rid of her! She sounds possessive and a bit of a psycho crazy girl. Not good. Things OK with me. Not seeing the wanker banker anymore. Long story. He was bad bad bad. I can actually joke about it now. I couldn't for a while. Anyway, let me know when you're next back in London/UK and we can have another catch up.

Rachel x

SUBJECT: RE: Brit Abroad
FROM: Johnny Buxford
<johnny_buxford@hotmail.com>
TO: Rachel Hortley
<sparkly_rachelhortley@yahoo.com>

Hi Rachel,

Cheers for your email. I think you're right. I do need to speak to her. I think her job has a lot to do with it but I feel she is spending more time with friends and psycho crazy girl than me. I think she prefers it. I can't say I've been that happy. My job is so dull. You were right. I should have questioned going back into the mundane world of corporate 9 to 5. Anyway, I'm sorry things didn't work out with the banker (who I'm assuming was a wanker). I will definitely get in touch when I'm next back in London.

Johnny x

The next day Johnny decided to do something about their relationship. He texted Suzi while at work to ask if she wanted to grab a meal that evening at a restaurant they often visited in Kowloon. She agreed in a reply a few hours later.

Johnny was already sitting at the table in the restaurant when she arrived.

'I ordered you a beer,' said Johnny waiting for an apology for her lateness. There was none.

'Thanks. What I needed after today,' replied Suzi.

'Not a good day?'

'No. You ordered any food?'

'No. I was waiting for you.'

'So, what did you want to talk about?' Suzi asked.

'OK. Here we have it. I feel that things aren't great between us,' said Johnny.

'I agree. They haven't been for a while.'

'I just don't feel like we laugh anymore. I don't feel we're that close anymore,' said Johnny.

'It's changed between us, yes, I agree.' Her answers were cold and terse.

Johnny's feelings were now venting out of him. 'Every conversation we have seems to turn into an argument. I feel like I'm walking on eggshells around you sometimes. Like I have to watch whatever I say, because you'll just get annoyed at me for saying something you don't want to hear. Look I know I haven't been a bundle of laughs, always moaning about my job. I'm trying not to do that. I know it's not nice living with someone who's always bringing you down. But you've hardly been on top of the world with your job.'

'I haven't. I constantly feel overworked and I can't keep up with it all,' said Suzi.

'OK,' replied Johnny, wanting to know more about how she had been feeling. Hoping in some way he could understand why they had got to this stage in their relationship.

'I'll be honest with you,' she said.

'Please do.'

'I've been thinking this for a while now. There's no easy to way say this, so I'm just going to say it. I don't think we should live with each other anymore,' replied Suzi.

'I wasn't expecting that,' said Johnny.

'I'm not asking to break up. I just think we need some time apart to like each other again. The apartment is small. I think we should just have our own places. Still see each other and see how it goes from there.'

'It seems as though you've already made up your mind,' he said.

Suzi didn't reply and she was avoiding eye contact with him.

'OK. Fine. Well. I'll start looking tomorrow,' said Johnny.

'I don't mean right away.'

'I mean is there really any point in having a relationship if we do this?'

'Johnny...'

'Well it's basically a stepping stone to breaking up. Why don't you ask Chloe to move in?'

'What? Come on what the hell has Chloe got to do with anything?!'

'Did she put you up to this?'

'No. She did not put me up to this! This is my decision!'

'Really?'

'Look I don't want to have an argument here!'

'You're right. In fact, I don't really want to have a conversation with you anymore!'

Johnny stood up to get the waiter's attention who wandered over.

'Hi. Sorry, I'll come up and pay for the drinks. We're leaving. Thanks.'

'So mature,' Suzi uttered to herself as Johnny left.

Suzi caught up with him as he walked towards the Star Ferry terminal by the Cultural Centre.

'Johnny, I know this is not what you wanted to hear. But neither of us have been happy living together. I mean for God's sake, we're in one of the most exciting cities in the world, and neither of us are enjoying it. We owe it to ourselves to enjoy our time here.'

'I moved here for you because I wanted to share this experience with you, and now you're just kicking me out when I'm the one who takes you out to talk about what's been going wrong!'

'If I'm mistaken I think it was Rachel who suggested it in her email, or am I mistaken?'

'You looked at my computer? At my emails?'

'You leave your computer on all the time, and yes, I did. I saw her name and I wanted to know why you were emailing her. Are you still in love with her?'

'I needed someone to talk to.'

'I've read the messages. You tell her things. Things you would never tell me and I'm your girlfriend Johnny. I read those messages, and it hurts me, the way you never let me in like you do with her. I know you lied to me. You met her in London.' Tears began to fall from her eyes.

'I met her once, for a drink.'

'And chose not to tell me. Why?'

'I don't know. Because I felt guilty.'

'Because it was wrong. It was more than a drink. You know that. Every time you talk about her you act differently.'

'We're not having this conversation.'

'You don't think I don't know you. I know you Johnny and reading those messages every time, it breaks my heart!'

She was falling apart in front of him but all he could do was walk away.

'Just go. Go home Suzi.'

When he was a good distance away he turned back to see she had disappeared. He sat down on a bench to try and take control of his emotions. He could feel his eyes well up. He hated crying.

He always had. It made him feel vulnerable and weak in a way he could never handle. He wiped his tears away, stood up and walked to the ferry which had just opened its doors.

The boat was empty as it left the harbour to make its way across the bay. The lights of the Hong Kong skyline looked fantastic. They always did at night, but all Johnny could feel was loneliness in this brightly lit city.

After he disembarked the ferry at the other side he made his way through a nearby shopping centre which was devoid of visitors. He walked to the tram stop, and waited a few minutes for the next one to arrive, and took a seat on the top deck to get a good view of his journey.

When he arrived back to the apartment he could see Suzi was asleep in the bedroom. He couldn't sleep in the same room with her anymore. A chasm had been opened between them. He went to the cupboard and got out the sleeping bag and pillow, and set up a bed for the night on the sofa.

He awoke the next morning as Suzi trotted around the kitchen, getting ready for work and left. He dragged himself out of bed and turned on the kettle. The thought of going to work filled him with dread. He needed to clear his head and think about what had happened the night before. He also needed to find a place to move to. Suzi had been right. They needed space. Things needed to change. But she had been optimistic about the status of their relationship. She saw hope. He didn't see any now. He waited until 8.30am before he phoned his manager in the office.

'Hi Matthew,' he said, surprised to find his manager in the office. Johnny lay down on the sofa, made his voice sound husky, as if he was losing it. He was a good actor when he wanted to be. 'I've just woken up,' he said. 'I really don't feel very well so I'm going to stay at home today. I just think I need to sleep this one off.'

'OK. Please let the others know in the afternoon how you feel and if you will be in tomorrow.'

'Sure. Will do.'

He put the phone down. It sounded plausible and it was the first day he had been sick since he started the job. He didn't feel bad. There were more pressing matters. He looked out of the apartment window at thick tropical clouds.

He went to his laptop and began looking at apartments on the internet. He phoned up letting agents to enquire about potential meetings. He was surprised by how many appointments he had booked in such a small amount of time. His first meeting was at an address in Fortress Hill.

The letting agent was waiting for him when he arrived. A dainty local woman in her late twenties who kept joking politely about the urgency in which he needed to find somewhere. The apartment wasn't that much different from the place he had been living in. A less impressive view but cheaper rent. It didn't take him long to make his decision. It ticked the box.

'I'll take it,' said Johnny

'Yes?' asked the letting agent, confirming his decision.

'Yes.'

'You take place very quickly,' she laughed.

'I do.'

Johnny was sitting outside on the balcony reading when Suzi arrived back that night. There seemed to be an element of calmness between them.

'Have you eaten?' he asked amicably.

'I met Chloe for food,' she replied, unpacking a carton of milk and orange juice which she had bought on the way home. 'Work go OK?'

'I didn't go. I said I was ill. I went to look at apartments instead. I've found somewhere to live so I'm moving out.'

'When will you go?' she asked while still unpacking.

'It's available now, so a few days. I'll take stuff over bit by bit, so I should hopefully be done by the end of the week. Will you stay here?'

'I think so.'

'It won't be cheap.'

She closed the fridge and folded up the plastic bag placing it on the kitchen surface in front of her. 'So, this is how it ends?' she asked turning to him with tears cascading from her eyes.

Johnny went over to hug her and held her there. Loving her as much as he could, but knowing it had never been enough.

'This is how it ends,' he replied.

Brighton, South Downs and London, UK

Rachel stood frying salmon and scrambled egg when her mother appeared in her dressing gown. She had lost weight, Rachel thought, and she was surprised by how attractive her mother now looked.

'You want some bread?' Rachel asked her mother, taking the frying pan off the Aga.

'Best not.'

'It's your wedding day Mum, you can ditch the diet for the day.'

'Go on then, you've persuaded me.'

Becca arrived in her pyjamas as Rachel served up their food onto plates.

'This looks great Rach,' said Becca as they sat down at the kitchen table to eat their food.

'Look I know this day can't be easy for the both of you,' said their mother, hesitating about what to say next. 'You probably think it's too soon since your father passed way, but Charlie and I, well, we wanted to do this, and I need you to understand that. He makes me very happy.'

'We know Mum,' replied Becca.

Rachel kept quiet. She had mixed emotions about her mother's wedding. It did feel too early but it was obvious Charlie did make her happy and she couldn't deny the subtle beam that appeared on her mother's face ever since Charlie had proposed to her. It was around this time she had finally made amends with her mother after months of not talking. She had to go along with this day, for her mother's happiness, no matter how she felt.

'I forgot the champagne,' said Becca, darting to the fridge to get out a bottle which she poured into their glasses with cranberry juice.

'This looks interesting,' commented their mother.

'I read this is a good wedding morning drink so thought we'd give it a go.'

'Well cheers to that,' replied their mother.

'Don't you think it is too soon?' Rachel asked Becca while putting on her bridesmaid outfit in the spare room later that morning.

'If I did what would be the point in making a thing of it? She worships Charlie. You can tell just by the way she looks at him. You know she never had that with Dad. Well certainly not when we were growing up.'

Becca fought hard to do up the zip on the back of Rachel's dress which fitted tightly around her.

'I guess I put on weight,' said Rachel.

'Mum's so happy you came you know,' said Becca.

'So what's Charlie like?' asked Rachel.

'He's nice.'

'Wow you're really selling him.'

'He's good for her. You'll see what I mean when you meet him.'

'It's kind of bad I haven't met him yet isn't it?'

'I think you could have made more of an effort, yes.'

'How to sound like an older sister.'

'You're the one that asked.'

After they had finished getting ready Becca went to help her mother get into her dress, while Rachel went downstairs to phone her brother to check that plans where coming together at the wedding venue. Her mother appeared shortly after wearing a subtle plain cream dress and a blazer with a small fascinator on her head.

'Mum. You look amazing,' commented Rachel.

'Not so bad is it.'

A Jaguar MK2 arrived at the house to pick them up. It was a short drive to the small stately home on the South Downs where the wedding was taking place. When they arrived they walked into the grand reception room of the house, turned left where the doors to the ceremonial room opened. Piano music played while Becca and Rachel walked their mother down the aisle.

Rachel spotted Charlie for the first time standing at the front of the room. He was more handsome than she had expected. She had only seen him in photos before. He had a slim physique, glasses, a full head of white hair and tanned skin; her mother was marrying a silver fox.

When the ceremony was finished her mother and Charlie waited by the door of the room to greet the guests as they came out.

'Charlie,' said her mother as Rachel approached. 'This is Rachel.'

'Good to finally meet you Rachel,' he said with a hint of an East London accent.

'Congratulations,' she replied, feeling unusually buoyant about the occasion.

They moved to a hall where light snacks and drinks were served. Rachel approached her brother who was standing awkwardly with his confident girlfriend, Vicky, who was talking to some elderly relatives.

'How's the new place?' Rachel asked Mark.

'Nice, except the family downstairs are a pain in the arse.'

'How come?'

'Oh, they just moan all the time. Claim we make too much noise.'

'And do you?'

'I spend most of my time playing computer games with my headphones on, while Vicky sews in the living room, so no.'

'What a great service. Your mum looked so happy,' commented Vicky with her soft middle-class North Midlands accent.

Vicky had surprised them all when she came on the scene. She was so normal and sane. It felt bad to think it, but the opposite of what her brother was. She was the breath of fresh air he had needed for a long time and his mental health had improved significantly as a result of this.

They sat down for the wedding breakfast where Rachel found herself sitting next to Charlie. She knew her mother had done this intentionally but she didn't make a big deal of it.

'I see you're the unlucky one who has to sit next to me,' commented Charlie as the starter was served.

'Well I guess it's a chance to get to know you better,' replied Rachel.

'Listen I just wanted to say it can't have been easy losing your father like you did, and then hearing about me.'

Rachel admired his honesty. 'It wasn't,' she replied.

'I only hope that one day we can all be friends or at least get on with each other.'

'I hope so too.'

They didn't talk much for the rest of the meal. Brief speeches, toasts were made, drinks consumed and food eaten. Most of the guests, who were older, made their way home after the meal was finished. Music had been arranged for the younger members of the wedding party who ranged from primary school age to late teens.

'So have you been seeing anyone?' asked Vicky, sitting down next to Rachel who sat alone at a table watching her older sister dancing with one of their younger cousins.

'Nope. Having a break,' replied Rachel.

'That's a shame. There must be plenty of choice in London.'

'That's if I stay there.'

'Are you thinking of leaving?'

'I don't know. I feel like a bit of a change is needed.'

'Where would you go?'

'Maybe go travelling again. Last time I was abroad it was cut short because of Dad dying. I wish I'd carried on but I decided to stay here.'

'That sounds exciting.'

'You've changed my brother, you know,' said Rachel. 'Meeting him I mean. God, he really needed to meet someone like you.'

'I think I needed to meet him too,' replied Vicky emotionally, putting her hand on Rachel's, thanking her for her comment.

'You think we should make a move?' Mark asked Vicky, approaching the table.

'Yes I think that might be a good idea,' replied Vicky.

'I don't feel like I've talked to you much Mark,' said Rachel standing up as they got ready to depart.

'You should come by the flat some time,' replied Mark.

'Definitely, next time I'm down maybe,' she said going to kiss him on the cheek.

'You take care of yourself Rachel,' said Vicky giving her a warm embrace.

Becca arrived to say goodbye, then sat down next to Rachel.

'Our twelve-year-old cousin is exhausting me. Are you not going up to dance?' asked Becca.

'Maybe later.'

'You OK?'

'Yeah. Just thinking about things.'

'Such as?'

'Oh, just thinking about what to do no next in the grand scheme of my life. Sorry, it's the booze talking.'

'Don't apologise. I have those thoughts on a daily basis. Then I realise I have a screaming child to look after. What are you thinking about?'

'I just feel like I'm stagnating. Like I need to do something.'

'Well you've got no responsibilities. What's to stop you? I envy you, you know that?'

'You don't envy me. You think my life's a mess.'

'I've never thought that Rachel.'

'Oh come on, you do. You should, I mean, look at you. You have an amazing family and you're settled. I'll probably never have that.'

'You don't know that. When the time's right, it'll happen, when you least expect it.'

'I'd be a terrible mum.'

'No you wouldn't. You'd be a messy mum, that's for sure. But I could see you with a few ankle biters, definitely.'

'Angels' by Robbie Williams began to play.

'Come on, I want a sister dance,' said Becca coaxing Rachel onto the dance floor.

The next morning Rachel woke early. She ordered a full English breakfast at the hotel restaurant, made small talk with relatives, then went to knock on her mother's hotel room door.

'You're up early?' said her mother answering.

'I wanted to get back to London fairly soonish.'

'Not too hungover then?' asked Charlie while placing their wedding presents into the corner of their honeymoon suite.

'I didn't really drink that much.'

'You all have a good time?' asked Charlie.

'Roger and Miles were practically on the dance floor to the bitter end.'

'These are Rachel's cousins. They were really going for it.'

Her mother went to give her a kiss and drew her into a hug. 'It was lovely seeing you Rachel. Be down soon, won't you?'

'I'll try,' replied Rachel. She always found these moments of intimacy with her mother hard to handle.

'Nice to meet you eventually,' she said to Charlie.

'You too Rachel, you too.'

They didn't hug but kept a respectable distance and shook hands.

After she had said her goodbyes to everyone Rachel caught a taxi to the village station to catch the next train to London and was back in her Stoke Newington flat by lunchtime.

When she entered the kitchen she saw a note from her Australian housemate, Fiona, next to her pile of dirty dishes. *Please clean Rach. It's been here way too long. F x.'* She put down her bag in the kitchen, filled the sink and began tackling the job she had been putting off. She could hear her other housemate, Nigel, watching football in the living room next door. When she had finished cleaning she didn't bother to see him as she wasn't in the mood for small talk. It would only be about football which bored her, so she walked upstairs to her untidy bedroom and lay down on her bed and fell asleep.

She awoke later on that afternoon. The sun was shining through the window. It always did this time of day if there were no clouds and it gave life and colour to the room. She got up, had a quick shower, dressed and headed out to the local park which was full of young families preparing to pack up and return to their homes ready for the working week. As she walked past them she began to reflect on her life and her reasons for not joining Johnny after her father died. It became clear now. It had been to help her mother and brother who both seemed to have moved on with their lives and finally found happy relationships. Her job was done so what was to stop her carrying on with her travels? Though it wouldn't be travelling as such, it could be more of an experience of working abroad again. It suddenly all fell into place as she returned to the flat that evening. This is what she would do. She would go to her room, go on her laptop, and begin planning out her next adventure.

Dubai International Airport, UAE

Johnny fought his way through the airport crowds, hoping that Rachel would still be waiting for him outside her departure gate. When he arrived, there was no sign of her. He stood there, scouting the area in the hope she would be still waiting in a shop nearby, trying to get back his breath back. There was a tap on his shoulder.

'Hello fellow traveller,' she replied.

'Thought you'd given up,' he said. 'Flight was delayed.'

'I saw it on the screen,' replied Rachel.

'And I had to re-scan my bag at the transfer queue. How long have you got?'

'About forty minutes.'

'OK. You want to go grab a drink?

'Sure.'

They made their way to the centre of the terminal building, past the many duty free shops, which made the place feel more like a shopping mall than an airport. They were both tired, due to the different time zones they had travelled from, but being in each other's company had woken them up.

'So you're off to Thailand?' asked Johnny.

'I am.'

'And I'm flying back to England. We never quite seem to be in the same country, do we?'

'We really don't.'

'This OK?' he said heading in the direction of an American style coffee shop.

'Perfect.'

'What d'you want? This is on me, for being late.'

'Go on, a tea then. Thanks.'

'You love your tea.'

'Would you want me any other way?'

'Most definitely not.'

Rachel sat down to check she still had her boarding pass for her ongoing flight. She had a habit of losing them on long haul journeys, but found it folded up inside her passport at the bottom of her bag.

'One tea and one cappuccino,' said Johnny, placing the drinks on the table, sitting down opposite her.

'So this trip was a recent decision I'm assuming?' asked Johnny.

'Yep.'

'Any reason you wanted to do it now?'

'I just realised there was nothing really stopping me. My family seemed to have sorted themselves out. I broke up with the guy I was telling you about. It just felt like the right thing to do.'

'So you're going to be a diving instructor?'

'It's kind of nuts, right?'

'Did you have to do much training?'

'I had to do a few more courses in Egypt which I did about a month ago. But you know I was fairly experienced. We did diving holidays when I was a kid so it's not like I'd never done it before.'

'It sounds great Rach. It really does'

'Well I wasn't really expecting to get the job so quickly. I went online about a week after getting back from Egypt and applied for it. A couple of days later I get this email asking for a phone interview and the next thing I know they're offering me the position.'

'It's always the way. Where are you going to be based?'

'It's an island in Eastern Thailand, towards the Cambodia border. It's a smallish resort, but I've got a tiny flat, which comes with the job.'

'Sounds like you've landed on your feet.'

Rachel sipped her tea with a subtle look of ebullience.

'So I'm sorry to hear about you and Suzi,' she remarked sincerely.

'Thanks.'

'Is that why you decided to head back to England?'

'One of the reasons, yeah. I just started to feel rather alone out there. After we broke up I realised a lot of the people I was hanging around with were pretty much Suzi's friends and they didn't really want to hang out with me anymore.'

'Did you like Hong Kong?'

'Yeah, it was a great. The weather was fantastic. You had this amazing city with different islands surrounding it with loads of stuff to do. I don't regret going out there. It's just a shame how it ended.'

'Your family will be pleased to have you back.'

'I think so.'

'How are they?'

'Fine. My sister's good. On silly money now. Got another promotion. Still working as a city lawyer. She's moved in with her boyfriend.'

'And your parents?'

'All good. Retired. Going away on holiday. A lot. A hell of a lot actually. On cruises. They like their cruises.'

'See. This is the life we get to look forward to.'

'Oh no, our generation are screwed. We're working well into our eighties. And probably ending work with no pension. No cruises for us.'

Rachel laughed.

'And yours?' asked Johnny.

'Really well actually. My brother has a girlfriend he's moved in with. My mum got remarried a couple of months ago.'

'And from what I recall you weren't so keen on your mum's fella?'

'True. So I finally met him at the wedding and I actually rather warmed to him.'

'And your sister?'

'Still being a mum.'

'You think she'll have any more?'

'I don't know.'

'You ever think about kids?'

'Sometimes. You?'

'Definitely. If I meet the right girl.'

'Little Johnnys.'

'Exactly.'

'Though you may have to drop the Johnny part if you're trying to conceive!'

He laughed.

'So what are you going to do when you get back home?' asked Rachel.

'Probably go back to York and scrounge off the parents.'

'Will you move back to London?'

'Maybe. Unless I get bored and head off to some other foreign destination.'

'Will you stay in touch with Suzi?'

'I was never one for staying in touch with an ex.'

'Well that's hardly true, you're here talking to me.'

'That's a very good point.' Johnny smiled at her wry response. 'I'll claim you as the exception. She was always jealous of you, you know that?'

'Jealous of me? She never even met me.'

'She knew about you.'

'Well, she needn't have been. There was nothing to be jealous about.'

Johnny cleared his throat while Rachel took out her ticket and passport.

'You OK for time?' asked Johnny.

Rachel glanced at the time on her phone. 'We should probably make a move, head to a few shops on the way?'

'Sure, which reminds me. I need to get some Toblerone for the parents. It's a family tradition, bringing home Toblerone if you've been abroad.'

'Which flavour is the family's preference?'

'White chocolate, every time. Once made the huge mistake of bringing back a fruit and nut. Didn't go down very well.'

They entered the chocolate section of the duty free store where each brand was neatly displayed in a museum like fashion.

'Here we go.' Johnny said finding a large pyramid sculpture made up of Toblerones. 'Dare I take one off? I'm worried the whole thing will fall down.' He carefully lifted a packet from the display.

'Subtly done.'

They walked to the counter where a girl at the till scanned his boarding pass.

'So are you going to do much travelling around Thailand while you're over there?' he asked.

'I think so. Though I've been told the job is pretty intense. Not much down time, which reminds me, I need to buy a travel guide.'

'Well hang on a sec.'

Johnny put down his rucksack and undid the zip.

'Have mine,' he said, taking out his travel book. 'You remember this?'

'How could I not? I feel bad taking your precious travel book with all those black arrows in it? '

'It's had better days,' he said, slipping in a couple of loose pages which had almost fallen out.

'Still going strong though. Won't you miss it?'

'Please, I'd like you to have it. I insist in fact. Come on, this book brings a lot of luck for us. We would not be here now if it wasn't for this book.'

'Very true.'

'Plus, I also think it's got a pretty good section on Thailand.'

'Well OK then, if you're really sure.'

He handed it over.

'You really don't think we would be here if it wasn't for this book?' she asked.

'This book put an end to two hard months of hoping to find you. Sorry, I didn't mean that to sound stalkerish.' He could feel himself blush.

'I never knew that. It feels like a long time ago now, meeting you there.'

He walked with Rachel towards her gate where a large queue was starting to form.

'I wish this had been longer,' Rachel said, stopping to face him.

'Me too. Time always seems to go quickly with you. Well I hope the job goes well Rachel.'

'You too. Bye Johnny,' she said giving him a fervent hug and as soon as he knew it, he was walking away from her, through the crowds towards the gate where he was due to leave in a couple of hours.

He had only sat down for a moment in a quiet corner, near a young Asian couple who were flirting with each other, playing with a set of headphones putting one side in each of their ears, when he began to feel a sudden feeling of loss. It gave him the sudden urge to get up and walk back to where he had come from, hitting people's shoulders as he made his way down the airport hallway. He picked up his pace, until he was lightly running in what felt like an eternity toward the departure gate at the other side of the airport where Rachel was standing in the queue, about to have her ticket checked.

She turned, abashed by his return. 'Johnny.'

213

'Can we talk?' he said, willing her out the queue.

'What is it?'

'Crazy idea. But I was just thinking, back there. What if I came to live with you in Thailand?'

'What are you talking about? You're going back to England.'

'As mad as it seems, saying goodbye to you back there and catching a flight in the other direction felt like the worst thing in the world to me. I had to tell you that, and now I have, so what do you say?'

She could tell he was nervous, utterly vulnerable by what he was saying and all she could do was go and kiss him, and as she did, the airport fell still for a moment, as if time had stopped to allow them to savour this moment and make everything around them feel utterly insignificant. She held his hand and looked at him. A feeling of relief on both sides.

'Well,' she replied, going to kiss his hand and holding it tightly. 'Maybe you should think about changing your ticket.'

Koh Chang, Thailand

'I'm excited. First day on the new moped!' said Johnny as he left the wooden bungalow he was now sharing with Rachel.

'Now promise me you're going to be careful.'

'I'll be fine.'

'Johnny I'm being serious. They drive like crazy people around here.'

'I'll be careful,' he said, kissing her lightly on the lips. 'And Happy birthday. Remember I'm cooking tonight.'

'I know.'

'Love you,' he said putting on his helmet and shooting off on his new toy.

Johnny could have taken the fifteen-minute walk to work but the excitement of owning a moped convinced him otherwise. Besides, he wanted to show off his new purchase to Ewan, his boss, the co-owner of the Barracuda Lounge; the island of Koh Chang's most popular backpackers' beach bar.

Ewan was an ex London city banker who ran the bar with his savvy Thai wife, Eve, who was twenty years his junior. Eve had started the bar from scratch, despite people assuming it was Ewan's money that had got it up and running. Ewan had only met her five years earlier while on holiday shortly after being made redundant soon after his fiftieth birthday. After marrying him, Eve had made him co-owner of the business.

Johnny had not warmed to Ewan the first time he met him for his interview. He had found him arrogant and sarcastic. After a few weeks on the job, he had learnt to appreciate his wry sense of humour.

'You're early,' remarked Ewan, while Johnny entered the bar. He was reading the most recent imported copy of The Daily Telegraph, his usual morning routine.

'I biked in,' replied Johnny.

'Bought one then I see?' said Ewan with a hint of disapproval. Ewan had tried to talk him out the purchase, having had a bad accident on a moped a few years earlier.

'I did.'

'Fucking idiot.'

'Why did I know you were going to say that?'

'Have you given Rachel ideas for your funeral?'

'Yes, I'm going to be cremated with my moped.'

Ewan smiled at Johnny's sharp reply. 'Well. It's your life. I can see you're happy with it.'

'I am.'

'Well I guess that's all that matters.'

'How did the pub quiz go last night?' Johnny asked, while checking the drink stocks behind the bar.

'I don't think we'll be using that quiz master again.'

'How come?'

'He was not very good. He seemed to think he was incredibly witty and funny, when he really really wasn't. And it dragged. Painfully dragged.'

'That's a shame. The other bars around here seemed to recommend him.'

'Yes, well, we won't be trusting their judgment again.'

'Well why don't you do it?'

'Me? No I'd be far too rude and inappropriate.'

'Isn't that how quiz masters are supposed to be?'

'Yes, but I'd be rude about things like my wonderful wife,' he replied as Eve walked up to the bar, holding a number of swimwear items on hangers. 'Wouldn't we my dear?!'

'You would what?' replied Eve, with her strong Thai accent.

'I said I'd be rude, take the mick out of you among other things if I did the pub quiz,' remarked Ewan.

'You rude to me all the time!' she replied while holding up an article of clothing in front of Johnny's face. 'What'd you think?'

'Yeah, they seem nice. What are they for?' asked Johnny.

'I open up new swim shop!' she replied.

'I'm sure Johnny would love to buy some ladies swim wear,' said Ewan smiling.

'I would not,' replied Johnny.

'They could look like speedos on you,' Ewan jested.

'I hate speedos,' said Johnny.

'British people do not like speedos,' said Eve.

'No they don't,' Johnny added. 'French people like them, but not the English.'

'This is because French people have good bodies because they are slim and British people are fat, yes?' replied Eve.

'Possibly,' said Johnny while laughing.

'Yes. Look at my husband. He is British and he is fat,' said Eve putting up the swimwear on the door of the bar storage room, which she was planning to convert into a new shop.

Ewan patted his large stomach. 'You wouldn't want me any other way.'

'Because British people drink too much alcohol and eat too many fried foods like burgers and fish and chips,' said Eve.

'She's very observant your wife,' said Johnny, turning to Ewan.

'I wouldn't want her any other way. She's the best Thai bride I could have ever have ordered.'

'I am no Thai bride!' snapped Eve. 'You are my mail order husband who I ordered at discounted rate.'

'See what I have to put up with?' replied Ewan.

217

Johnny smiled.

'So what are you doing for Rachel's birthday?' asked Ewan.

'I'm cooking.'

'Do we trust she will be well in the morning?'

'Hey, I'm a good cook now I'll have you know. Been learning how to do all these Thai dishes.'

'Johnny, you give Rachel a birthday present,' said Eve, looking through her new collection.

'Oh. Thank you.'

'She should be a small size, no?'

'Possibly. I don't know.'

Eve handed over three swimsuits.

'You take these home and she can choose which one she wants. She can also tell her friends that this is the new place to buy swimwear in town.'

'That's really nice Eve. Thanks.'

'I am nice person. You tell my husband I am a nice person!'

'Ewan your wife's a nice person.'

'Good thing I paid such a high rate for her on the Thai bride website,' replied Ewan while turning the page of his newspaper.

'Not funny!' she replied slapping his shoulder.

'Ewan thinks I'm an idiot for buying a scooter,' Johnny texted Rachel while she was preparing for her afternoon trip with her diving clients.

'You are. I'm pleased I'm not the only one who agrees! What are we having for dinner tonight?'

'It's a surprise.'

'Looking forward to it x.'

Rachel tucked away her phone in her rucksack.

'We really need to get some of these wet suits replaced,' added Emily, Rachel's Australian diving colleague.

'You try telling that to management. They won't replace them. They don't have any money.'

'I mean half these suits have bloody holes in them! It gives off such a bad impression. Especially if we're competing with all the other diving schools in the area.'

'How did your date go last night?' asked Rachel.

'Yeah, he seemed like a nice guy, but he's leaving in a couple of weeks. Downside of dating a backpacker. They screw you then leave you.'

Rachel liked Emily for her coarse no-nonsense Australian personality which she found both crude and entertaining in equal measure.

'So are you going to see him again?' asked Rachel.

'Yeah. Probably. He was hot.'

'Who was hot?' said Elliot, their nosy South African work colleague approaching them.

'Emily went on a date last night.' Rachel regretted telling him the minute she mentioned it. She could tell Emily did not feel comfortable with Elliot hearing about her love life. There had been a minor fling between them a few months earlier and a lot of tension since.

'Really?' replied Elliot. 'Are we seeing more of him?'

'Maybe, I don't know,' replied Emily coyly, while also making it obvious she did not want to discuss this any longer with him.

The five divers that Rachel had been teaching approached consisting of a nervous Dutch mother, her two precocious teenage daughters and a heavily tattooed English couple.

'Hey everyone,' said Emily addressing the group. 'If you'd like to collect your wetsuits, snorkels and fins, and we'll make our way over to the boat!'

They helped get their clients onto the dive boat which had other groups on board from surrounding schools.

'OK guys,' Rachel addressed her group. 'So we've arrived here at the reef. Emily and I are going to enter first while Elliot and the

219

other instructors will help you one by one into the water. Have a great dive, see you down there.'

Rachel pushed herself back off the boat into the water, then waited for her pupils to swim towards the buoy. They used the rope to guide themselves down to the correct spot on the ocean bed.

The water was exceptionally clear and there was an abundance of fish swimming around the reefs. It made a change considering the water had been particular murky over the last few days. When they reached the bottom they congregated in a group for a few moments, then slowly headed off around the reefs. Rachel enjoyed these trips as she could tell the group gained more confidence the more time they spent underwater.

By the time they had got back to the diving office Rachel was surprised to discover that the Dutch mother had agreed with her daughters to carry on with completing the PADI course for an extra two days; she had wanted to pull out earlier despite being the one to show the most promise out of the entire group. It felt good when this happened Rachel thought, to see a pupil carry on to the next stage, despite being so anxious to start off with.

After the guests had departed they washed all the diving gear and filled out all the necessary paperwork before closing up for the day.

'So can we treat you to a birthday drink Rachel?' asked Elliot.

'Sounds good. Johnny's cooking so it's got to be a quick one.'

They headed to a bar next door, a slightly shabby establishment which they often visited for after work drinks. They handed Rachel a present which she unwrapped; a blue t-shirt with a silhouette of a diver and the words below it, *'I love to go down.'*

Rachel laughed.

'It was the most tasteless t-shirt we could find,' remarked Emily.

'Well it certainly is that. Just to say I won't be wearing it while I'm with clients, but maybe I can wear it as my new sleeping t-shirt. Thanks guys. This is the first day I've actually enjoyed being at work on my birthday. And I'll be honest, I could do this job forever.'

'I'll remind you of this in the future when you've been doing this job as long as me,' replied Elliot.

'How long have you actually been a diving instructor?' asked Emily.

'Longer than I like to admit.' Neither of the girls were sure of his age. Rachel assumed he was in his late thirties.

'Fifteen years,' Elliot admitted.

'Wow. That's a long time,' said Rachel.

'I know. I came here travelling and I never left,' replied Elliot.

'Isn't that every diving instructor's story?' Emily said.

'Yes, it probably is,' he replied.

'You ever think you'll go back to South Africa?' asked Rachel.

'Yeah, I think so. I've got to grow up eventually. Get a proper job.'

'What? Like this isn't a proper job?' said Emily, offended by his comment.

'Yes it is, but the money's not great,' replied Elliot. 'Got to follow in the family business, haven't I?'

'Oh, forgot you were a rich kid,' said Emily.

'I'm not a rich kid,' contended Elliot.

'Isn't that what all the trust fund kids say?' she replied.

'What's the family business?' asked Rachel trying to placate the situation.

'Dad makes suits,' said Elliot.

'Expensive ones. Doesn't he supply them to a heap load of celebrities?' added Emily.

'Yeah, he's supplied them to one or two.'

'You think you can go back to something like that after this?' asked Rachel.

'Yes, make a bit of cash. Definitely,' replied Elliot. 'Teaching diving's great, but not something you want to do for the rest of your life.'

'How about you Rachel? Are you going to stick this out for much longer or do you think you'll head back to the UK?' asked Emily.

'For a bit longer, definitely,'

'What else would you do?' asked Elliot.

'I always wanted to design greeting cards. Do something with my degree.'

'Yeah, Rachel showed me some of her drawings. You should totally pursue it,' remarked Emily.

'Oh you're an arty farty sort?' replied Elliot.

'Don't be rude,' said Emily.

'Who's being rude?' asked Elliot. 'I'm just saying she's artistic. Do you think Johnny would want to move back to England?"

'I don't really know what he wants. I think he's happy at the moment but I can't see him wanting to work behind a bar forever.'

'So what's Johnny got on the menu tonight?' Emily asked.

'Not sure.'

'Something romantic to celebrate your birthday?'

'Hopefully. In fact, I should probably get going,' she said looking at her watch. 'I don't want to be late.'

'Cool. Have a good one babes,' said Emily, giving her a hug. 'Happy birthday!'

'Thanks. Bye Elliot.'

'Have a good night,' he replied.

Rachel arrived at the flat to find a strong coriander smell coming from the kitchen.

'Hey!' she said putting down her work rucksack in the living room, flinging off her sandals and walking into the kitchen.

'How's the birthday girl?' he said, going to kiss her.

'Something smells good,' she said looking hungrily at the food. 'Green curry. Amazing.'

'Thought you'd like it. So I've put some white wine in the fridge if you fancy it?'

'Great. Elliot says hi.'

'Oh. Right. Elliot. How is Elliot?' he replied attempting to put on a South African accent.

'Wow, you made him sound Jamaican.'

'I sound South African bro,' he replied accentuating his accent. 'Can't you hear my South African accent bro, it's genuine.'

'How was the bar?' Rachel asked, opening the bottle of wine and pouring out two glasses.

'Not bad. So Eve's set up a ladies' swimwear shop.'

'Bloody hell. That woman is a force to be reckoned with. More to add to her business empire?'

'She insisted you had something from there for your birthday.'

'Oh right.'

'It's in the bag on the table. You can choose one.'

Rachel went to look in the bag.

'I actually quite like all of them,' she said holding up the different designs.

'You can try them on now if you want?' Johnny said with a smouldering look in his eyes.

Rachel smiled. 'Maybe I will.'

'And your sister Skyped about half an hour ago.'

'Cool. I'll phone her back at some point.'

'I think she wants to speak to you today.'

'OK.'

'I'm being serious.'

'Fine, I'll do it now!'

'Well dinner's going to be a bit longer. I'm just saying, you're always really rubbish getting back to people.'

'OK. Look. I'm Skyping her!' she said going over to the laptop in the next room and opening up the Skype icon on her desktop. 'Internet's being really slow again!'

'You're the one that wanted the cheap package!'

Rachel's sister picked up on the other line.

'Hey!' replied Becca.

'Hey. Can you hear me?'

'Yes. Happy birthday!'

'Thanks.'

'How was your day?'

'Good. Been at work. Just had a quick beer and now Johnny's cooking.'

'Hi Johnny!' replied Becca.

'Hi Becca,' he shouted from the kitchen.

'How's Lola?' asked Rachel.

'She's good. Speaking a lot and her vocabulary is really coming along, you'd be surprised.'

'Can I see her?'

Becca bought her on the screen. Rachel was shocked to see how much she had grown. She was starting to look like a toddler.

'Hey you!' said Rachel.

'Can you say hi to Auntie Rachel?'

'He-wo Auntie Rachel,' replied Lola slowly while playing with her toys.

'She was practicing her singing of 'Happy Birthday' yesterday but I think her toy tea set has proved more exciting,' said Becca.

'I really miss her,' said Rachel.

'Well she really misses you. We all do.'

'Have you seen Mum?'

'Yep. She came over with Charlie for dinner at the weekend. You should call her. I'm sure she'd like to talk to you.'

'Did she say that?'

'No, but I can tell she misses you.'

'How's Mark?'

'He's OK. I think he's going to buy a flat with Vicky.'

'It's getting serious.'

'Well I think Vicky's on a decent wage so it makes sense.'

'I should speak to him.'

'You should, and it would be nice for us to speak more often, yes?'

'OK, point taken. I do work all the time.'

'I know, but we're all busy.'

'Johnny tells me I'm rubbish as well so I get the grief from all sides.'

'She is!' Johnny shouted from the kitchen.

'So Johnny's cooking for me tonight.'

'I wish Lawrence did that for my birthday. Very jealous. Well I will leave you both to it. Are you going to say bye to Auntie Rachel, Lola?'

'Bye Lola!' Rachel said.

Lolo appeared on the screen. 'Ba bye.'

'Oh my God she's so cute! Bye bye. Love you!'

'See you later,' said Becca.

The Skype call terminated as Johnny came out of the kitchen.

'Were you not pleased you did that?' he asked.

'Yes, I was pleased I did that.'

'Thought we'd eat outside.'

She followed him out onto their patio where he had put a white cloth on a tatty fold-up table, and on top of it he had placed a lit candle.

'You didn't have to make this much effort,' Rachel said.

'Well I have.'

Johnny poured them some more wine, then returned to the living room where he brought out a dish which was covered with a plate warmer.

'Well. Enjoy,' he said sitting down, prompting her to lift up the plate warmer, which she did to reveal an empty plate, where, written in tomato sauce was the message, *Will you marry me?*'

225

Rachel looked up with an incredulous grin. 'Well, I did not see that coming.'

'I know this might seem quick,' he said coyly. 'I mean we've only been back together three months but I just feel like this works. We work. You and me. If you need time to think about, by all means....'

'Yes,' replied Rachel suddenly. 'My answer, I think, is yes.'

'Are you sure?' Johnny said.

'Yes! I cannot truly believe this is happening.'

He reached over the table, narrowly missing the flame of the candle, and kissed her.

'I know this isn't the fanciest proposal in the world,' Johnny added

'This is amazing.'

'And I promise to get you a nice ring. In the meantime, you may just have to make do with this.' He went into his pocket where he bought out a smart biro which he used to carefully draw an engagement ring around her finger.

'Do you think you can manage that?' he asked.

'That's the nicest engagement ring I've ever seen,' Rachel quipped. 'Was there actually a real starter?'

Johnny laughed. 'No, we are actually just having a main course.'

Rachel laughed. 'Damn. So disappointed.'

Johnny went to stroke her hair and kiss her lips again. 'Thank you.'

'For what?"

'For saying yes. You don't think this is crazy? You and me?' asked Johnny.

'Nope,' she replied. 'I don't think this is crazy at all.'

Phuket and Khao Lak, Thailand

It was lunchtime by the time Johnny and Rachel arrived on a large speedboat at Ko Panyee; a fishing village that stretched out into the sea on wooden stilts.

'OK,' said Buddy their amiable Thai tour leader addressing the group as the boat docked. 'We stop here for one hour. You have lots of food for lunch, for buffet lunch. We meet back here at 1.30pm.'

Johnny helped Rachel step off the boat and they walked up the wooden pier to the restaurant where a buffet of different Thai foods had been prepared for the guests. Johnny and Rachel sat down with a German couple of similar age who had recently moved to Kuala Lumpur for work purposes and were visiting Thailand for the week. They made small talk with them where they compared their different experiences of living abroad.

After lunch Johnny and Rachel headed into the village centre, where shaded narrow corridors lay between the village buildings, lined with market stalls where persistent salesmen bartered over handmade fabrics and local merchandise with visiting tourists.

'I might buy a top. You going to help me barter?' said Rachel, looking through one of the stalls.

'Why am I going to haggle?' asked Johnny.

'Because you're better at it than me. I always feel bad trying to get the prices down.'

She went to look at a blue scarf which had small white elephant designs sewed onto it.

'You like?' said the middle-aged Thai saleswoman wearing a baseball hat. 'Five hundred.'

'Two hundred,' said Johnny intervening. They had been offered a scarf at this price earlier.

The woman was silent as she looked away to think. 'Four fifty,' she said.

'Two fifty.'

'Four hundred.'

Johnny shook his head. 'Three hundred,' he said.

'Three fifty,' she replied.

'Three hundred', Johnny said, sticking to his figure, about to walk away.

'Three hundred,' the woman agreed and took the scarf to wrap it up.

'Where did you learn to barter like that?' asked Rachel.

'I don't know. I kind of enjoy it.'

'You're too good at it.'

They carried on walking towards the edge of the village, past a sign for the local mosque, a football field and a school. They could occasionally see gaps between the buildings where they noticed the muddy and littered sea which lay stagnant below.

The guests arrived back at the boat and they headed south out of the village back into the open sea. Buddy sat down on a tub cooler opposite Johnny. He grabbed four different coloured straws from a bag, attached two, and did the same with another two, repeatedly wrapping them around each other until he had eventually made a plastic looking multicoloured flower ring. He handed it to an American teenager in the group.

'Your go,' Buddy said offering Johnny the bag of straws.

'You don't want to ask me,' said Johnny resisting the offer. 'I'm terrible at these kinds of things.'

'Go on. You try for her. Look.' He took out four more straws and repeated the technique for Johnny to watch.

Johnny grabbed four new straws and attempted to copy him. He could sense the entire boat watching him and he knew he was going to look like an idiot. He tried to focus, doing his best to complete the task ahead, but as he wrapped the straws together his flower ring was beginning to look more like a deformed mushroom!

Buddy took the straws from him and unfolded them in his hands. Rachel turned away to get a camera out of her bag and while she did, Buddy jokingly passed Johnny the most recent flower ring he had made, which Johnny handed to Rachel.

'Right. Of course you made that one,' said Rachel.

'Talented aren't I?' replied Johnny.

She kissed him and slid it on her finger.

'If I only believed you,' Rachel said.

Buddy approached the other guests and taught them the same technique until they arrived at a beach on the next island of Koh Lawa, where the group disembarked the vessel.

After a quick swim in the sea Johnny and Rachel sat down to sunbathe and read their books.

'Johnny?'

'Yep?'

'When are you going to tell me where we're going for Christmas?'

'I'm not. Not until we get there.'

'I hate surprises. You do know that?'

'I don't think you'll hate this one.'

'How do you know that?'

'I just have an inkling.'

They returned to the boat around 5.30pm and made their way back to Phuket where the trip had begun earlier that day.

'Hey man,' said Buddy as Johnny stepped off the boat. 'You're English right?'

'Yep.'

'What team you support?'

'Err...I'm not really a massive football fan. But my dad supports Newcastle so I guess that would be team of choice. You?'

'Manchester United man.'

Buddy gave him a high five. 'You have a fun time.'

'Was a great trip. Thank you,' said Johnny handing him a four-hundred baht tip, before following Rachel to the car park to catch the minibus back to their hotel.

Due to heavy traffic it was an hour back to Patong Beach. Rachel had not approved of the location. She had found the resort seedy, especially the many bars along Bangla Road, full of young girls making popping sounds as they sold tickets to ping pong sex shows.

'Why do they keep coming up to me and making those disgusting noises?' Rachel had remarked.

'Because maybe they think you'll enjoy it.'

'I feel like going up to one of them and telling them to get a job away from here. It must be so depressing having to sell tickets for such a horrible show.'

'I don't think it's as easy as that.'

'I know, western point of view, but still.'

They left the hotel the next morning and caught a taxi north over the Sarasin Bridge and onto the Thai mainland where the coastline became flatter, the traffic quieter and the landscape more rural. They drove for two hours to a resort on the outskirts of Khao Lak where Johnny had arranged for them to stay over the Christmas period.

'How much did this place cost?' asked Rachel as they stepped out of the taxi in front of a large white colonial styled building with vast grounds surrounding it.

'A fair whack.'

'Johnny. This will have been expensive.'

'Mum and Dad might have helped a bit.'

'I thought they were mad at you for not spending Christmas with them?'

'They came around, and they said they wanted to treat their son and future daughter-in-law as we weren't going to be in England.'

It still felt exciting and fresh Rachel thought, the idea of being someone's wife and daughter in law. A reminder of a new chapter of her life which was steadily approaching.

Two young Thai bellmen appeared in shorts and carried their luggage to the lobby. While Johnny checked in, Rachel walked to the back of the reception area where large doors opened onto elegant gardens which led down to a private beach. She could hear 'Santa Claus is Coming to Town' being played at a low volume on the hotel speakers. It felt odd considering the weather. It was the first time she had spent Christmas in a warm climate.

They followed the bellmen down the corridor and outside through more gardens, past a pool area, to a detached white wooden ground floor bungalow in a more secluded part of the complex.

Their suite was contemporary but with traditional elements, dark brown laminate flooring, cream walls, a large four-poster bed, contemporary Thai art hung up on the wall and a large patio area at the front.

'What do you think?' asked Johnny. 'You think we can spend Christmas here?'

'I think we'll manage,' she said, carefully picking up their towels from the bed which had been wrapped in a way to look like elephants, which she placed on the dressing table.

'I've stayed in worst,' she said, wrapping her arms around him as they both looked out of their hotel room window at the turquoise ocean.

'You liked the surprise?' he asked.

'I liked the surprise very much.'

They headed to the hotel buffet that night and sat outside, surrounded by families and couples of all different ages.

'So I was thinking,' Rachel commented while they ate. 'Now that you've passed your PADI open water, how about we head out on a dive tomorrow?'

'Aren't you tired of diving?'

'No. I'd like to go. Just the two of us. No annoying tourists to babysit.'

'You'll be babysitting me.'

'I don't mind babysitting you.'

'I was kind of hoping to just laze around the pool and then watch crappy Christmas films on the telly.'

'Come on Johnny. You can do that on Christmas Day.'

'Alright. You win.'

She smiled winningly. 'Always do, don't I?'

Rachel used her contacts to hire some cheap equipment the next day and book them on a low cost boat which would take them to a nearby reef.

'Darling, your mask is all steamed up,' she said as the boat docked. 'How did you pass the test again?'

'Watch and see,' he replied, spitting onto his mask to wipe away the mist. They stepped backwards off the boat and descended towards the ocean bed.

Each party from the boat went in opposite directions, respecting each other's space, leaving Johnny and Rachel diving alone together with the vast ocean surrounding them. It was the first time she had dived with just Johnny. He was more confident than she had expected and she felt surprisingly relaxed in his company as they moved amongst the tropical reefs.

'Better than watching Christmas movies?' she asked him when they returned to the boat.

'Alright. Point taken,' he replied.

That evening they got dressed up and headed into the local town for pizza at a local restaurant, followed by drinks at a nearby Rocky Mountain themed bar.

'Happy Christmas Eve!' said Johnny bringing some shots of tequila.

'Oh Johnny. I'm going to have a stinking hangover tomorrow!' deplored Rachel jokingly.

'That was the intention. Come on. Drink up.'

They both downed their shots.

'OK, I'm getting cocktails. You want one?' asked Johnny.

'Sure,' said Rachel, looking at the drinks menu and beginning to slur her words. 'Get me a… Khao Lak Sunrise. Thanks.'

After they had finished their next round, they carried onto the another bar, a smaller establishment where they were seated opposite a Thai band who were singing Johnny Cash songs on a small stage in the corner.

'I love it,' said Johnny.

'What?' asked Rachel.

'He actually sounds like him. Amazing. A Thai guy singing with an American accent.'

'Oh my God!' said a concerned drunk Johnny looking at her finger.

'What?'

'The engagement ring is fading!' he replied looking at the latest design he had drawn a week earlier. They had agreed to keep drawing them until Johnny had enough money to buy her a proper one.

'I'm getting a pen,' said Johnny.

'Only if it's a nice one!' she insisted as he headed to the bar.

'What's the nicest pen you own?' Johnny asked the young female Thai bartender.

'What?'

'Have you got a smart pen?'

'This one?' the bartender said grabbing a tacky black biro she had found near the till.

'Cheers.'

He returned back to the table.

'OK. This biro is nothing fancy but it's all they had. Hold your finger still.'

'Johnny, let's do this tomorrow, when you're not so drunk.'

'This is going to be the best ring you've had. Just wait and see.'

'If it's rubbish, I'm washing it off and you're doing it again.'

'It won't be. Hold still!'

He tried to focus while drawing it.

'There you go.'

She looked at the frivolous bling design he had drawn on her finger with little lines surrounding it to show off the ring's shine.

'That is hideous,' she noted.

'But amazing,' he added.

'Fine. I'll keep it for the night.'

On Christmas Day they slept in late and opened their presents just before lunchtime. Johnny opened his first, unwrapping a pair of Ray-Ban sunglasses which Rachel had bought him.

'These will come in handy, absolutely,' said Johnny.

'Well put them on.'

He did as he was told and went to look at himself in the mirror.

'Loving it. Your turn,' he said passing her a smaller present which she unwrapped to reveal a small designer purse.

'You remembered. This isn't the one in Bangkok right?'

'I may have sneakily gone back to buy it.'

'You cheeky sod. I love it. Thank you. Though shouldn't we be saving for an engagement ring?'

'You'll get your ring. I promise.'

After they had finished handing over presents they headed to the hotel restaurant for lunch which had a large selection of Western and Thai foods on offer.

Later in the day they went to the main pool to sunbathe, then returned to their room early evening so Johnny could Skype his parents.

'Hi sweetheart,' said his mother picking up.

'Hi Mum. Merry Christmas!'

'You too.'

'How is everyone?'

'Fine. Your sister's upstairs. James has popped out. Your dad's just in the kitchen. How's the hotel?'

'Amazing.'

'Let's see the room.'

He moved the laptop around to show her.

'Oh. Looks lovely. Let's see outside.'

He headed onto the patio.

'You can't really see much because it's getting dark.'

'I can see bits and bobs. So have you already eaten?'

'Yep. The hotel put on a big buffet at lunchtime.'

'I hope you had turkey?'

'Yes, had some turkey.'

'Good. I suddenly had a thought last night, you can't celebrate Christmas without a turkey. Must be weird with it being so warm out there.'

'It's just different.'

'How's Rachel?'

'Yeah, she's good.'

'Hi Pam,' Rachel said appearing behind him.

'Oh hi love, I hear the hotel's nice?'

'It's really really nice. Thank you so much for helping out towards it. Johnny told me what you did.'

'Oh it's our pleasure. We wanted you to have a good time seeing as you weren't going to be here with us. Just a shame we couldn't be out there with you.'

'Well you know Mum, flights are expensive, especially at Christmas.'

'I know, I know. So your dad and I are thinking of coming out to see you sometime soon. Possibly in April?'

'OK. Great. Well you can always sleep on the sofa bed if you guys want to stay in the flat?'

'Oh no. We'd get a hotel. You wouldn't want us staying with you. So what time is it over there?'

'I think we're seven hours ahead.'

'I thought it was something like that.'

'So who have you got coming over this year?'

'Not a massive one this year. We've got Aunty Jane and Uncle Philip coming around so I better get on with cooking the dinner as I don't trust your father in the kitchen.'

'Fair enough.'

'But it's been lovely talking to you.'

'You too Mum.'

'Hang on. I think your sister wants a word. Claudia!' she shouted. 'It's Johnny and Rachel!' She turned back to the screen. 'Alright sweetheart. Speak soon.'

'Love you.'

'And I you. Bye for now.'

'Hey,' replied a perky Claudia appearing on the screen.

'Hey. You alright?'

'Good.' She checked to see if her parents had left the room. 'Just wanted to check they were gone. Good. So I have something to tell you.'

'OK.'

'Is Rachel there?'

'Yeah.'

'Do you want me to go?' asked Rachel clearing up some leftover wrapping paper from the floor.

'No no, it's fine, you'll find out eventually. Here it is. So I went for a scan recently,' she said presenting an ultrasound image.

'Oh my God. Are you pregnant?!' replied Johnny, noticing the smile of joy on her face. 'Oh my God!'

'Wow. That's so exciting!' said Rachel.

'I can't believe this. I take it Mum and Dad don't know, hence the secrecy?' asked Johnny.

'No, I haven't told them yet. I'm going to tell them later on so keep your voice down.'

'James must be pleased.'

'He is.'

'I didn't even know you guys were trying.'

Claudia gave no reply.

'So how many weeks gone are you?'

'Coming up to twelve.'

'This is amazing. By far the best Christmas news ever!'

'Just to say I am thoroughly jealous of you guys being out there.'

'Yeah, well you won't be going anywhere like this for a long time with a baby to look after.'

'Johnny!' said Rachel.

'Well I'm just being honest. Babies are expensive.'

'Thanks for reminding me Johnny.'

'Honestly Sis. I'm made up. Big style.'

'I think Dad might want a word.'

'OK. I'll speak to you soon.'

'Dad, it's Johnny for you!' she shouted.

His dad headed over and appeared on the screen.

'Hi love. Can't talk long. I've been bloody well put in charge of the kitchen,' his dad groaned.

'No worries. Just wanted to say Merry Christmas.'

'Merry Christmas to you too!'

'All going well?'

'Yes, despite your mother driving me nuts with all this cooking, everything's fine.'

The Skype connection suddenly froze.

'Hello? Hello Dad?' said Johnny, trying to relaunch the application but it wouldn't reload. 'You'd think for an expensive hotel like this the connection would be half decent.'

'Well at least you spoke to them.'

'I'll phone them tomorrow,' he said shutting the laptop.

They sat outside later that night with some wine, playing cards on the patio, while Phil Spector's *A Christmas Gift For You* played in the background.

'Bloody hell. She's pregnant. My sister is pregnant.'

'You're going to be an uncle. Uncle Johnny. I love it.'

'I did not see that coming.'

'It was a nice end to the day.'

'I feel ill from the amount of food I've eaten. Definitely going on a run tomorrow.'

'I will not be joining you. I will be sleeping in.'

'Listen, I've been thinking.'

'This sounds ominous.'

'I think I'm ready to go home.'

'OK.' Rachel said calmly. 'When were you thinking?'

'Late spring or early summer?'

Rachel looked woefully at her pack of cards.

'Say something. I take it you don't feel the same?' he asked.

'No, it's not that. I knew this was never going to be forever. I just didn't think it would be so soon. Where would we go?'

'We could give London another go?'

'Really?'

'Yes.'

'What would you do?'

'Don't laugh but I think I'm going to train as a teacher. Nice holidays.'

'It's not as easy as you think it is. It's not about the holidays so please don't go into it on that basis.'

'I'm not. They will be a nice part of it. Look, I know it won't be easy. I've got friends who say it's the worst job in the world but I think I'm willing to give it a go.'

'OK.'

'I've got to do something with my life. It's not insurance and I know that now. I would like to settle down and get some sort of career going eventually.' He paused for a moment. 'But whatever happens, whatever I do, all I care about is that I do it with you.'

As Rachel lay with Johnny that night she realised, she felt happy. More than she had in a long time. How long this would last, she did not know, but she promised herself she would appreciate this moment.

Johnny woke early the next morning and got quietly out of bed to put on his running gear. He turned to see Rachel asleep in the bed. She always looked so beautiful this time in the morning. As he closed the door Rachel awoke. She saw the empty space next to her, and rested her hand on the sheet. She lay there for a while then got herself up, put on some shorts and a t-shirt and headed out onto the patio to take in the morning air. She quickly noticed there was something different about this morning. There was an eerie quietness in the air. Then came the sound. A horrendous overwhelming sound of snapping trees and buildings collapsing in an instant. Then she saw it. A rise in the water, which charged towards her. This was going to kill her she thought. She was too young to die. She wanted Johnny to be there, somehow he would make this all seem better, but there was nothing she could do but let this water take her, smash her against the wall and plunge everything she knew into darkness.

26th DECEMBER 2004.
THE INDIAN OCEAN EARTHQUAKE AND
TSUNAMI.

TEN YEARS LATER

Heathrow Airport, UK

Suzi Ley sat on the Piccadilly Line looking exhausted as the busy tube made its way towards the end of the line. After a long day attending a teaching conference, Suzi was not looking forward to catching a twelve-hour flight to Thailand.

When she arrived at Terminal 3 she was met by hoards of passengers fighting their way through check in while joyful Christmas music played on the airport speakers. She meandered her way to one of the ticket machines which refused to scan her passport.

'Can I help you madam?' asked a helpful curvaceous airport assistant.

'It seems to dislike me.'

'They're a bit temperamental sometimes,' she replied, taking hold of Suzi's passport and unsuccessfully scanning it under the reader. 'Nope. They install these machines at our busiest time of year and they don't bloody work! You'll have to go to the counter. Sorry about that.'

'OK. Thanks,' replied Suzi, trying her best not to sound too aggravated by the ineptitude of the airport's technology.

While she waited in line at the other queue she looked at her smartphone to see a message from her cousin Eric on Facebook. *'Hey Suzi. I just got to the hotel. The room is awesome. Resort is sweet. Hope to see you guys tomorrow. Let me know if arrival time changes. E x.'*

There was always something uplifting in her cousin's tone which instantly put her in a better mood.

She willed herself through security, wrapping lotions and perfumes in plastic see through bags, taking off jewelry for the scanning machine; she had done this so many times as a frequent traveler it felt like a military operation.

She made her way through the shops to the nearest bar where she ordered a pint of lager, and sat down to read a copy of The Guardian which she found on a spare table.

'You look like you needed that?' asked a bald man in his mid-forties sitting close by, wearing a rugby shirt.

'Pardon me?'

'I said it looks like you needed that beer.'

'Oh. I did. Very much so.'

'Where are you heading?'

'Thailand. And you?'

'Hong Kong. Off to see my brother for Christmas.'

'Oh. I used to live there.'

'Any good?'

'Really good. It was a while ago. I often think about the city.'

'My brother moved out there in the summer. Whereabouts in Thailand are you off to?'

'Khao Lak.'

'You off with anyone or going by yourself?'

'I'm meeting a friend shortly. We're flying out together. She's just running a bit late.'

'Weather should be nice over there.'

'I hope so. Warmer than here.'

'Where's the accent from?'

'Vienna.'

'Not been there.'

'You should go. It's beautiful this time of year. Yourself?'

'London.'

'Well.' He said finishing his pint. 'Merry Christmas'

'And to you. Enjoy your vacation.'

'Won't be hard,' he said giving her a smile, 'See you later.'

It felt nice Suzi thought, to still have strangers strike up a conversation in public. It was a reminder she wasn't just an invincible body, caught up in a fast paced world. She picked up her newspaper and found a magazine sandwiched in the middle of it. Its covering story which was titled *The Indian Ocean Tsunami: 10 Years On'*. A part of her didn't want to read it but she had the urge to turn the pages. The magazine was made up of different stories from people across the world who'd lost their loved ones in the disaster. The first article was about a boy, aged twelve years at the time, now twenty-two, whose entire family had been swept away in the Aceh region of Indonesia. Another report was about a German woman, aged fifty-five, whose husband and daughter had been killed by the wave. Her son had been the only family member to survive.

While Suzi read, her mind wandered off, as she recalled the first moment she heard about the event, while back in Vienna, shortly after her return from Hong Kong. She had found a note which her mother had left on the kitchen table when she'd come downstairs for breakfast. *'Big tidal wave in Thailand and other surrounding countries. Many dead,'* it had read. Her mother had done a similar thing on the morning of the death of Princess Diana. The thought of someone she knew being involved in the disaster had never even crossed her mind. It was only when she got the phone call from Johnny's sister a few days later, she was told the news that both Johnny and Rachel were missing. It had surprised her how calm Johnny's sister had sounded. Suzi had thanked her for letting her know, then sat there in shock, holding the phone in her hand, even after the conversation had ended. It had felt as if the call had never happened. After half an hour of trying to come to terms with the news she had left her mother's house and walked for several hours in the cold, unsure of where she was going, but all the time pining for Johnny to be close by. A deep longing for him that didn't feel appropriate considering they were no longer in a relationship. When she had finally returned to the house she had laid on her bed and cried until her eyes had stung.

'I'm sorry,' said an American voice at the airport bar.

Suzi looked up to see a dark haired girl in her early thirties.

'I hope you don't mind me asking but did you teach at Pardale College?'

'Yes. Yes I did,' replied Suzi.

'You probably don't remember me. I was in your Puritan Literature class. Abigail Salou.'

'Oh. Hi,' replied Suzi. She did not recognise the student but hid it well.

'Are you flying back to The States for the holidays?'

'No. Going to Thailand.'

'Wow. I'm jealous.' There was an uneasy silence. 'Well it was really nice talking to you. I thought I should come over and check to see if you were who I thought you were. '

'Thank you.'

'Happy holidays.'

'You too.'

She turned to look at her phone. Her inbox was clogged up with work emails. It was getting close to the time she was meeting her friend. Suzi turned back to the article to carry on reading but was interrupted by a familiar voice.

'Suzi?'

The girl looked so different from the last time she had seen her. Mature. Wiser. How could she not?

'Good to see you Rachel,' Suzi said, embracing her warmly.

'Sorry I'm late,'

'You're fine. They haven't even announced the gate yet.'

'How was your conference?'

'Oh. Boring. Same as last year.'

Suzi tried to move the article away but Rachel had already seen it.

247

'You read it?' she asked.

'Started to.'

'There's so much coverage at the moment.'

'I know.'

'It's good. It reminds people. It would be the worst thing if people forgot.'

'I don't see that happening for a long time.'

'I'll go see if there's a gate yet,' said Rachel restlessly heading towards the screen while Suzi finished her pint.

'Gate 19,' Rachel said returning quickly. 'You want to head over? Sorry. I'm rushing you.'

Suzi downed the last of her beer.

'All good, I'm done.'

'I was trying to remember how long it was since I last saw you?' asked Rachel as they walked down the long airport walkway.

'It will have been ten years. Just under.'

'Right. That makes sense.'

'Are any of your family coming?'

'My sister was going to come but she's got my nieces, plus her husband just broke his leg. It wouldn't have been a great idea.'

'Doesn't sound good. How did he do that?'

'Football. I think he's realised he's not as flexible as he used to be.'

'It's scary how your body can start to give up on you when you get older. How old are your nieces?'

'Lola's twelve and Hannah's seven. And my brother just had a baby last week so he can't make it either. All these things seem to happen at once.'

'It sounds it. So where are you living now?'

'I'm in Horley. In between Brighton and London.'

'You're managing a marketing company now, right?'

'Yeah.'

'You like it?'

'It's good. I just bought a flat down the road from work so it's easy to get to, cuts down on transport costs which is good as I'm practically broke after paying silly amounts to buy a flat.'

'I get so shocked when I hear about the house prices in this country. How anyone can afford it is beyond me.'

'I know. Personally, I had to borrow some money from my mum to help me out. I don't know how people do it alone.'

They arrived at the gate and sat down.

'So I'm sorry to hear about your mum's husband,' said Suzi.

'Thanks. He was in a lot of pain by the end of it. I just think it was a relief. It was hard but I think my mum's slowly getting used to it. She really wanted to come out too but I just think it would have been hard. Saying that, I'm kind of pleased she didn't. It would have just been a challenge having her around. We have a tricky relationship a lot of the time.'

'So I got a message from Eric. He's arrived and says he loves the room at the hotel.'

'Great. You know I haven't seen him in years. Since Hawaii. It's just so good he wanted to come. Like you. It's a long way.'

'Hey, I wasn't going to miss this. I couldn't.'

'The thing that gets me is the fact it's been ten years. It feels like only yesterday, I was there standing on that patio outside the hotel room thinking I had the whole world, and in an instant, I had nothing. But I know I had to do this. To bring some closure to my life. To finally say goodbye to Johnny.'

'Well, you know what,' replied Suzi. 'I have a feeling this trip might just help you do that.'

Khao Lak, Thailand

Rachel and Suzi arrived at Phuket Airport the following day where there were met by a long queue for immigration. After an hour of queuing they walked outside to flag down a taxi and negotiate a decent rate to take them north.

The journey back to Khao Lak reminded Rachel of the taxi ride she had taken with Johnny the days before the wave had struck. It surprised Rachel how much the area had been rebuilt. Modern buildings had been constructed. New roads laid down. Fields of palm trees had been planted at the side of the road to replace the old ones destroyed by the disaster.

Eric was waiting for them at the entrance to the hotel when they arrived. He had shorter hair now and a clean-shaven face; still handsome Rachel thought but with more manly features which made him seem very different from the surfer boy she had met in Hawaii all those years ago.

'Hey!' he said going to hug Suzi as she got out of the taxi.

'Long time no see,' she replied.

'Hi Rachel,' he said unsure whether to shake her hand.

'Hi Eric,' she replied patting him gently on the back. 'Good to see you.'

'Time goes way too fast,' he replied.

Rachel and Suzi checked in at the reception, then headed to their separate rooms. Rachel's hotel room was on the first floor with a balcony and a sea view room. The room had been pricey but she had saved methodically for it. She unpacked her suitcase and connected her phone to the Wi-Fi so she could WhatsApp Claudia to let her know she had arrived. She got a reply straight back.

'Hey Rachel. Do you want to come to the room in about an hour? Just got back from the pool. We're in Room 425 x.'

'Sure. See you then x.'

Rachel had a quick shower, slipped into something more comfortable, then trotted down towards the beach in front of the hotel to walk along the ocean. The water was calm and the beach was full of tourists enjoying the Christmas sun. After she had got an idea of her surroundings she walked back up to find Claudia's room which was in a smaller building separated from the main hotel. She knocked on the door.

'You're here,' said Claudia buoyantly answering it, wearing bikini bottoms and a t-shirt. 'Come on in. Adrian should be back any minute, he made some friends by the pool.'

It felt good to see her, Rachel thought. They had formed a close bond ever since Johnny's death. A vast change from how they had been with each other in Mexico.

'You want a drink? I have fruit juice? Or coke? Or a gin and tonic?'

'I'll have a coke. Thanks. So I heard you met Eric?'

'I did, put a face to the name finally. He was telling me all these crazy stories about him and Johnny on that boat they worked on in New Zealand.' She handed over her drink. 'He's a character.'

'He certainly is that. Different from how I remember him.'

'How so?'

'I don't know. More mature. He grew up like the rest of us.'

There was a knock on the door so Claudia answered it. A tanned Australian woman in her early forties was standing there.

'Hey. Here he is,' she said.

'Hi darling. Thanks for looking after him,' replied Claudia.

'No worries. Merry Christmas.'

'You too.'

A skinny nine-year-old, with short dark hair entered wearing Marvel themed swimming shorts and a Batman top.

'How was the pool?' asked Claudia.

'Good,' the boy replied.

'Look who's here, are you going to say hello to Rachel?'

'Hello stranger,' said Rachel.

'Hi Rachel,' he replied reservedly.

'Haven't seen you in a few years.'

'Time flies, doesn't it?' said Claudia. 'Now can you go have a shower and hang up your shorts in the bathroom to dry?'

He nodded his head and did as requested.

'So what's the plan for tonight?' asked Claudia.

'I didn't know if you guys wanted to meet for food in the restaurant? I know everyone's probably going to be pretty jet lagged.'

'That would be nice. Gives everyone a chance to catch up. What time were you thinking?'

Rachel got a text from an unknown number on her phone.

'Hey. In the bar if you fancy a drink? Eric.'

'Sure. Be down in 10.'

'Sorry. It's Eric. I think we're meeting around 7.00pm,' said Rachel looking up.

'That'll work. Gives me enough time to have a shower and get ready.'

'Great. Well I'll leave you guys to it then.'

Rachel went down to meet Eric who was sat by the bar wearing a white shirt and smart cream trousers. The sunset was in the distance, creating a golden light which reflected soothingly onto the hotel bar.

'I could get used to this,' remarked Rachel. 'These sunsets are a normal thing in Hawaii, right?'

'Yeah, most days, but this is nice.'

'So I just met Claudia,' Rachel said. 'I cannot believe how much Adrian has grown. Last time I saw him he was little toddler running around.'

'They grow up quick. So where's Claudia's husband?'

'They divorced about five years ago.'

'I didn't know. Amicably?'

'Not really. I think he'd been seeing someone else, which wasn't great.'

'That's got to be tough. Bringing up a kid alone.'

'I think she's doing OK. So tell me, what are you up to these days?'

'I teach high school.'

'I didn't know that. That's a bit of a change from being in the sea every day. What made you decide to do that?'

'Oh there's only so many times you can meet the cast of *Finding Nemo*.'

'You like teaching?'

'Some of the kids are challenging. I do like it, yeah.'

'Are you still in the same place?'

'No, I moved to Honolulu. Went there a while ago and it's where I did my teacher training.'

'So you've totally packed in the diving?'

'I get out every so often. The advantage of living somewhere where you can do it. How about yourself, you dive much anymore?'

'No. I didn't really go back to it after everything that happened.'

'That makes sense. So you're still living in London, right?'

'A small town just outside.'

'It's funny. I was going through some photos the other day, just before I caught the flight out here in fact. I came across photos we took when we all went to the volcano, remember?'

'Of course I remember! I still have nightmares about that night. I still can't believe we did that. The fact we were so close to the crater.'

'It was kind of insane. But those are the moments you remember, right?'

'What's this you're talking about?' asked Suzi, looking attractive in a black dress, her hair down and without her glasses.

'Oh, hey. We were just talking about this volcano we went to in Hawaii when Johnny and Rachel came to stay,' said Eric.

'I remember Johnny telling me about this. You cooked popcorn on one of the vents, right?' asked Suzi.

'I think that was the crazy tour guide with his 'I Love Lava' t-shirt!' said Rachel.

'That t-shirt was awesome!' replied Eric.

'Hello everyone,' said Claudia, appearing in a smart blue dress with Adrian who was wearing a flannel shirt and shorts.

'Hey. How's it going?'

'Good.'

'Did you have fun in the pool Adrian?' asked Eric.

Adrian nodded his head.

'He made some Australian friends, didn't you?' said Claudia. 'Oh my God Suzi. I didn't even recognise you there. You look amazing.'

'Thank you. You too.'

'Hey. Let me grab some seats for you guys,' said Eric going to bring some over from a neighbouring table.

After they had chatted at the bar they were taken to a table where they sat down for their evening meal.

'Well everyone. I'd like to propose a toast,' said Eric raising a glass or Prosecco they had ordered. 'To Rachel, for organising everything.'

'Here here,' said Claudia.

'And lastly, I wanted to bring up the reason why we're all here. To remember someone who we all loved. To Johnny.'

'To Johnny,' they all replied, raising their glasses.

When the meal was finished, Claudia and Adrian went back to their room while Eric, Rachel and Suzi walked to a bar down the road.

'Well what are we having?' asked Eric. 'Cocktails? It is Christmas Eve after all.'

'I could go for a cocktail. I think it may have to be a Screaming Orgasm,' said Suzi smirking to herself.

'Mojito for me,' said Rachel.

'This round is on me ladies,' Eric said heading off to order.

'Does he ever sound unhappy?' asked Rachel.

'Eric. No? I wish it was contagious,' said Suzi. 'That endless positivity. I wish I had it.'

'You ever think about returning to The States?' asked Rachel.

'Some days. Sure,' replied Suzi. 'I do feel like I'm too old now.'

'You're never too old.'

'I want to settle down soon. Maybe have kids. So it's probably not the best time to uproot my life. Who knows.'

'But you're happy in Vienna?'

'Yeah. I'm like most people. I could always be happier.'

After they had finished their cocktails a jet lagged Suzi returned to the hotel while Rachel and Eric went for a stroll along the beach.

'I have to ask. Whatever happened to that girl you were seeing when Johnny and I came to visit you? Colleen, that was her name, right?'

'I forgot you met her. We broke up. Man she was hard work. One of those people who always liked to be the centre of attention. It just got exhausting. Plus, I think she found me a bit of a bum. Which I kind of was back then.'

'Are you seeing anyone at the moment?' asked Rachel.

'I was seeing this girl for about four years. She was a teacher, but we decided to end it at the start of the year. It was hard.'

'Sorry to hear that.'

'And yourself?'

'No. It took me a long time to start dating people. I mean there has been the odd guy. Just nothing serious.'

'I wish I'd come to Johnny's memorial service in England after it happened. It's just with the price of the flight and I was doing my teacher training back then.'

'It wasn't like it was down the road. At least you're here now.'

'He was a good guy Rachel. I'm just sorry. So sorry about what happened.'

'Me too,' replied Rachel, hearing Christmas music playing in the background from one of the hotel bars. Rachel looked at her phone. It was just gone midnight.

'Oh. Merry Christmas,' she said.

'Merry Christmas Rachel.'

△△△△

That night Rachel had a dream she was lying on rubble, shortly after the wave had hit. Two figures hovered over her. As her eyesight returned she could make out two young local Thai boys. She could feel a large cut on her shoulder, and another one on her leg. Her body ached all over. There was movement as she was suddenly lifted up and away on some sort of stretcher. She fell in and out of consciousness until she was aware she was in a hospital. A foul stench of blood, dirt and chaos surrounded her. She looked up at a white cracked ceiling where the occasional lizard would show up then disappear. She could sense her mother next to her but she was too weak to speak to her, until she finally gained enough energy to turn to her mother and ask her where Johnny was.

'We'll find him. He'll be alright,' she had replied. Her mother was renowned for making promises she could never keep.

△△△△

The next morning Rachel awoke and went to Claudia's room to unwrap presents. When she arrived Adrian was playing with a lightsaber that his mother had bought him.

Rachel handed Claudia her present which she opened; a framed photo of Claudia and Johnny in Mexico. Claudia sat down and put her hand to her mouth after she had looked at it.

'What's wrong Mummy?' Adrian said going to hug her.

'I'm just a little tearful. Looking at the picture with Uncle Johnny. That's all.' She put her arm around Adrian and kissed his forehead.

After the group had eaten lunch at the hotel restaurant, Rachel went for a walk with Suzi up to the main town.

'I hated you, you know that, for many years,' Suzi said as they walked along the main street. 'You don't mind me being honest with you?'

'You can be honest,' replied Rachel cautiously.

'Although I'd never met you, I always felt threatened by you. The girl Johnny had met in the Gili Isles. Then I borrowed his travel book when I met him in Australia, to look up things to do in Sydney. There was your number, written above the opening paragraph. I woke him up that night to tell him. You should have seen the look on his face. He'd found you.'

'He moved to Vienna, to Hong Kong with you. You must have meant something to him.'

'I did. But then he would meet you and email you, when we were still going out. It used to drive me mad.'

'Look I did a lot of things back then which I'm not proud of.'

'I don't want you to apologise. And you're right, he did love me, as much as he could. But it was never going to be enough, and the strange thing is I knew that, that deep down the inevitable would happen. And it finally did.'

'I didn't appreciate him. Not until the last few months together and then he was gone. He was going to be my husband and I never really understood how much that meant to me until he wasn't there any longer and that gets me everyday. So please don't think our relationship was a bag of roses Suzi because it really wasn't.'

'I didn't say this to make you feel bad. He chose you after all, which was the right decision, and I'm thankful he did. I certainly don't hate you now. When I met you, I wanted to, but I couldn't. Not seeing you there at the memorial service after it had happened. I just needed to say this, because after all, we both loved him so much when he was alive.' She instantly regretted what she had said. 'I'm sorry. I shouldn't have said that. Making this about me.'

'You're being honest.'

'No. It was wrong. Selfish.'

'Suzi. It was in the past.'

'Look I'm pretty tired actually, all that food I ate, so maybe I'll head back to the hotel.'

'Suzi.'

'I'm fine. I'll see you tomorrow. OK.'

Suzi walked back and Rachel watched her go. She could have persuaded to stay but she knew Suzi needed some time alone after venting her feelings. Rachel carried on walking to the main street. It was strange she thought. She could have been annoyed about what Suzi had said, but she wasn't, she had appreciated her honesty.

Early the next day Rachel met the rest of the group in the hotel reception. Everyone wore smart casual clothing; Rachel had insisted that no one wore black. They walked down to the beach where the Tsunami remembrance ceremony was taking place, by a large collection of rocks on the beach where a blue plaque had been attached on the largest one with the date of the incident.

A local man played the flute while people from all walks of life, all nationalities, laid down different articles such as photos, bracelets in jars and flowers in remembrance of their loves ones which they placed below the rocks. Speeches were given and a two-minute silence was held at the time when the first wave had hit.

After the ceremony had finished, Rachel turned to the group as they walked back to the hotel.

'Guys, you don't mind heading a bit further north up the beach do you? Make it a bit more personal for Johnny.'

The group agreed and walked half a mile up the coastline where they stopped to form a circle as Rachel spoke to them.

'So I wanted to come here because, well, this used to be where the hotel was, where we stayed.' Rachel wiped her eyes. 'I didn't want to cry. I promised myself I wouldn't. I don't know what to say apart from the fact that over the last ten years I've wanted Johnny to walk into the room, to come back from his run, but I know now that's never going to happen. So I'm left with no other option but to let him go. To finally say goodbye to him, to a boy who we all loved. Adrian has created a wreath which we're going to put out to sea. I know I asked you to write some words about Johnny. If you wouldn't mind folding up your messages and putting them into the wreath, and then we'll let it go.'

Adrian went around the group as they all folded up their slips, Rachel got out a piece of paper, which was the page on Sydney from Johnny's travel book where she had written her number, which she folded and put deep down into the wreath. When they were all done, Adrian took it down to the water where he let it go and they all watched it drift away into the distance.

△△△△

It had been three weeks after the wave had hit when Rachel convinced her mother to take her back to the spot where her hotel had once stood. She had been discharged from the hospital. Rachel had prepared herself for the worst. The area was unrecognisable. A desolate landscape with only a few remaining buildings.

'Rachel?' said her mother. 'Be careful.'

It took Rachel a while to make her way over the ground. It was when she almost tripped she saw it. A bag of hers, battered, covered in sea weed, laying on the ground. She lifted it up and looked inside to find a collection of her items which included headphones, an empty sunglasses case and there at the bottom, Johnny's travel book which was still intact. She held it in her hand and she noticed her engagement finger, still displaying the wedding ring that Johnny had drawn though it had more or less faded away now.

She put the book back in her bag and placed it on the ground. She grabbed a piece of rubble below her feet and threw it towards the ocean, picked up another piece, threw it, and another one, again and again, until she had lost all the energy to throw anything else towards the empty horizon in front of her.

Khao Lak, Thailand and Gili Isles, Indonesia

Johnny had felt energised that Boxing Day morning when he left Rachel sleeping in their bed. There was something about being in a tropical climate which made it easier to get the body moving in the morning.

Johnny ran from his room, through the hotel gardens, past a family making their way down to the pool, through the lobby and out into the car park. He turned left through a small pathway which led down to the beach where he ran along the shoreline where the sand was hard and easier to run on. He headed north and after fifteen minutes he stopped to turn to look back at the view of the flat coastline he had made his way along. It was tricky to pick out his hotel, hidden amongst the palm trees that lined the back of the beach. There was something odd, the tide seemed unnaturally far out, exposing rocks and seaweed normally hidden by the water and there were several tourists heading out into the bay to explore this area of exposed land.

Johnny ran inland, through a small car park and up along a narrow road full of mopeds and souvenir shops which eventually joined up with the main street of Khao Lak town. Then came the screams, people running up the road towards him. He was unaware of what they were running from but then he saw the dark muddy water shoot down the street, flipping mopeds over on their sides. He ran as fast as he could but the water quickly caught up with him, swallowing him whole and keeping him under its surface. He felt an impact, a ripping pain as sharp objects flowing in the water jabbed into him, again and again, like a pinball stuck in a machine. He tried to reach the surface for air but the currents were too powerful, and as much as he fought, he had never fought for anything so strongly in his life before, his lungs filled with water and his mind drifted away. He felt himself floating to the top of the water. Warm sunlight was beaming down when he reached the surface and he was aware of being in a different place, a day in the past where the water was calm and he was swimming along a boat which had bought him from the island of Bali towards the dock of Gili Meno.

He swam to the shore where he collected his bag. A local man offered him transport on a cart and donkey to take him to his hotel. He had heard ominous stories about the way they treated their animals, so he declined and made his way to the hotel alone.

The journey took him through the centre of the island, passing through a local village established on flat arid farmland. He headed north until he reached the north side of the island where his hotel was situated.

'Hi. I've got a reservation,' he said to the attractive female Australian working behind the desk.

'What name is it?'

'Buxford. Johnny Buxford.'

'First time to Gili Meno?'

'Yep. It's the best hotel on the island, right?'

'We're the *only* hotel on the island.'

'So what's good to do here?'

'Well that's the beauty of the place. There's not really that much you can do. There's of course the diving. I hear there's the full moon party tonight.'

'Sounds good.'

'So I just need your signature here and we're all good to go.'

He scribbled his name down and she handed him his key.

'Room 8. Out the door, right, last building at the end. Enjoy your stay.'

'Cheers.'

The room was dated, but had everything you needed for a hotel room. A TV, a decent sized bed, and a bathroom.

It was beginning to get dark as Johnny left the room, wearing a crumpled shirt he taken out of his rucksack. He walked along the coast of the island under coloured fairy lights which dangled from different trees. As he headed further south more buildings appeared along the pathway, hostels, bars and small shops in wooden shacks selling toiletries, handmade gifts and second hand books.

He arrived at the main hub of the island where the beaches got larger, the crowds bigger, where more restaurants and bars were located. He sat down on an outside table at one of the main restaurants on the beach, where he ordered a beer and a tuna steak meal. He was the only one sitting alone amongst the different groups of people surrounding which made him feel uncomfortable. He had forgotten to bring a book. It was one of the best pieces of advice his dad had ever given him, 'always take a book with you when dining alone, it always looks less awkward.'

He looked further down the beach where preparations were being made for what he assumed was the Full Moon Party; local workers were constructing a stage, putting up lights and placing torchlights into the sand.

After he had eaten his meal he walked down to watch the workers work.

'You want a go?' said a local man, showing him a sky lantern.

'I'm good.'

'It give you good luck.'

'How much?'

'You have US note?'

He had bought some US money with him as well as Indonesia rupiahs as his travel book had recommended bringing both currencies.

'Five dollars.'

'Go on then.'

Johnny handed him his money. The lantern was lit and Johnny held it with the man as hot air filled the inside of it. Johnny noticed other people surrounding him holding their lanterns ready to let them go.

'OK, we release!' said the local man. Johnny let go of his lantern and along with the others he watched them rise into the sky.

'Very bad for the environment, but of course very pretty,' said a voice next to him. How had he not noticed her before?

'Are they really that bad?' replied Johnny.

'Well first of all, there's the wire in them which can land anywhere and isn't biodegradable, and it can also get caught around animal's necks, all very bad things. And then of course there's the fire risk.'

'Well, we're obviously not in Mother Nature's good books tonight then are we?'

'Probably not.' The girl smiled which enriched her eyes.

The lanterns were in the distance now, when suddenly they vanished as their lights burnt out, taken by the sky.

'Are you off to this party tonight?' he asked her.

'I think so. My friends were keen. You?'

'Not sure. This is my first day here.'

'Oh. A Gili virgin. How long are you here for?'

'A week.'

'Are you coming?' said the well-spoken Englishman in the group to the girl.

'That's what everyone says, but they carry on staying and they never ever leave,' she said walking off with the group.

By this point Johnny hadn't been sure if he had wanted to stay out. But the girl kept him there. He had to speak to her again. He subtly followed her to the bar she'd gone to and ordered another beer while reggae music was switched on at the stage nearby and torchlights were lit on the beach.

'So how long have you been here for?' he asked the girl when she approached the bar.

'Two weeks.'

'Was that planned?'

'No. It was originally a couple of days. You should come join us.'

He did what she said. The alcohol calmed his nerves.

'Everyone this is…?'

'Johnny.'

'Johnny. This is Rob,' she said pointing to the preppy male who had spoken to her earlier.

'Ness,' she said introducing him to a girl with braided hair.

'Nigel, Arthur, Mimi and George,' she said pointing her finger at different figures in the group. 'The rest of them I have no idea of their names. So there you have it. My Gili family.'

'And you are?'

'Right. I didn't tell you that. Might have been helpful. Rachel.'

A drunken man walked past their table crashing into it and knocking over several drinks.

'Mate, that's a whole load of drinks you've spilt!' Rob shouted.

'Hey man, not my fault,' said the inebriated American walking away.

'Well who's fucking fault is it?' said Rob standing up aggressively.

'Rob!' Rachel said intervening, trying to placate the situation. 'It's all good.' She turned to the American and quietly replied, 'if I was you, I'd just walk away right now.' He followed her orders.

Rob sat down to talk to his friends while Rachel turned to Johnny. 'What is it with boys and alcohol?' She leant towards him and spoke softly in his ear. 'You fancy heading out, just the two of us? I'm not really in the party mood anymore.'

265

'Where do you want to go?'

'Lets go for a walk. I need some air. Besides, it's still early.'

'OK.'

'I'm going to love you and leave you guys,' announced Rachel, leaving her group who looked on with rejected faces.

They both walked south along the main path.

'So you know those guys well back there?' asked Johnny.

'Not really. I met them on the first night I got here.'

'You came here by yourself?'

'I did.'

'Me too. I sort of like travelling alone.'

'It kind of makes it easier to talk to people. Though it does get lonely at times.'

They headed past an outdoor cinema where they could hear a film playing.

'They have a cinema here?' asked Johnny.

'They do. I wanted to go tonight, but the group insisted we start drinking early. It's old movie night.'

'What's the film?'

'*Blue Hawaii*.'

Johnny looked at the poster. 'Not seen it.'

'Elvis Presley. We used to watch it all the time when we were kids. I like the setting. Made me always want to go there.'

'Where?'

'Hawaii.'

'Sorry. Stupid question.'

'You want to go in? We don't have to stay, we can just pop in, besides, the film will probably have started by now.'

'Sure.'

They sneaked into the back of the field where the film was playing. Johnny could see the crowd was full of backpackers sitting down on the dry grass watching the movie on a white projector in front of them with the beach and the sea behind it, and a cloudless sky above it.

The film was playing a scene where Elvis Presley was singing to an older lady 'Can't Help Falling In Love With You'.

Rachel suddenly lay her head on Johnny's shoulder and linked her hand with his, and as they watched the film Rachel turned to Johnny and kissed him slowly. He was shocked at first, surprised a girl like her was showing such an interest.

'You OK?' he said as she broke away from the kiss.

'Come on,' she whispered, 'I don't really fancy sitting here now.' She stood up restlessly offering to take his hand.

'Where we going?'

She smiled mischievously. He took her hand, they got up, they ran through the audience and left the cinema. They ran in between tall trees, snapping twigs as they headed down to the beach where the crowds were gone, but as soon as Johnny got there he realised he was not with Rachel anymore. He was alone with the music of the film fading away in the distance. There was a chill in the wind. He soon became aware of a family close by to him. His family. Something dreadful was about to happen. He looked at them. There was his dad sitting in his usual corner armchair. His mother anxiously standing by the fireplace. His cousins. His aunt and uncle. His favourite grandmother who had died when he was eighteen. And then there was Claudia, pregnant, with tears in her eyes, trying to keep herself together but she couldn't. He wanted to speak out to them all, to tell them that everything was going to be alright but he knew somehow it wasn't. And then he felt Rachel next to him, her hand going to hold his firmly. It was the comfort he needed at a time like this as he took his last breath under the water that morning as the wave rushed inland as far as it could, then retreated back into the ocean, taking with it everything it had stolen that morning.

Khao Lak, Thailand

Rachel felt galvanised when she woke up on the morning of her penultimate day in Thailand. As if the beginning of a new chapter of her life had begun.

She shot out of bed, put on her swimwear and headed down to the pool for a morning swim. She always enjoyed this time of day, before the guests arrived and noises filled the pool. She lost count of how many lengths she completed, each time she touched the side of the pool she felt more energized, edging her on to tackle another lap.

They had all agreed to head to a National Park that morning just south of the resort. They met in reception later that morning and made their way up the hill out of the town towards the park.

'So I wanted to say I'm sorry. For what I said at Christmas, all that stuff about my relationship with Johnny,' said Suzi approaching Rachel.

'Suzi you don't need to apologise.'

'I feel I should do. I was his ex-girlfriend who had some issues and I shouldn't have just poured them out on you the other day.'

'You had your reasons.'

'True. But I don't want it to be weird between us. You're a friend. So I hope we're OK?'

'Of course we're OK.'

Rachel looked ahead to see a sign at the side of the road which read '*Khao Lak-Lam Ru National Park.*'

'I think we're here,' she shouted to the group.

They walked to the entrance, each paying 300 baht to take the coastal trail which took them south along the rugged coastline towards a small isolated beach.

'You do much hiking in Hawaii?' Claudia asked Eric as they made their way down some steep steps, over-hanging tree branches which had fallen down onto the pathway.

'Some weekends I try and get out.'

'I'd love that. Having the weather to do that whenever you like.'

'A thing you guys lack in the UK, right?'

'You could say that. So when do we get the invite to Hawaii? No hints.'

'Whenever you like.'

'I want to go to Hawaii,' said Adrian.

'Well maybe we will someday darling,' replied Claudia.

'Well there's a spare room in the house if ever you guys come visit.'

'Thanks Eric. We may just take you up on that.'

They arrived at the beach an hour later where they put down their towels on the white sand and set up base for the hour, while Eric and Adrian ran towards the sea to play with a frisbee.

'I don't know how my son's going to cope when Eric's gone at the end of this holiday,' said Claudia watching them both. 'Suzi you have a very cool cousin by the way.'

'I know,' replied Suzi applying sun lotion on her face. 'I wish he didn't have to live so far away.'

'So I have a friend who's getting married in Spain in the summer so I was thinking I may turn it into a big European trip,' said Eric to Rachel while they packed away their things. 'I was going to see Suzi in Austria and then maybe head to London afterwards. It would be around the end of July. You think you'll be around then?'

'It just depends on work really, it gets pretty busy in July,' replied Rachel.

'I'm sure she can fit you in,' said Claudia who had been listening in on the conversation.

After they had returned to the hotel, Claudia spotted Rachel reading a book in the hotel gardens.

'Mind if I join you?' asked Claudia.

'Sure.'

'You know it is OK to accept an offer when someone is making it blatantly obvious they'd like to see you again.'

'You're talking about Eric?'

'I am.'

'You do know he lives on the other side of the world?'

'And who knows what could happen. You have to start living your life again Rachel. Johnny would want that.'

'Its funny you should say that because I woke up today and for the first time in a long time I felt like I was ready to do that. But when Eric said that today I froze up. I felt like I had to make an excuse not to see him.'

'Well when he asks you again, you need to make sure you don't do that. Look I'm not saying it's as easy as that. I just worry about you Rachel. We all do. You deserve to be happy again.'

Rachel took a walk alone along the beach that evening, past the site where the memorial had taken place. She turned to look at the ocean and she knew this would be the last time she would see this place again. She was ready to say goodbye to it.

They had a meal together that night. Made plans to get together again, while underneath knowing this was probably the last time they would see each other.

After they had finished for the night, Eric accompanied Rachel back to her room.

'So I was thinking you could maybe come stay in the flat if you do come to England,' said Rachel. 'Though I have to warn you, my flat is tiny.'

'I can cope with that.'

They stopped to look at a small water fountain.

'Why do these trips have to go so quickly? I was dreading this trip,' Rachel said.

'That's understandable.'

'And now I don't really want to go home. But I don't think I'll ever come back here. That's the thing.' She sat down by the fountain ledge.

'Really?'

'I don't want to return here. It needs to be a place of the past.'

'I think it's good you've made that decision.'

'I appreciate the lift tomorrow by the way.'

'Well I'm going there anyway, so it makes sense.'

'And now I have to pack, which I loathe. I should go back.'

They carried on walking to her room.

'Well. This is me,' she said, turning to look at Eric.

'Goodnight Eric,' she said going to peck him on the cheek.

'Goodnight Rachel.'

They looked at each other. A sudden urge drawing them together which was cut short by Rachel moving to her room, smiling at him and closing the door shut.

Rachel lay in bed early the next day, unable to sleep. There was one more job she had to do. She turned to look at her rucksack placed on a nearby chair. She pulled herself up, slung on a hoodie and shorts and left the room, taking the bag with her.

She arrived at dawn at a secluded area which looked onto the beach. She picked up twigs around her until she had created a small pile for a fire. She withdrew a lighter, putting the flame to the twigs below it. She went into the bag and took out Johnny's travel book and placed it on the fire. It barely resembled a

271

readable book these days; every page had more or less faded away. She sat down looking at the waves in front of her as a breeze swept towards her, bringing life to the flames which eventually engulfed the book, darkening the curved edges, gradually shrinking it, until all that left was left was a pile of blackened ashes.

'So I spoke to Mum and Dad,' said Claudia greeting Rachel in the lobby as she prepared to leave. 'They mentioned you coming up some time to see them?'

'I would definitely be up for that,' said Rachel giving Claudia a warm embrace.

'Thank you for doing this.'

'You're welcome,' said Rachel, turning to face Adrian, 'Do I get a hug?'

Adrian smiled and wrapped his arms around her.

'Please stop growing so much,' she said ruffling his hair.

'This week has felt very cathartic. Thank you,' said Suzi appearing next to her.

'I'm pleased.' They gave each other a warm hug.

'We will talk again soon,' said Suzi.

'No doubt about it.'

'Bye Eric,' said Claudia hugging him goodbye. 'Lovely meeting you finally.'

'And you,' he said, before going to give Adrian a high five. 'See you later buddy.'

'Your new best friend,' said Claudia.

After they had moved the luggage to the hired car, Rachel and Eric waved goodbye to the group and drove south towards Phuket Airport where they both sat in silence.

'So have you got a long wait?' asked Rachel as Eric maneuvered her suitcase onto the pavement outside the terminal building.

'A couple of hours. Drop the car off. Read my book.'

272

'I can't believe this is all over.'

'I know. But this was a good trip Rachel. And you did this. You should be proud of that. Johnny would be. So I'll see you in London?'

'I will see you in London.'

'Well I'm going to go now. I'm never good at saying goodbye,' said Eric walking back to the driver's door smiling at her. 'Safe trip.'

'You too,' she said before entering the terminal building.

It was on the plane that night that Rachel fell asleep and dreamt about Johnny for the last time. In the dream she had woken in Johnny's hotel room in Gili Meno. She had looked at the alarm clock. It was just gone 7.00am. Johnny was asleep next to her. There was something telling her to feel guilty about this moment because of Ross who she was supposed to be still in a relationship with. But she liked this boy. More than she had liked a boy on the first night of meeting them. There was something safe, secure, but not entirely dull about him. She slowly pulled herself out of bed and went to put her clothes on over her swimwear. He still lay asleep in the room, displaying a smooth youthful back. She went into the bathroom to wash her face. She had forgotten that salt water even came out of the taps on the island and it didn't feel as inviting as the usual water you got in normal hotel rooms. She walked into the bedroom. She knew she had to leave, but on her way out she noticed his travel book lying on the table; the one they had looked through the night before. It was open on a page about Sydney. She looked around and saw a pen. She grabbed it and did something she probably would have done on a boy's hand at primary school. She wrote down her name followed by her number. She turned to Johnny still sleeping. She closed the book. It was time to say goodbye. She went to kiss him on the cheek and he did not move an inch. She went to open the door, looked back at him sleeping peacefully in the bed and then quietly slipped away into the early morning light. She would miss this boy. Oh how she would miss him.

ACKNOWLEDGEMENTS

A massive thank you to Dr Jocelyn Chatterton, Rosanna Whitehead and Laura Sleep for their proof reading and editing skills.

ABOUT

This is Matthew Peacock's first novel. He works in TV Production and lives in Leeds and London.

Find out more about Matthew at:

www.matthewpeacock.co.uk

Printed in Great Britain
by Amazon